Tom Holt is a post-graduate student at Oxford University, specialising in Ancient Greek History. A passionate admirer of E.F. Benson's original *Lucia* novels, he set out to create a new adventure for the residents of Tilling that followed on from where their creator had left off. Although he has published some poetry and magazine articles in the past, *Lucia in Wartime* is his first novel.

Also by Tom Holt

LUCIA TRIUMPHANT

and published by Black Swan

Lucia in Wartime

Tom Holt

Based on the characters created by E.F. Benson

BLACK SWAN

LUCIA IN WARTIME
A BLACK SWAN BOOK 0 552 99202 X

Originally published in Great Britain by
Macmillan London Limited

PRINTING HISTORY
Macmillan London edition published 1985
Black Swan edition published 1986
Black Swan edition reprinted 1989

The map of Tilling shown on pages six and
seven is adapted from *E.F. Benson: Mr
Benson Remembered in Rye*, and the *World of
Tilling* by Cynthia and Tony Reavell
(published by Martello Bookshop, Rye) and
is reproduced by kind permission of the
authors.

The author acknowledges with gratitude
the permission kindly granted by the Estate
of K.S.P. McDowell to base this novel on
the characters created by E.F. Benson

This book is set in 11/12 pt Mallard

Black Swan Books are published by
Transworld Publishers Ltd., 61-63
Uxbridge Road, Ealing, London W5 5SA, in
Australia by Transworld Publishers (Aust.) Pty.
Ltd., 15-23 Helles Avenue, Moorebank, NSW 2170,
and in New Zealand by Transworld Publishers (N.Z.) Ltd.,
Cnr. Moselle and Waipareira Avenues,
Henderson, Auckland.

Made and printed in Great Britain by
The Guernsey Press Co. Ltd.,
Guernsey, Channel Islands.

Acknowledgements

My thanks are due to:
— Robert Smith, for help and encouragement;
— Sylvia James, who typed out the (almost illegible) manuscript;
— my mother, who first introduced me to Lucia.

TILLING

To Station and
the Coalmerchant

MALLESON STREET

Woolgar
and Pipstow

Dr.
Dobbie

Stationer's

Post Box

Fruiterer

WEST STREET

Irene
(Taormina)

Hopkins'
(Fishmonger)

Wyses

PORPOISE STREET

Captain
Puffin

Dentist

Major
Flint

Mallards

The Garden-Room

Poppits

Mallards Cottage

Suntrap

Trader's Arms

CURFEW STREET

Viewpoint Terrace

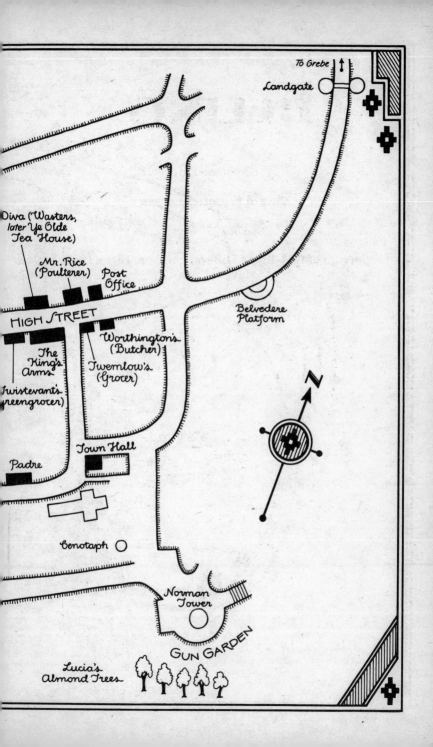

To Grebe

Landgate

Diva (Wasters, later Ye Olde Tea House)

Mr. Rice (Poulterer)

Post Office

HIGH STREET

The King's Arms

Worthington's (Butcher)

Twemlow's (Grocer)

Twistevant's (Greengrocer)

Belvedere Platform

Town Hall

Padre

Cenotaph

Norman Tower

GUN GARDEN

Lucia's Almond Trees

Dedicated to

Edward Frederick Benson

1867–1940

'Servant of God–Brave Sufferer–Author–Three Times
Mayor of Rye'

1

It might have been supposed that the outbreak of war
would have broken the spirit of Mrs. Emmeline Pillson,
formerly Lucas, née Smythe, always Lucia, three times
Mayor of Tilling. Nothing could be further from the
truth. Had not Lucia been forced on many occasions to
fight desperate battles to retain her rightful position as
Queen of Tilling society against the awesome figure of
Elizabeth Mapp-Flint? Had not her little realm on so
many occasions been overrun, as Hitler had overrun the
Sudetenland, and had she not always risen phoenix-like
from the ashes of her supposed defeat and triumphantly
driven the pretender and the infidel in full flight? Hitler,
be he never so formidable, could scarcely be as savage,
as unprincipled an opponent as dear Elizabeth (three
times Mayoress of Tilling).

The enemy had, of course, started with many advantages. Given the international situation, Italian –
which it had never been conclusively proved that Lucia
could not speak fluently – was banished from the
dinner-tables and Bridge parties of Tilling. Mozart –
celestial *Mozartino!* – was a German, as was
immortal Beethoven, and the transcendent beauty of the
slow movement of the Moonlight Sonata was almost
forgotten in the garden-room at Mallards. This
unexpected treason on the part of her most trusted
allies had left Lucia momentarily at a disadvantage; but
her unquenchable spirit was only scotched, not slain.
Where Mozart and Beethoven had reigned, there would
be Elgar, Dowland and Purcell. Instead of Italian she

would punctuate her conversation with. . . .

Certainly the outbreak of war had upset the social order of Tilling. The Wyses, linked by marriage with the Italian aristocracy, were little better than uninterned aliens. But Major Benjamin Mapp-Flint, the town's only resident warrior, enjoyed an *estime* even greater than had been his when, on one never to be forgotten occasion, he had briefly (and erroneously) been clothed in the glamour of the desperate duellist. The fact that both participants in this affair of honour had sought to escape to London by the early morning train and had converted their *rencontre* into a round of golf in no way diminished the antique splendour of the incident. His opinions on strategy and tactics were eagerly solicited at every Bridge party and the somewhat vague and enigmatic manner in which his oracles from the shrine of Mars were delivered only served to augment his reputation. Also, when he carried his wife's shopping basket in the High Street, there was the slightest trace of a limp attributable, no doubt, to a war wound, although in which leg it was not quite certain.

It was this aspect of her husband's many-faceted character that engaged Elizabeth Mapp-Flint as she addressed her patriotically frugal breakfast of toast and home-made plum-jam one morning at Grebe, their house near the marshes outside Tilling.

'Such a pity, dear,' she said thoughtfully, 'that the foolish War Office cannot find some use for such an experienced and illustrious soldier as yourself.'

A letter had arrived yesterday from that criminally short-sighted body, thanking the Major for his public-spirited offer to take charge of his old command but evincing a rather naïve belief that Hitler could be crushed without him. This had not completely exasperated the indomitable old soldier; his military career, although spanning some twenty-five years, had been mercifully free of any involvement in actual conflict.

'Yes, girlie, I know,' he said, shaking his head sadly,

10

'always were damn' fools in Whitehall. Couldn't recognise a good man then, can't recognise one now. Still, that's that, eh?'

'That most certainly is not that. I simply won't have your talents going to waste at this crucial point of our nation's history. Why, it's as bad as burning food, or pouring petroleum into the sea. We must find some work for you – air-raid warden perhaps, or training such able-bodied men as are still here in the town into a proper Home Guard, capable of offering resistance in the event of an invasion. Or watching for German aircraft or parachutists.'

The Major had not thought of that. Of course his duty to his country must come first, and ever since the sand-dunes on which he had been accustomed to play golf had been draped in barbed-wire and signboards warning the public not to proceed beyond this point he had had to spend more time under the eye of his dear wife than he would have chosen himself. Watching for enemy barges, however, perhaps in the company of another golf-playing patriot, would surely entitle him to access to the forbidden zone; and there was that spartan but nonetheless inviting little public-house opposite the tram-stop, where an old soldier had been wont to fortify himself against the delights of domestic life. But training – attempting to train – the farm-labourers and chemists' boys of Tilling to hurl the Hun back into the sea – that was a different kettle of fish altogether.

'Air-raid warden?' he said hopefully. 'Surely a younger man?'

'No, Benjy, such a responsible duty calls for a man of authority, a man respected in the community. Can you imagine dear Mr. Georgie, in his cape, strutting round Tilling bawling "Do put that tar', some light out!" or some such thing? Or Mr. Wyse perhaps? Or the Padre? Why, no one would understand him, for he would be sure to shout in Scotch! No, Benjy-boy, you are the only man in Tilling who would be up to the task. I wonder what is the proper authority to apply to.'

Benjy scowled at the teapot, which these days tended to supply a particularly anaemic fluid. The national emergency had enabled Elizabeth to ascend new pinnacles of frugality.

'I suppose you'll want me to hang about in all weathers outside Mallards, in case Lucia – I mean Mrs. Pillson – happens to break the black-out regulations. 'Pon my word, girlie, I don't think a matter of vital importance should be entrusted to an old man already worn out in his country's service. I would have thought Twistevant's young lad – he's got flat feet, you know – or one of Twemlow's boys. . . .'

'The defence of Britain is not to be left to tradesmen,' said Elizabeth grandly, surprising herself almost as much as her husband. 'Besides, if you don't do it, that woman will get herself involved in it somehow. You mark my words.'

Elizabeth took a savage bite of her thin toast. The defence of Britain was under no circumstances to be left to Lucia.

Strangely enough the same national issues were engaging the mind of the Pillsons in Mallards.

'Mark my words, Georgie, she'll try and get that husband of hers involved in some important war-work, and that I could not allow. I feel a deep responsibility for our little town, having carried out its most onerous public duties for three consecutive years. And what would Major Benjy do to further our security? Challenge Hitler to a duel on the sand-dunes perhaps, and then run away to London by the first train? No, Georgie, I feel that it is up to us, as Tilling's leading citizens, to shoulder yet another burden on behalf of our community. Air-raid wardens, Georgie, and collections to raise money to build Hurricanes, and digging for victory. And Grosvenor and Foljambe must go and make munitions or parachutes or something.'

The horror of this awful idea struck Georgie dumb for a moment. Never in their married life had Lucia

12

suggested anything quite so dreadful. Do without Foljambe! What, he wondered, was the point of fighting this tar'some war if all vestiges of civilised life were to be abandoned in the process?

'You, Georgie, you must put your name forward immediately for some responsible position. And we must have some evacuees to live here. We must not be selfish. We must give of ourselves to the utmost.'

'I won't do without Foljambe, and that's flat. And I won't have evacuees. Why, they'd steal my *bibelots*. And I'm sure I don't know what I could do. Really, Lucia, you mustn't let yourself get carried away like this.'

'Oo vewwy naughty Georgie not to answer Country's call in time of Emergency,' said Lucia, lapsing into the baby-talk she so often used to deal with Georgie when he was troublesome. 'Oo surely not leave ickle Lucia to face frightful Germans on her own?'

'We do have an Army, Lucia, who I am quite sure are perfectly capable of dealing with Hitler without any help from us. I'll tell you what – we can get together a concert party to entertain the troops – music and *tableaux*, and Irene doing impressions of Goering and Himmler. I'm sure that will achieve much more than depriving ourselves of the bare necessities of survival.'

'We shall see, Georgie, we shall see. And now, perhaps, a quarter-of-an-hour of immortal Elgar, and then to the High Street. We must not allow the horrors of war to come between us and contemplation of the Eternal. Dear Elgar! So quintessentially what we are fighting for.'

Except that dear Elgar, although so quintessentially English, was rather more difficult than Georgie remembered, so that he played many false notes, and went forth into the High Street in a very dark frame of mind.

They met Godiva Plaistow in the queue at the butcher's.

'Sausages,' she she in her telegraphic style. 'Supposed to be pork, but presumably breadcrumbs. Haven't seen a sausage since Paddy had that fight with a Scottie.

Don't suppose I shall recognise one when I do see it.'

'No!' said Lucia, her high-minded concern for strategy eclipsed by the thought of pork sausages. 'And are there any left?'

'Don't know. Wyses were here at crack of dawn. Left draped in sausages on their tricyles. I wonder how they knew?'

'You know, dear Diva, I sometimes wonder whether our dear Tilling has yet grasped the need for community spirit at this critical time. I, for my part, entirely disapprove of the virtual ostracism of our dear friends the Wyses, simply because they have connections with a hostile country. Yet I do not believe that they will help their own cause by. . . .'

'By hogging all the sausages. Still, they were here first. Would have done the same myself in their shoes, I expect,' said Diva magnanimously. She could see that the couple at the counter had quite incredibly failed to buy any sausages, so that she was now certain to get some. 'I hope there's some scraps for Paddy!' she added, more hopefully than realistically.

Quaint Irene Coles, attired in a flying-jacket and blue serge trousers, braked her racing-bicycle beside the kerb and shouted, 'What are you queuing for?'

'Sausages, dear,' said Lucia, 'although I fear you might be a little bit late.'

'Never mind,' said Irene. 'What's a sausage or two between sisters-in-arms? Besides, Henry can probably get me some from the Officers' Mess if I ask him.'

With that bombshell, more explosive than anything hurled by the long-range guns of Germany, she raced off towards the Landgate.

'Henry!' said Diva, thunderstruck. 'Officers' Mess! Fancy.'

And so deep was she in thought that she almost forgot to ask if there were any scraps, although, since there were none, this hardly mattered.

Outside the shop she met the Reverend Kenneth Bartlett, known to all Tilling as the Padre.

'Sausages,' she said to the Padre, 'and Irene's got an officer from the Harbour who can get her all the sausages she wants.'

'No!' said the Padre. 'An officier of the soldiery. I ken he must be one of yon Staffordshire Regiment. A godly company o' Christian knights I ween they are, too.'

This macaronic dialect had been a playful whimsy to start with, but, like a child who had ignored his mother's warning, he had 'stuck like it', and now the accents of his Midlands birthplace manifested themselves only in times of great excitement.

'Henry,' said Diva, 'and all those sausages.'

'Wait till I tell wee wifie. And are ye no coming to take tea with us this afternoon, Mistress Plaistow? Very well then, till four-o'clock.'

He hurried off towards the butcher's, in time to see the last sausages disappear into Lucia's basket.

One might have thought that Tilling was a nest of enemy spies, to judge by the number of its residents who could be seen later that day walking past the small infantry camp at Tilling Harbour, furtively regarding it and occasionally, when they thought they were not overlooked, peering at it through opera-glasses. Lucia and Georgie, with the smallest of her first husband's telescopes concealed in a copy of the *Hastings Chronicle*, had suddenly been seized with a desire to take their bicycle-exercise as near to the sea as the barbed-wire allowed them. Major Benjy too was filled with a nostalgic wish to gaze upon the scene of his former golfing triumphs, his binoculars no doubt being essential to pick out the details of the long seventh hole; and the Padre, who had previously been content to leave the spiritual guidance of the troops to the uniformed cleric attached to them, had clearly heard the call of pastoral duty, for he went down to the Harbour with fifty copies of last week's parish magazine. But there was no sign of Irene, or her bicycle, or Henry, or sausages. Had they troubled to look into the dining-room of the Traders' Arms, they would have seen the object of their espionage having lunch with a short, balding man in the uniform of a Captain of the Staffords, discussing the latest trends in the European *avant-garde* (for Henry was none other than Henry Porteous, the painter) with a parcel of what might easily have been sausages on the table in front of her. As it was, all Tilling risked arrest, denunciation and the firing-squad without any result.

But the incident had set off a train, a veritable Flying Scotsman, of thought in Lucia's mind: she must have an officer too, who would come to Mallards (with or without sausages) and be inspired by the beauty of Purcell and Elgar before venturing forth, a knight wearing her favour, to do battle with the infidel. In fact, more than one officer. There must be a whole Round Table of the Knights of Mallards, the goodliest company of chivalry ever seen on the Sussex coast. When she had established her short-lived *salon* in London, she had been seeking selfishly to enthrone herself queen of that glittering city of shadows; so unworthy of one who had since devoted every fibre of her being to the public service. How better could she assist the nation's war-effort than to instil in its leaders of men (or at least such of its leaders of men as were currently in Tilling Harbour) the true essence of their struggle against barbarism. Also, said the old Eve at the back of her mind, how better to put dear Elizabeth in her place than by trumping her retired Major with a couple of real live officers still on active service?

Actually getting hold of a job-lot of assorted officers was a different matter. She could not order them from Twistevant's ('Good morning, Twistevant, and have you got any Colonels today? Four then, please, and send them to Mrs. Pillson, Mallards'). The Army had kept itself to itself, confining its activities to the Harbour and the Sebastopol Arms. Occasionally, a uniformed male had been seen about the streets of Tilling with a camera or a sketching-book, but she could not seize such a man by the elbow and drag him off to the garden-room to listen to madrigals, arranged for four hands on the *pianoforte*. Presumably they were under orders to keep their distance from the townsfolk on account of some military secrets that they might disclose in an unguarded moment.

Baffled but by no means despondent, Lucia returned to Mallards with her day's trophy of two lamb-chops. On her way, she passed Elizabeth and Major Benjy in deep conversation with the Padre and his wife Evie. The Major was apparently confiding to his enraptured audience that a counter-attack, via the Faroes and Iceland, was so inevitable as to be a foregone conclusion, and the only question over which Whitehall was still agonising was whether to establish the final bridgehead at Oslo or Copenhagen. Smiling in such a way that she could grind her teeth at the same time, Lucia turned up West Street and propelled her bicycle up the cobbled slope.

'Georgino – I mean Georgie,' said she, as soon as she had reached home. 'I have an idea.'

Georgie raised his eyes from a snuff-box he had been engaged in polishing. His poor *bibelots* had gathered dust in the last few days, for his soul was full of horrors. Foljambe had declared that, since her husband Cadman was away at the wars (he was slightly too old for military service, and had gone to work at the Transport Headquarters at Hove, where he spent most of his time polishing the motors of Generals and Cabinet Ministers, and in sundry other ways devising the downfall of Hitler), she ought to be doing her bit by making bombs at the Ordnance Factory. As a result, he had neglected his *bibelots*, left a chair-cover, on which he had been embroidering Britannia ruling the Rother Estuary, abandoned half-finished in a cupboard, and lain awake two nights in a row tormented by nameless fears.

'Well,' he said, 'what is it?'

'Officers, Georgie, from the Harbour. Think of them, pacing up and down their dusty barrack-rooms in the evenings, dwelling on the perils of war, the dangers that

17

lie before them. Allowing their morale to sink into the depths.'

Georgie shook his head. 'I thought they had a nice little Officers' Club in the old Customs House where they can play billiards and. . . .'

'Billiards, Georgie! What sort of occupation is that for a man who is about to confront the horror of the battle-field? What they need is somewhere where they can refresh their souls with music and poetry and intelligent conversation, to inspire them to go out and fight for the values of civilisation and democracy, where they can get a final taste of what England really means.'

'You mean the Institute?' asked Georgie, puzzled.

'No, no, Georgie. Why, don't you see? A *salon*. Here. At Mallards.'

'Lucia! You can't.'

'Why not, pray?'

'But really! They'll drink whisky, and laugh at my embroidery.'

'No, dearest, you are mistaken. Not all soldiers are like poor Major Benjy, boozing and making up vulgar stories about the Pride of Poonah. Imagine, Georgie, if you were an officer stranded in an unknown town, how your heart would yearn for the company of kindred souls, the refreshment of the mind. Oo not be unkind to officers, Georgie, make them play billiards all evening.'

'I believe you only want them about the place to score off Elizabeth and Major Benjy. And I'm sure they won't want to listen to us playing duets or watch us doing *tableaux* when they could be drinking beer in the Sebastopol Arms.'

Even as Georgie said this, a light had dawned in his brain, a light as brilliant as the first rays of the morning sun. If they were to entertain officers at Mallards, surely they would have need of at least one permanent member of staff, to wit Foljambe. Even that conscientious person would have to admit that ministering to Lucia's officers was as much war-work as making bombs at the Ordnance Factory. Foljambe, in other

18

words, would go to sleep in her own little room again.

'And anyway,' he said cautiously, 'how do you plan to get hold of all these officers? They don't come into the town very much.'

He knew, of course, that Lucia would manage it somehow, through some stroke of luck or Machiavellian effort. Had she not, in the space of a few months in London, filled her house in Brompton Square with duchesses, politicians and flute-playing prizefighters?

'Me must fink,' said she. 'But you agree in principle, don't you? Of course, there will be no question of Foljambe leaving if we do start entertaining in this way. Why, it would be almost like war-work!'

Every man has his price, thought Georgie, and the value of a parlourmaid-*cum*-valet like Foljambe was far above rubies. Nonetheless, it would not do to be over-enthusiastic. Lucia must not be over-encouraged in her personal war against Germany; really, she was being even more insufferable now than she had been in the first few weeks of her Mayoralty.

'Oh, very well then. But *you* must catch the officers, and *you* must entertain them.'

'Thank you, dear, a thousand times. So noble of you. Now we must put our heads together and make our plans. How splendid it is to be doing something at last!'

Elizabeth, meanwhile, unaware that her military monopoly was so gravely endangered, was sitting in the drawing-room of Grebe. She had found an old pair of velvet curtains which, with a little imagination and a great deal of application, could be turned into an evening-dress. It would, of course, be very heavy and cumbersome, but the thought of appearing in a new costume of red velvet reconciled her to any degree of physical discomfort. Poor Diva had been forced back on chintz roses again, regardless of the disasters that had attended their first appearance, and little Evie Bartlett was now not only a mouse, but a church-mouse as well. Let Lucia attempt to steal this advantage from her if she dared – very fine she would look in an evening-gown of figured damask. . . . But the heavy material was hard to cut and her fingers were becoming quite sore where the scissors bit into them; and the lines were not really straight, even when the pile of the velvet was taken into account. . . .

She turned her mind to the matter of Irene and the enigmatic Henry. Who was he? An officer evidently, and therefore one of the Staffords from the Harbour. But did this mean that Irene had at last fallen victim to the litle gentleman with swan's wings and such cruel arrows, whose marksmanship had (albeit in a rather restrained manner) accounted for Susan Wyse, Emmeline Lucas and herself? Could Irene, she of the moleskin trousers and short clay pipe, have fallen in love? Such an event would indeed be outstanding in the chronicles of Tilling. And would love, that softener of the hearts of tyrants, disarm the tongue of Tilling's most dreaded mimic, in terror of whom Elizabeth had lived for so many years? She was still young enough, and admittedly still attractive enough, if one disregarded the fishermen's jerseys; war is a great foster-nurse of love, even between the most unsuitable of people.

'Benjy,' she said as he entered the room, 'it's no use, I shan't get a moment's rest until I am certain that dear quaint Irene isn't exposing herself to the most terrible danger.'

'Riding that bicycle of hers so fast down Porpoise Street?' hazarded the perplexed Major.

'No, no, I mean allowing herself to fall into the clutches of an unscrupulous man. You know what you wicked soldiers are like for breaking poor female hearts.'

'Well, I don't know about that, Liz, old girl. But there's something I must tell you. There's been a spy arrested in Hastings.'

'No!' screamed Elizabeth, wide-eyed. 'In Hastings! Benjy, is this true?'

'I heard it from the Padre,' said he, simply. 'Apparently he heard it from Twistevant, whose cousin's brother-in-law keeps the Seven Stars in Hastings. Anyway, some fella with a funny accent came knocking on the door of the Plough and Harrow, which is just down the road from the Seven Stars, at seven-o'clock yesterday morning, asking for a bottle of Franklin's Ale. Now, not only is it funny that a chap should think he could get a drink at seven in the morning in England, but old Franklin sold up two years ago. So the landlady said she was going down to the cellar to fetch his bottle of ale, and went and telephoned the police. They took him away in an armoured car. Well, what do you think of that, girlie?'

'Benjy, how terrible. German spies just along the coast – why, we shall all be murdered in our beds. What shall we do?'

'Well,' said he, 'I'm going to dig out my old service revolver. If anyone comes asking for beer at the King's Arms at the crack of dawn, they'll get the shock of their lives!'

And with this ferocious speech the old soldier went and rummaged about in his desk. Instead of his service revolver, however, he found a flask of whisky, the existence of which he had quite forgotten, and he paused for a moment to stiffen his resolve before arming himself to await the onrush of the hordes of thirsty barbarians.

News of the spy in Hastings spread through Tilling like wildfire, and its inhabitants, who had never been reluctant to observe their fellow-creatures from windows, street-corners or the doorways of shops, redoubled their efforts in the interests of national security. A German agent, entering Tilling from the sea coast, would have had to pass first the sentry-post of Grebe; supposing he managed to get past the untiring eyes of Elizabeth Mapp-Flint, and had gained the Church Square without being discovered, he would have to find some way of bypassing the Vicarage and the searching gaze of wee wifie. Even if he was successful thus far, he must then evade the garden-room of Mallards, towering like a hilltop fortress above the narrow street, before passing on to the High Street and certain detection by the ladies of Tilling queuing inside Twistevant's, or the vantage-point of the front window of Diva's house, Wasters. Had he as many shapes as Proteus or the ability, like Oberon, to make himself invisible at will, he could never pass by so many eyes without the need of strong refreshment. In order to obtain it he would have to encounter the scrutiny of Major Benjy, who had taken up a regular post at the bar of the King's Arms; the next German to make the slightest slip in the ordering of alcoholic refreshment would undoubtedly go the way of his predecessor. For his part, the Major had thrown himself heart and soul into this form of war-work, for which he was undeniably well suited. The only doubt left in his mind was whether he would be able to claim reimbursement from the War Office for the occasional whisky-and-soda he was forced to consume from time to time in order to maintain his disguise.

While on sentry-go in the garden-room one morning, Lucia was allowing her fingers to stray over the keys of her piano when an idea dawned in her mind.

'Georgie,' she said (for he was there also), 'an idea!'

'Officers?' said Georgie gloomily. He had heard many ideas about officers lately.

'No, dearest, just a thought. How shall I put it? You remember how, before Italy removed itself from the circle of civilised nations. . . .'

'Yes,' said he, 'go on.' He, like Lucia, missed the easy Italian phrases they had been accustomed to slip into their conversation. They had experimented briefly with a number of alternatives of varying difficulty and elegance. French was barred to them, for had not dear Elizabeth once used it to parody Lucia's Italian? Classical Greek had had a short vogue ('Diva dear, what a *kalon himation*! and now I must just pop *epi* Twemlow's and see if they've got any *allanta* for our *ariston*'), but

22

had been abandoned since it rendered their talk completely unintelligible not only to everyone else in Tilling but frequently to each other as well.

'What better decoration for our speech than the language of our dear Polish allies? Such a mellifluous tongue, Georgie, and so much a mark of respect to our intrepid comrades-in-arms.'

'But I don't know any Polish,' replied Georgie, 'and Elizabeth would be sure to tell everyone it was Russian, and I can't remember if they're on our side or not.'

'Nonsense, Georgie. I shall send for a Polish phrase-book at once.'

At this moment Grosvenor entered with the post. There was but the one letter, addressed to Mrs. Pillson. Lucia opened it and presently she almost screamed with pleasure.

'Lucia, what is it?' said Georgie.

'It's from Tony Limpsfield – you remember, I made his acquaintance in London. Listen!

My Dear Lucia,
    As you may have heard, I have been able to secure a commission in the South Staffordshire Regiment, which is stationed in your divine Tilling. My dear, how marvellously fortunate! To be able to spend a few hours of civilised relaxation, listening to the Moonlight Sonata or wonderful Mozart, before going out on to the battlefields of Europe. Do say that I can call on you while I am in Tilling, and perhaps bring a few fellow-souls with me.

                                        Your devoted
                                        Lord Tony.'

'No!' said Georgie, profoundly moved. Although he and Lord Limpsfield had not been introduced when the latter had stayed with Lucia in Riseholme while she still lived there, that turbulent weekend when all Riseholme had turned against Lucia, he knew him by sight, and of course he was a friend of his adored Olga Bracely.

'Officers, Georgie! Officers from heaven!' said Lucia,

23

almost incoherent with joy. 'At last we shall be able to do something beyond depriving ourselves of butter and sending our sauce-pans to be melted down!'

'And what price Major Benjy now?' said her husband. 'why, all he'll be doing is boozing and watching for spies in the King's Arms.'

They were both silent for a moment.

'Can he really mean Beethoven and Mozart?' said Georgie. 'And to think we've been doing without them all this time, and having to make do with beastly Elgar and madrigals. Why, it's worse than having to make do with powdered eggs instead of real ones!'

'And to think that I believed that those wretched weeks I spent in London were all wasted when in fact they were simply laying the foundations of this vital work that lies before us. It was Destiny, Georgie, Destiny. I feel that my actions in the past have been guided by a greater providence. We must practise as never before, for we shall be playing – how does dear Virgil put it? – not for light or trivial rewards but for the life-blood of our country.'

So it was that Elizabeth and the Major, passing under the garden-room as they walked into Tilling, heard German music being played there once again.

'Ah,' said Major Benjy, 'there's Mrs. Pillson playing Elgar, no doubt. A great improvement on all that frightful German twaddle she used to make us listen to, eh, girlie?'

'No, Benjy-boy, that is the frightful German twaddle she used to make us listen to. Sometimes I wonder if dear Lucia's patriotic displays – so forceful, don't you think? – may mask some slight sympathies towards the enemy. Of course, I would never suggest that she was an active sympathiser. . . .'

Major Benjy's jaw set in an implacable line. If he ever caught Lucia trying to buy bottled beer at the King's Arms at seven-o'clock in the morning, he would shoot first and ask questions afterwards.

*   *   *

Captain Anthony, Lord Limpsfield, called at Mallards the next morning. Elizabeth, as it happened, was passing at the time, and she saw the dark-green military car nosing its way along the narrow street and stopping outside Mallards, and the uniformed man step out and ring the bell. Her heart leapt up with involuntary optimism as she recalled how the soldiers had called to take away the Hastings spy in an armoured car, but when the door opened and she heard the rapturous greetings and Dear-Lord-Tonyings that followed, her heart was at once sent plummeting into the pit of her stomach. Who was this terrible officer, calling on dear Lulu and being greeted as an old and intimate friend? Better, she thought, to have German *Panzers* in Porpoise Street than British Humbers outside Mallards. . . .

'My dear,' said Tony Limpsfield, 'who was that large woman who passed by just now? Such a smile, my dear. I thought she was going to swallow me whole.'

'Poor Elizabeth!' said Lucia. 'One of my dearest friends in our little Tilling – Mayoress three times – but such a jealous nature. She cannot bear that anyone else should do anything to help the war-effort. But such a character, and married to the most comical old Major. You shall meet them both, I promise you; they are quite as ludicrous as Queen Charlotte's mittens that you saw in that dear little Museum in sweet Riseholme. And now, perhaps, a little *musica*, and then you must tell me all about what you are doing and how the war is going. But, wicked Lord Tony, to encourage me to play Beethoven and Mozart, for are they not German composers? Surely we should be listening to Elgar and sweet Delius?'

'Delius was a German, come to that,' said Tony Limpsfield, 'so you can't have him. I don't care a fig if you play Wagner, so long as I hear something other than "Rule Britannia" and "Land of hope and glory", or American jazz, which is all I've heard in the last month.'

'Poor Lord Tony! How wretched is the soldier's lot. Very well then, no more talk, but some delicious Mozart.'

Lord Tony immediately assumed the listening-to-music face that had been the badge of the secret society of the Luciaphils during those heady days in London, while Lucia flexed her fingers and began to play. . .

On his return to the camp in the Harbour, he ran into his fellow-officer Heny Porteous, who was engaged in making a highly stylised sketch of a three-ton lorry.

'I met your lady love in town today,' he said.

'If you are referring to Miss Coles,' said Porteous, 'she's nothing of the sort. We admire each other's work, that's all. Her picture last year – Bellona in arms on the South Coast – a marvellously sardonic treatment of British jingoism. That brilliant face she put on it – everything that's wrong with this country today. That stupid, complacent smirk! What an artist!'

'From what I gather,' said Lord Limpsfield, 'it wasn't meant to be ironic at all. That brilliant face was based on my friend Mrs. Pillson. Apparently quaint Irene – I mean Miss Coles – regards her as an embodiment of all that's splended in the British character in wartime. Serene but dogged resistance.'

'But she looks so damned smug!'

'I know. She's that too! Listen! You must come and meet her, she's colossal. I made her acquaintance in London before the war. She lived in a little village called Riseholme in Worcestershire and she was trying to break into London society. She didn't so much climb as rise effortlessly, like one of those mediums who practise levitation. And such a snob! She went after duchesses like a gundog!'

'She sounds quite frightful.'

'Oh she is – but she is magnificent and I adore her, and I want her to have as many officers in Tilling as she had duchesses in London, if not more. And your Miss Coles adores her too. Lucia introduced her to me in the High Street, like a queen scattering largesse to the mob!'

'Oh very well then, since she's the original of Miss Coles's Bellona,' said Henry Porteous, scowling. 'But I won't take her any sausages, or eggs, or parachute silk, which is all that women seem to be interested in these days.'

Meanwhile Lucia was practising the Moonlight Sonata, deep in thought. She must not repeat the mistake she had made when she had entertained Lord Tony in Riseholme. She had invited all her London friends there one weekend and, foolish woman that she was, had kept them to herself, taking them to laugh at the new Museum and not introducing them to any of her subjects, even Georgie. As a result Riseholme had rebelled against her, and she had been hard put to it to regain her crown. This time she would allow Tilling to meet her officers, although she would have to ration them, as everything is rationed in wartime. An occasional lunch or Bridge party, at which an honoured Tillingite would be permitted to be present. On no account should Elizabeth be allowed to annex any of her officers. On that point she was adamant.

With these elements of strategy firm in her mind, she closed the lid of the piano and looked out of the window in case any German spy, entranced by the music of his countrymen, should be standing beneath. Having satisfied herself that her lure had attracted nothing, she took her bicycle and cycled down to the High Street to order a Polish phrase-book.

She had not gone far when she saw something that caused her to skid violently and almost collide with a lamp-post. There, outside Irene's house Taormina, was the quaint one being kissed by a short, balding man in uniform. Covered in confusion she righted her machine and pedalled furiously into the High Street.

She had not been the only witness of this most un-Tillinglike event. Diva, walking her dog up towards Church Square, observed it also and immediately turned round and walked briskly back towards the High Street, almost colliding with Elizabeth in her anxiety to escape from the remarkable display of emotion.

'Irene,' said Diva breathlessly. 'Soldier. Kissing outside Taormina.'

'No!' said Elizabeth. 'Are you sure?'

'Saw them myself just now,' replied Diva. 'Probably still at it.'

'Fancy! What was he like?'

'Short, balding, spectacles. It must be Henry.'

'I was saying to Major Benjy just the other day how morality is remarkably lax in wartime,' said Elizabeth proudly. 'And now this! The poor child. She must be protected against herself.'

'I wouldn't worry about that,' said Diva crossly. 'I just hope it *was* Henry, that's all. If there are two of them after her, they might go and fight duels over her in the sand-dunes. You know how military men tend to fight duels over women.'

Elizabeth decided to ignore the deadly irony of this remark.

'Hardly likely, dear. Even if he did have a rival, I doubt whether they'd be able to have a duel in the sand-dunes. Mines. Patrols. Military police. Someone would be sure to stop them.'

'Be that as it may,' said Diva, more red in the face than ever, 'you're not to go interfering. Besides, love might be good for Irene. Stop her wearing fishermen's jerseys and riding her bicycle too fast. And I don't see how you could stop it, unless you walked up and down outside Taormina ringing a dinner-bell.'

With this brilliant allusion, Diva scuttled off to impart the news to the Padre and wee wifie, who were queuing outside the fishmonger's in the pretty belief that he might sell them some fish.

2

Lucia's first officers' dinner was an outstanding success, for Lucia if not for the officers. There was lobster *à la Riseholme* (albeit with rather more Riseholme than lobster) and raspberry fool (rather more fool than raspberry) and a quantity of sound port. This was followed by Beethoven and *Mozartino*, Elgar and Purcell, by readings from Shakespeare (Henry V to the troops at Harfleur – Lucia was Henry V) and Pope's *Iliad* (Hector's farewell to Andromache – Lucia was Hector). As the two Humbers rattled away down the hill in the rain (one of them pausing outside Taormina to release quaint Irene) Lucia waved them goodbye from the blacked-out window of the garden-room and then retired to bed, gloriously happy. Four officers, including a peer of the realm and a notorious *avant-garde* painter, and Irene as a witness that it had actually happened.

Irene was not slow in performing her *rôle* as messenger, for by marketing time in the High Street next morning Elizabeth had heard all about it from Evie Bartlett.

'There were two Humbers,' said the mouselike one 'Lord Limpsfield and Captain Porteous in one and Captain Oldshaw and Lieutenant Custard in the other. They arrived at six and they didn't leave until after twelve. Fancy that!'

Elizabeth smiled. 'I wonder what they can have been doing all that time?' she said cheerfully. 'Ah! Of course. I see it all. Dear quaint Irene has been misleading us, for clearly it was not Lord Limpsfield and Mr. Porteous the painter – such daubs, dear Evie, no form at all – at Mallards last night, but Mr. Churchill, the First Sea Lord and the head of the Air Force, all come to seek our dear Lulu's advice. After all, if you recall, in peacetime all the leading lights of the Stock Exchange, and no doubt the Treasury as well, were accustomed to hang on her every word,' (Lucia had been known to say occasionally that Mammoncash, her broker, had come round to her way of thinking) 'even though those shares she recommended me to put all my money into did so very badly. Well now, we must hope she gave the Government rather better advice than she gave me.'

Evie waited patiently until this bitter, although confused, tirade had subsided.

'I don't think so, Elizabeth dear, or there would have been more than two cars, and I don't think dear Irene would have been asked. I would have thought Mr. Churchill was capable of conducting the war without *her* help, even if he can't do without Lucia's.'

Despite the shock of apparently being savaged by a mouse, Elizabeth found a gleam of comfort in this reply. Was Evie just the slightest bit resentful that Lucia had invited quaint Irene Coles to the inaugural officer-feast, rather than one of the more senior members of Tilling society?

'I expect he wanted to meet our brilliant young painter. Perhaps,' she said, echoing the hopes of her own unconscious mind, 'he intends to send her abroad as an official war artist.'

Poor Elizabeth! Lucia might well have been taking lessons in strategy from the Chiefs of Staff, for she had forestalled all disaffection by brilliant generalship. Evie, on her return to the Vicarage, found an invitation waiting for her; dinner, for the Padre and herself to meet the officers at Mallards the day after tomorrow. Clearly Tilling would get its ration of officers, although as with all rationing there must be some standing in line and waiting of turns first. And so it proved, for, with the exception of Irene, who was invited every time that

30

Henry came, thus securing his presence, each and every Tillingite of note received their invitation in turn, even including the Wyses; all that is, except the Mapp-Flints. For word of Elizabeth's fury had reached Lucia's ears, and she had concluded that if Elizabeth expected to meet Mr. Churchill at Mallards she would be sadly disappointed, and had better not come at all.

So Elizabeth was thrown back upon two miserable alternatives. Either she must sue for peace, and upon wretched terms, or else she must make up her mind to ignore Lucia and her officers and her magnificent gesture towards the war-effort (for, in order to feed so many officers so well and so often, she and Georgie must, between dinners, be living on fresh air and rainwater) and pretend that neither she nor the Staffordshire Regiment nor indeed the whole British Army existed. This would be wellnigh impossible to do, for all Tilling now lived and breathed officers; the latest despatches from the Mallards front were awaited with breathless excitement in the High Street next morning – how Lucia had addressed Lord Limpsfield as 'Lord Tony'; how Irene and Henry Porteous always sat next to each other and exchanged furtive glances which, to the innocent ladies of Tilling, looked remarkably like smouldering passion; how the tall, lean officer from Yorkshire, Captain Oldshaw, had admitted in strict confidence that he had been across the Channel in a small boat to inspect the German barges, and how he thought that they were mostly like to sink before they got half-way. To ignore all this was to ignore life itself. She had nothing left with which to fight back; Major Benjy might specify the exact fjord in Iceland where he thought the counterattack most likely to land and no one would pay the slightest attention. She must find *something* or else submit utterly.

Her mind was filled with these horrible imaginings as she walked briskly up through the Landgate and up the High Street one morning in search of eggs, although for all the luck she was having she might as well have been looking for phoenix eggs, which the Arabian fowl lays only once every thousand years. She would have, she realised, to go and virtually prostrate herself at the feet of the odious Mr. Rice whom, in happier times, she had so often broadsided with the full batteries of her eloquence, and this wretched thought so filled her mind like mist that she utterly failed to notice Lucia, hurrying along towards her with her eyes downcast as if wishing for once to avoid attention. Of course, even if Elizabeth had seen Lucia, she would have failed to notice her (Lucia and her officers and her merry little dinners did not, needless to say, exist), but she would not have collided with her quite so sharply, knocking the basket from her hand. Filled with furious remorse she stooped to pick up the contents of the basket, but Lucia stooped more quickly than she and began to hurl provisions back into their container without bothering to replace their newspaper wrappings. She was also trying to screen those provisions from Elizabeth's sight, and in this she was imperfectly successful.

'So sorry, dear, let me help you,' cried Elizabeth, frantically scanning Lucia's upset hoard. There was sugar and eggs, one of which was broken, its golden essence seeping away between the cobbles, a whole leg of lamb, from a lamb the size of a horse, and – ye gods! – four oranges!

'Not at all, not at all,' replied Lucia, and there was mortal fear in her eyes. 'Nothing broken.'

'Such lovely things, Lulu dear. Leg of lamb, surely?' purred Elizabeth.

'So fortunate. A food-parcel from dear Lord Whitby in America. All these treasures!' And the petrified woman almost ran down the High Street and up towards Mallards. Elizabeth stepped back and felt something against her heel. There, evidence of Lucia's undoubted crime, was an orange.

She thought quickly. Would it be better to hold it above her head and call out in a voice that all Tilling would be able to hear, 'Lucia dearest, you've dropped one of your oranges!', or should she bear that unimaginable prize back to Grebe to use as the main exhibit in Lucia's trial, as it were, when she came to broadcast this episode, complete with Lucia's ludicrous story about food-parcels, to the entire town? Strategy and the thought of the dramatic effect that could be obtained from skilful use of that orange caused her to slip the treasure into her pocket and continue on her way, murmuring as she went a prayer of thanksgiving to the God that she had believed only that same morning had utterly forsaken her.

Lucia, her heart pounding, finally managed to regain the safety of Mallards; she closed the stout front-door and, to make sure, put on the chain. What could have possessed her, she thought, to return from the interview with the seedy little man at the railway-station with all her eggs (and sugar and lamb and oranges) in one eminently insecure basket? She had been simply inviting this disaster, and that foolish, foolish lie about Lord Whitby in America and food-parcels had surely sealed her doom for ever. Had she merely dropped the basket and run, she might conceivably have come up with some convincing explanation; now she was as good as convicted of black-market trafficking. And that it should be Elizabeth Mapp-Flint – Liblib of all people – who had discovered her! The Padre or Diva or the Wyses might have had mercy on her, for had they not eaten her salt (most of it from the same source) and dined with her officers, in aid of whom she had steeped herself in sin in the first place? But, of all Tilling, Elizabeth alone had not partaken of these illegally provisioned banquets, and she alone was under no obligation to keep silent. Perhaps, just conceivably, it might all be put down to the forgeries of jealousy; it all depended. Perhaps her guests had already reached the conclusion that all the culinary glory laid before them had not been earmarked by King George for Lucia's use, and had decided to turn a blind eye. Perhaps not. . .

She hurled the evidence of her guilt into the secret

cupboard in the garden-room where, so Tilling folklore related, Elizabeth, at that time the proud owner of Mallards, had once hoarded food during a coal-strike while condemning hoarding to others as a particularly nasty form of treason. To think that she, three times Mayor of Tilling, could have sunk as low as dear Liblib!

Already the secret cupboard contained riches beyond the dreams of wartime avarice, gleaned from the gratitude of the Staffordshire Regiment or her own unlawful enterprise. Besides tea and sausages, there were eggs and jars of honey and bags of sultanas; three bottles of whisky, seven tins of peaches, nine tins of salmon. There was bacon, butter, lard (in incredible quantites), nutmeg, cinnamon and cloves. To this she added the leg of lamb, the eggs, the sugar and the three oranges. . . .

Three oranges! Numb with fear she stared at them, and in her imagination they replied with wide, Elizabeth-like grins of mocking triumph. One of these detestable objects must be still there in the High Street, or else in the possession of that awful woman. Suddenly she remembered the sight of an orange-coloured thing glimpsed out of the corner of her eye as she stooped down, rolling away behind Elizabeth's foot. It seemed inevitable now that Elizabeth had that orange.

She dashed out of the garden-room and into the house. Georgie was sitting in the drawing-room, working on his chair-cover (Britannia had turned out splendidly, but the Rother Estuary resembled nothing so much as a sleeping python).

'Georgie,' she cried, 'the most appalling thing has happened. As I was returning from the station that woman crashed into me – she must have done it on purpose – and spilt everything in the basket all over the ground. And I think she's got one of the oranges.'

'No!' said Georgie, the chair-cover falling forgotten from his hand.

'We've been found out, Georgie. Everyone in Tilling will know by now. Oh! How could I have been so foolish? And to make it worse, I told her it was a food-parcel from

Lord Whitby in America. I can't imagine what made me say that, but it was the first thing that came into my head.'

'We must think,' said Georgie, pulling himself together with an effort. 'Are you sure she's got it?'

'I can see it now, rolling behind her foot. It would be a miracle if she hasn't got it.'

'There's only one thing we can do,' said Georgie. 'You must invite her to the next dinner and let her meet all the officers. That's if she hasn't told everyone already.'

'That's true,' said Lucia. 'Perhaps she'll wait for the best opportunity. I'll write the invitation at once; she might possibly be bought off that way. Georgie, you must go down to the High Street and find out if she's told anyone yet.'

'How will I know?' he asked.

'Oh, I shouldn't worry about that,' said Lucia gloomily. 'If she has, no one will speak to you. Ever again.'

With this miserable prospect before him Georgie set off for the High Street. To his unutterable relief he found that he was still counted as a member of the human race; Diva angled for an invitation, Susan Wyse admired the new hat which he had obtained only recently and which he had been saving for a great event – but in the panic of the moment he had seized the first hat that came to hand. . . . Clearly Elizabeth had held her peace for the moment. He collected the Polish phrase-book which had just arrived and returned home. He told Lucia that they were safe for the moment, and was sent forth again to walk out to Grebe and deliver the invitation that Lucia so profoundly hoped would serve as Danegeld.

Brennus the Gaul, receiving ransom from the Romans for their city, weighed down the scale with his sword and, laughing, cried, 'Woe to the vanquished!' Even so did Elizabeth laugh, and would undoubtedly have made the same exclamation (had she thought of it) as she

35

opened the envelope and extracted one of the distinctive invitation cards that these days had the power of Royal Commands in Tilling. Why else, after all, had she spared Lucia so far? Only a stay of execution, not a reprieve, for the orange would keep for quite some time if stored in a cool, shady place, and could finally be used when she had made her bid to subvert Lucia's officers and transfer them to Grebe. She was not quite sure how to do this, but she felt absolutely confident that justice would prevail. . .

Of course. How foolish of her not to have thought of it before. How on earth could those dear soldiers, engaged as they were in a desperate struggle with a merciless enemy, consent to continue to break bread with a woman who, by engaging in such contemptible conduct, was virtually stabbing them in the back? They would spurn her as if she were a leper, and turn their Humbers towards Grebe.

'Dear Lulu's invited us to go and meet her officers,' said she to Major Benjy. 'How sweet of her! And I can tell you exactly what we'll have to eat. Leg of lamb, Benjy-boy, and I dare say orange *soufflé* to follow.'

'That'll be nice, Liz,' said he. 'But how can you tell?'

'Because I bumped into her in the street this morning and she upset her basket. And what do you think was in it? Three guesses? Very well, I shall tell you. Leg of lamb and four oranges. And now you must tell me where she got them from. Now, she told me that it was a food-parcel from dear Lord Whitby in America, but why, pray, should she unwrap the parcel and carry all those eggs and oranges down the High Street? To show them the fine Georgian houses, no doubt, and point out other features of antiquarian interest. Food-parcel fiddlesticks! Black market, Benjy.'

And with this alliterative outburst she sat down with the air of one who has realised some long-held ambition.

''Pon my soul!' exclaimed the Major. 'Mrs. Pillson fooling about on the black market. I wouldn't have believed it of her. Mayor three times and all that. Most out of character.'

'Nonsense, Benjy, it's just the sort of thing she'd do. How else do you suppose she's been feeding bevies of officers and making herself so conspicuous, without resorting to the black market? I say it is entirely in character – snatching food from the lips of starving orphans in order to impress the likes of Diva Plaistow and Susan Wyse! Quite contemptible, but entirely in character.'

'I don't think we should accept her damn' invitation in that case,' said the Major. 'Eating black-market food is almost as bad as buying it.' He paused and reflected for a moment. 'Mind you, leg of lamb. Can't remember when I last saw such a thing in this house.'

There was some point in this, for even in peacetime leg of lamb had been a rare visitor to Grebe. Other slightly less prized parts of the animal had been more usual.

'Spoiling the Egyptian, Benjy,' replied Elizabeth, who would eat human flesh in return for a chance to humiliate Lucia, let alone black-market lamb. 'Of couse, Tilling must know about this disgrace sooner or later, but I can see no reason why you and I should not enjoy ourselves at dear Lulu's expense and meet "her" officers, as it pleases her to call them – clearly His Majesty had better take care, or all his troops will transfer their allegiance to Mrs. Pillson. And I'm sure those dear soldiers will be interested to know where their sumptuous meals are coming from.'

'I say, Liz, that's a thought. They won't go back there in a hurry.'

'Indeed, Benjy-boy; and then we might do some entertaining of our own – for the good of morale, of course. Meanwhile I've written to the A.R.P., and they say they'll send an invitation to interview in a few days.'

Major Benjy froze with horror at this casual disclosure. Such awful treachery on the part of the wife of his bosom was as unexpected as it was fearful.

'I'm not so sure about that, Liz old girl,' he managed to say. 'The old wound's been playing up a lot over the last few weeks – difficult to get from one end of the room to the other some days.' (There was some truth in this, although the cause lay not with a *jezail* bullet buried in the Major's flesh, but with a hip-flask buried in his desk.) 'Wouldn't do to entrust such vital work to an old wreck of a retired soldier already wellnigh crippled by his nation's enemies.'

'Nonsense, Benjy,' replied Elizabeth, 'you're just trying to wriggle out of your responsibilities to Tilling and to Britain in her hour of need. I shall have to find a white feather and send it to you anonymously, you dear shirker.'

'Steady on, old girl,' said the Major. 'That's putting it a bit strongly, isn't it? If you feel like that I shall certainly allow my name to be considered. It's just that – well – when you're as anxious to do your bit as I am it hurts the old pride a bit if you're turned down, you know, on account of age, or injury.'

'But they won't turn you down, Benjy.'

'Well, you know, they might,' sighed the Major. He was more than afraid of refusal, he was sure of it, even if he had to feign a cardiac arrest during the actual interview. 'Still, even if the A.R.P. don't want me, I might find something else. Anyway, thank you for applying for me, Liz. Didn't quite have the nerve myself.'

'It was nothing, dear, nothing at all,' said Elizabeth, rather puzzled at this collapse of resistance. Her dear Benjy-boy, as she had occasionally observed in the past, was never more dangerous than when appearing to be obedient.

Meanwhile, the criminal gang were sitting in gloomy silence in the beautiful panelled front-room of Mallards, where, so legend had it, an early member of the house of Hanover had taken tea after his cavalry escort had lost their way *en route* from Hastings to London. But what use were the notable services rendered to the nation by their predecessors in the house, if they themselves brought shame on it with their own miserable crimes?

'There's no guarantee that she won't try and poach

our officers and then produce the orange,' moaned Lucia. 'That would be so like Elizabeth.'

'Surely by then it would be all mildewed and horrible,' replied Georgie, 'or perhaps Major Benjy might eat it when she isn't looking.'

'It's no good, Georgie. I appreciate your trying to raise my spirits but I fear that all is lost. I have no alternative now but to confess the whole business to Lord Tony and see how he reacts.'

'No!' said Georgie, thrilled by her courage. 'My dear, how brave of you. But surely it could ruin everything. And perhaps Lord Tony might never find out otherwise.'

'With Elizabeth and Major Benjy coming this evening? Do you think she could resist such an opportunity to make mischief? No, I was wrong to invite her in the first place. Better that Lord Tony hears it from my lips, directly, then from Elizabeth's. If he's terriby offended, I shall cancel all further dinner parties and have influenza for a month, and you will have to go and stay with Hermy and Ursy until it's safe to come back.'

'I think I'd rather stay here and be ostracised than spend a month with my sisters, if you don't mind. Oh look, there's a Humber coming out of Church Square. It's Lord Tony, and he's getting out. He's coming here. Do you think he can have heard already, from Irene or someone, and has come to say he's not coming – oh, you know what I mean,' he concluded crossly.

There was a knock at the door, and presently Lord Tony, attired as ever in spotless khaki, was shown in by Foljambe. He had a parcel in his hands, wrapped in brown paper.

'My dear,' he said to the trembling pair before him, 'I've just popped in to give you these. Four tins of salmon, Canadian I'm afraid, but fresh salmon is terribly tricky, isn't it? I couldn't get any through the N.A.A.F.I., so I had to consult a most unpatriotic little man who lives near the railway-station.' He paused and consulted Lucia's expression, which was rather strange. 'My dear, you aren't horrified, are you? I hope I haven't

39

offended your principles by offering you black-market fish.'

Lucia's first reaction was to say, 'No, of course not, there's nine more from the same source in the garden-room cupboard,' but she restrained herself and smiled.

'Dear Lord Tony,' she purred, 'do you suppose a poor civilian like myself could provide a square meal for four hungry soldiers from the Government ration? Very well then, let us not mention the horrid subject again.'

'Well said!' exclaimed Lord Limpsfield. 'Some people are so stuffy and silly. But I always say that it's all fair in love and war, and there's a war on, and I love salmon *mousse*, so that's fair enough. *Au reservoir!*'

'Well, that's something,' said Lucia as the Humber bumped away over the cobbles.

'There's still Elizabeth,' replied Georgie. 'Even if she doesn't frighten off the officers, she can make us horribly unpopular in the town. I don't believe that Tilling will be so broad-minded, even if they know that Lord Tony thinks it's all right.'

'We shall have to wait and see, I suppose. After all, it's not such a terrible crime. If we didn't buy it, all that food would go to waste, and that would be a crime. It's only for the officers, not for ourselves, and besides, it's rather dashing to buy black-market food to give to the troops. Like Robin Hood, stealing from the poor to help the rich – I mean the other way round.'

That, however, remained very much to be seen, as Lucia welcomed her guests the next evening. There was Lord Tony, and the dashing Captain Oldshaw; no Henry (and therefore, mercifully, no Irene) but instead there was Lieutenant Custard, an excessively shy young man with large pink ears who before the war had been that sophisticated playwright Grant Fever, author of the scandalous play *Hollow Shells*. There was also David Ashby, who was an anthropologist and had been to many quite extraordinary places. All in all there never had been such a brilliant gathering of officers at

Mallards, but it was not the *enfant terrible* of the British stage that Lucia fixed her attention upon, nor yet the discoverer of five quite unknown African tribes. Rather, it was Elizabeth Mapp-Flint that she observed the most closely, as no doubt Major Benjy in his youth had studied a tiger which was in the act of deciding whether or not to spring. In theory Lucia was safe from anything Elizabeth might do; in practice, however, anything might happen. Certainly the arrival of the salmon *mousse*, greeted with cries of rapture by the rest of the table, seemed to twist some nerve in Elizabeth's face, so that she winced as if forcibly restraining herself from some violent exclamation. As for the leg of lamb, Thyestes could not have looked so shocked when, duped by his foes, he ate his own son's flesh. Yet still Elizabeth kept her silence, contenting herself with a savage smile that caused Georgie, who intercepted it on its way to Lucia, to spill his glass of wine. As the meal dragged on, Lucia almost wished that she would make her move, but still she chatted to Captain Oldshaw about Napoleon and Ilkley Moor.

The leg of lamb departed and was replaced with the orange *soufflé*. It was a fine specimen, light as a feather and tall as a steeple, and it seemed to fascinate Elizabeth like a hypnotist's watch. She felt the blood pounding through her veins, and began to speak.

'Lulu, dear, what a particularly splendid *soufflé*. How clever you are – such flavour!'

Despite the wine, Lucia's palate was dry. She tried to speak but could only manage a broad smile.

'My congratulations, Mrs. Pillson,' said Captain Oldshaw. 'Haven't tasted anything like this since before the war. Mind you, my sister in Harrogate makes a very fine orange *soufflé*. Not as fine as this, though.'

'And so clever of you to have managed to find all the ingredients,' continued Elizabeth remorselessly. 'I haven't been able to get any oranges for simply ages.'

'Oh, you can pick them up in the High Street from time to time,' replied Lucia, without thinking what she was saying. This seemed to urge Elizabeth towards the kill.

41

For her part, Elizabeth smiled, showing all her teeth. 'Really, dear? You must tell me where you get yours, then, for I'm sure I haven't seen any such thing in the shops myself.'

'I don't know about you or Mrs. Pillson,' said Lord Tony, 'but I can usually find one or two on the *marché noir*, although the price is exorbitant. Such a benign institution, if one doesn't mind risking the condemnation of a few narrow-minded souls. But really, if one refused to eat anything that couldn't show its papers, so to speak, one would grow as thin as a rake, and anyone can see by my deplorable figure that I don't get by on Army rations.'

Elizabeth had been engaged in swallowing a spoonful of *soufflé*, as he said this, and a sort of minor explosion occurred in her mouth, followed by some violent coughing. From malicious joy her expression had changed to outraged innocence (for despite her scrupulous honesty she had managed to preserve her ample shape; if stoutness was equated with black-marketeering, she must be accused) and as soon as she was clear of *soufflé*-shrapnel she exclaimed, 'Oh, shame on you, dear Lord Limpsfield, encouraging us civilians to indulge in such unpatriotic activities! I would never dream of doing such a thing.'

'Well now, Mrs. Mapp-Flint,' replied Lord Tony with a twinkle in his eye, 'I'm sure you wouldn't, but in that case I'm equally sure I would never come to dinner at your house – Grebe, isn't it? – for I'm afraid I like my food, and if I'm to be called upon to drive Hitler into the sea at a moment's notice I would hate to have to do it on Army fare. Isn't that so, Oldshaw?'

'Quite right, Limpsfield. I'm sure the Hun has no such compunctions. Stuffing himself with all that French *cuisine*, I shouldn't wonder. Wouldn't like to face a storm-trooper stuffed with *crêpes suzettes* on an ounce of boiled beef and two carrots.'

' 'Pon my soul, Liz,' said Major Benjy, whose perceptions may have been clouded slightly by Lucia's excellent wine, 'I couldn't have got through my spell in

42

His Majesty's service – India, you know – ' (they did) 'without a square meal inside me. Come to that, we're not so blamless ourselves.'

'What do you mean?' cried Elizabeth hoarsely.

'Well, when I was looking for a handkerchief the other day,' he replied, eager to ally himself to the band of dashing buccaneers, 'I came across an orange in the drawer. Now I dare say that that never saw the inside of Twistevant's, eh, old girl? Went down a treat, as well.' And he winked broadly.

Elizabeth cast down her napkin and stood up.

'Come now, Benjy, we must be going home. Such a long way back to Grebe in the black-out. Thank you so much for our delicious dinner, Lulu darling. So sweet of you to ask us. Come, Benjy.'

'But I haven't had any coffee,' said Benjy, as the excellent wine began to assert itself. 'A cup of coffee and a li'l spot port with my friend Lord Tony Limpsfield. Spot of coffee, cup of port, li'l rubber of Bridge. Don't want to go back to Grebe yet. Want spot port and cup of coffee.'

'My driver will run you home in the Humber, Mrs. Mapp-Flint,' said Lord Tony. 'You mustn't dream of leaving us yet.'

'No, dear Lord Limpsfield, I couldn't allow Army petrol to be wasted on us. Benjy!'

Bitter and dark as any cup of coffee were Elizabeth's thoughts as she strode back to Grebe through the gathering gloom. It was just as well, she thought to herself, that she had declined Lord Tony's offer; anyone who had seen her riding home in the Humber would no doubt assume that she had been arrested for black-marketeering and was being taken off to prison. Major Benjy, having got over the disappointment of not having any coffee, declared that he wanted to go down to the Harbour and inspect the troops, and Elizabeth had a job to prevent him, so carried away was he by contact with soldiers. Arriving at last at Grebe, she took two Aspros and went to bed. Meanwhile, at Mallards, Lucia was playing the opening bars of the Moonlight Sonata. . .

3

Breakfast was a dour meal at Grebe next morning, for both the Mapp-Flints were feeling wretched, though for entirely different reasons. The Major sat toying with an enormous cup full of boiling water (faintly tea-stained), his mind divided between resentment and fear. His better part of valour (and Major Benjy's valour was largely composed of the better part) told him that a show of submission, such as becoming an air-raid warden, was demanded of him in order to keep peace and tranquillity in the home; but the old tiger-slaying Adam, nagging away like toothache, insisted that the slavery endured by occupied France was as nothing compared to his own subservience in not insisting upon his inalienable right to a little cup of coffee and a glass of port on the rare occasions on which he was able to dine out. Elizabeth, for her part, could think only of the humiliation she had suffered at Lucia's hands, the need for revenge and the difficulty of procuring it, and, of course, the loss of the orange.

From the military circles of Tilling she was utterly banished, without a shadow of a doubt. In the horrid confusion of the previous evening she had snatched defeat from the jaws of victory, and by some process she could not, even now, reconstruct, Lucia's crime had been transferred to her. Thank God no other member of Tilling society had been there to witness it.

As to Lucia's exposure and condemnation in the eyes of the town, as distinct from the Harbour, she was still in two minds. Every fibre of her being urged her to hasten to the High Street and broadcast the crime in plain, unambiguous English. But how could she be certain of being believed? And even if she were, was it not possible that all Tilling was infected with the same deplorable attitude to black-marketeering as Mallards and Tilling Harbour? Finally, if this last possibility proved to be the case, the thought that she had been depriving herself of such little luxuries as a few additional eggs and spoonsful of sugar bit into her soul like an ulcer.

Furthermore, her social exclusion, instead of being ended by her encounter on the road to Twistevant's, had been consolidated, for now she could not dream of joining (and so leading) the officer-based culture that now constituted all social activity in the town. Well, if she could not join them she must beat them. Courage and faith in her own abilities she had never lacked, but the scale of the task appalled her. She must hold her hand until she had established Tilling's views of the *marché noir*, as Lord Limpsfield had so glibly called it. Meanwhile she must cast about for some secret weapon. . .

Her reverie was interrupted by the arrival of the post. A letter each. Elizabeth opened hers and read it distractedly, for her mind still moved upon high strategy, so that only after she had put it back in its envelope and replaced it on a side-plate did she realise what it said.

'Benjy!' she exclaimed, but the Major interrupted her with a cry of 'Liz, old girl!'

'Well?' she demanded impatiently.

'Marvellous piece of news,' he said. 'You know Phillipson, the bank manager? He's been transferred to Folkestone!'

'Benjy, how wonderful,' said Elizabeth in a voice loaded with irony. 'I must say that has cheered me up considerably.'

'The best part is yet to come,' said he obliviously. 'He was the Officer Commanding, Tilling Home Guard. Dashed silly if you ask me. He couldn't lead an ace of diamonds, let alone a platoon. Anyway, they've offered

45

me the job. Old soldier. Highly respected in the community. No one else available.'

'No!' exclaimed his wife, and the joyful contents of her own letter melted from her mind like snow in the sunshine. 'Benjy, how marvellous.'

'Not half, old girl. I shall only be a Lieutenant – reduced to the ranks, ha! – but I'll have a platoon of trained men equipped with – now let me see – Ross rifles and a Lewis gun, whatever that may mean, and be solely responsible for the defence of Tilling in the event of an invasion; that's if there aren't any Regulars here, of course.'

And since, of course, there would be, he reflected, the job would be a sinecure, but attended with all the respect and dignity he so sorely lacked at the moment. A retired Major could be deprived of his coffee only too easily; a serving Lieutenant was an entirely different proposition. . .

'I wonder if I can still get into my old uniform,' he mused. 'Should be able to – kept in trim after all, all that golf and walking that infernally long distance into town every day. I'll go and try it on immediately.'

'Better still, Benjy. Listen to this. I've had a letter from my cousin Herbert, my aunt Elizabeth's grandson. The Lancashire branch of the family I seem to recall.' (The letter was post-marked 'Liverpool'.) 'He is an officer in the Royal Air Force, he tells me, and he's going to be stationed very near here, although he doesn't say exactly where – oh Benjy, that must mean his work is top secret, some dear new fighter or something – and he hopes he may come and call on me. There! Isn't that splendid news?'

Benjy had never met Cousin Herbert, of the Lancashire branch of the family (neither, in all honesty, had Elizabeth), but a fellow-soldier must be an ally.

'Excellent, Liz. We'll show Mrs. Pillson how troops ought to be entertained. Keeping morale up, eh?' He winked broadly. Elizabeth smiled. 'Yes, old girl, no stuffy music at Grebe. A good dinner, a glass of wine, a few rubbers of Bridge. That's the stuff to – ah – give the troops.'

Elizabeth sensed danger here. The presence of troops at Grebe wuld not lead to any relaxation of the strict licensing laws that prevailed in the house. She decided, however, not to press the point. Nothing should mar the joy of this unexpected good fortune, following close upon the heels of disaster.

'Go and try on your uniform, Benjy. Why, I declare I shall be quite in awe of you. And you must come with me to the High Street wearing it. Hurry up now.'

It is a sad fact of life that the material from which military uniforms are made tends to shrink alarmingly with the passage of the years, especially in those areas that encircle the waist. Even the belt and the boots seemed to have grown smaller, so that the only article of Benjy's uniform which had not shrunk was the cap, which seemed, if anything, to have grown (or could it be that the Major's locks had thinned as the rest of him had increased?). Another effect of the passage of time had been several attacks of moth. Nonetheless, Elizabeth decided he did look rather more striking in his uniform than in the antiquated tweeds that were his usual attire. Even so, it would be wise to allow certain repairs and alterations to be carried out before parading the new Officer Commanding, Tilling Home Guard, in the public streets; perhaps it would also be wise to conceal the news of Benjy's new honour, and the imminent arrival of Cousin Herbert, so as to have her best cards in reserve. Lucia's exposure was still to come. Should by any disastrous chance this manoeuvre backfire as well, she would have riches to fall back on. They were dining this evening at the Wyses (barley water as well as wine to be offered to the guests), with Diva, she recalled. She also recollected that the red-velvet evening-gown, so recently a pair of shabby curtains but soon to be the envy of all female Tilling, was almost ready. In all the excitement of the last few days, with pinnacles of hope being built and turned into pits of despair, she had forgotten all about it and the sensation it must inevitably cause. With a broad smile, she shouldered her basket like a shield and went forth to do battle in the High Street.

There she met the Padre and wee wifie, triumphantly bearing a short string of sausages out of Mr. Worthington, the butcher's. She bore down on them as the Spanish galliasses did upon the English ships of Drake.

'Padre, dear, and Evie – a new hat surely, or is it the old straw hat with some pretty ribbons? – what a glorious day. It's hard to believe in the horrid war when the sun is shining so brightly. Sausages,' she said, and a bitter thought crossed her mind, 'how very fortunate. Any left?'

'No,' said Evie.

'How disappointing. I shall have to give my poor Benjy fish again today, if there's any to be had.'

'There's nair a bittie o' fish to be had in a' Tilling, and there's yon ocean, that teems wi' the guid Lord's plenty. War is a terrible thing, begorra.' The Padre sighed.

'Oh dear. Well, an omelette perhaps. So nourishing.'

'And as for the wee eggies, 'twill be a miracle indeed if we see mair than wan or twa o' they before Michaelmas Eve. 'Twud be a hard thing for our Lord to feed the five thousand now, for where would he be after gettin' the three loaves and the twa wee fishes, with the shortage of food and the Government rations?'

Evie squeaked with horror at this blasphemy from the lips of her husband. Elizabeth smiled, for it was a perfect opening for her pitiful tale.

'Oh, but Padre, you must consult our dear Lucia on that score. Why, she could feed the five thousand from the contents of her market-basket. A new miracle, perhaps, for did not my Benjy-boy and I dine at Mallards last night, and was there not orange *soufflé* set before us – and such an orange *soufflé* I declare I never have

48

seen. So light! So dainty! I'm sure there must have been a lot of eggs in that, even if there are none in the shops.'

'No!' exclaimed Evie. 'Orange *soufflé*!' Her face lit up as if she had heard angel voices singing.

'And salmon *mousse* to start, and a leg of lamb,' continued Elizabeth. 'What a banquet it was to be sure. Yet I wasn't a bit surprised, for I had suspected as much.'

'Did ye now, guidwife Mapp-Flint? And pray tell us why ye thought that.'

'I was walking along this very street only the other day,' said Elizabeth, warming to her theme, 'when who should bump into me but our dear Lulu? And what do you suppose was in her basket, which fell to the ground and spilled itself at my feet? Three guesses? No? Very well, I see I shall have to tell you. There was a leg of lamb, and a pound of sugar, and a dozen eggs, and four oranges. Now, where do you suppose all these treasures came from? And no doubt you've been to dinner with dearest Lulu and her lovely officers, and had roast pork and lemon *sorbet*, or boiled beef and figs in honey, and where would they all have come from? It's a puzzle to me, I must confess. My poor brains can't fathom it, for poor Major Benjy and I have difficulty in feeding ourselves on the rations we receive.'

'And what did she say?' enquired Evie impatiently.

'I asked her of course, and oh! the lucky thing, for she had received a parcel from America, no less, with all those gorgeous things in it. Fancy that now! But I thought to myself that parcel must have fairly raced across the Atlantic for the eggs and the lamb to have stayed so perfectly fresh.'

'That'll be it, then,' said the Padre, relieved. He too had wondered how Lucia managed to procure such delicacies, and his conscience had troubled him with thoughts unworthy of his cloth. ''Tis a wonder how our valiant merchant seamen do cross those turbulent oceans like swift birdies. Now I'll confess, Mistress Mapp-Flint, that I had ma wee doubts that mebbe some of those fine viands had been bought on the black market. Ah, but what it is to have so little faith in human nature.'

Elizabeth was stunned by this reply. In desperation she cast aside all pretence of ignorance.

'And why, pray, should she unwrap her parcel and trot about the streets of Tilling with them in her basket? Answer me that.'

Both Evie and the Padre thought deeply for a moment, until a look of reverent illumination spread over the Padre's face, as if yet another aspect of Lucia's saintliness had been revealed to him.

'Isna that no so like Mrs. Pillson the noo! Sithen she gets a wee parcel o' viands she canna rest until she's been to the hospital or the home for the auld folks and shared her guid fortune wi' the aged and infirm o' Tilling. You enquire of her, Mrs. Mapp-Flint, and I've no doubt but that'll turn out to be the cause of it. Mind you, from what I know o' our Lucia, she wouldna dream o' mentioning the fact. She is an example to us a'.'

'And so lucky,' Elizabeth almost screamed, desperate to counter these horrible allegations, 'to have such good friends who send her so many parcels that she can virtually feed all Tilling and the Staffordshires as well. Why, there must be a whole fleet of ships standing by to rush provisions to her past the U-boats. Fancy!'

' 'Tis fortunate indeed she's after being, and so like her tae share her fortune wi' others, keeping no a morsel of it for hersen. What an inspiration to the parish.'

So profoundly inspired did Elizabeth appear to be that she hurried off down the street without a word, no doubt to devote the rest of her life to being worthy of such a fellow citizen.

It was with some trepidation that Diva rang the ponderous bell of Starling Cottage. The dusk was gathering in Porpoise Street, but not sufficiently to hide the evidence of her crime, which was literally all around her, for her rotund form was dressed in it. A large acreage of bottle-green *crêpe marocaine* to be exact, shaped into an

50

evening-gown and topped with a white Bridge-coatee. The coupons for all this splendour, needless to say, had not originally been issued to Mrs. Godiva Plaistow. Torment had wracked her soul for the best part of the week, and she was sure that she had lost pounds of weight through sheer worry. In a mad, reckless moment she had listened, like Adam in the Garden of Eden, to the serpent-like temptations of her maid Janet's nephew, who had offered her a sheaf of coupons for the gigantic sum of thirty shillings. But if Diva had a weakness (and she had more than one) it was for dress; those coupons were the passport to green pastures of *crêpe marocaine* and, being a weak and foolish old widow, she had (after a little haggling) succumbed. The horror of exposure had caused her to lie awake at night; the thought of wasting the stupendously elegant cloth had tortured her during the day. She had wracked her brains for some explanation: an old roll of material she had bought years ago and forgotten all about – no, for not a soul who knew her would believe that she could forget all about a roll of *crêpe marocaine*. An old dress, newly cleaned and refurbished – no, for who could have forgotten such a glorious creation? The very splendour of the garment would convict her. She pictured herself in a few weeks' time, sewing not *crêpe marocaine* in Tilling but mailbags in Holloway.

With a trembling heart she entered the drawing-room. There, in front of the broad fireplace, stood Mr. Wyse, dressed in a magnificent and undoubtedly new suit of mohair with a silk cummerbund, while his wife was a vision of royal-blue lace. A glorious relief flooded over all three.

'Why, Mrs. Plaistow,' said Mr. Wyse, 'such a beautiful dress, if I may make so bold as to say so. And such a delightful shade of green.'

'Your dress-suit. Mohair,' said Diva. 'How splendid, and a silk cummerbund too. And blue lace! Gorgeous.' She paused. It was a time for mutual confession, a cleansing of the soul. 'Janet's nephew. Had some black-market coupons. Couldn't resist.'

'Alas,' said Susan, 'in a moment of utter weakness I too succumbed. A new suit for my Algernon, a new gown for myself. Oh, Mrs. Plaistow, what will become of us? What will Elizabeth say?'

'Something nasty I expect, but we won't take any notice. If she acts all high and mighty about it, she can go home and leave us to our sins. Highly worthwhile ones in your case. Wish I'd thought of blue lace. In any case, I bet she's dabbled in the black market herself before now. Everyone does,' she added hopefully.

'It is not,' said Mr. Wyse, 'as if we are stealing, or depriving others of their share. If some people believe that they can do without additions to their wardrobe in exchange for a little extra income, that is their own choice. No doubt they are poor people who could not afford to spend money on clothes. In return for their coupons they receive money, which is of far greater use to them. I call it a fair, indeed helpful, system and not in the least like the pernicious black-market trade in foodstuffs, which I would be the first to condemn. We simply provide others with what they require in return for what we are prepared to pay for.'

This elegant sophistry, worthy of a leading K.C., served to close the unseemly discussion, and the conversation turned to more amenable topics such as Lucia's last officers' party, until a ring at the door signified the arrival of the Mapp-Flints.

'Good evening, Mr. Wyse, Susan – blue lace! Such a pretty colour, and so flattering – and dearest Diva – is that a new Bridge-coat dear? – so many dear friends and such elegance. I'm afraid my Benjy-boy and I must look like church-mice in such company. Now, I have some rather shocking news that I must tell you at once, for I declare that if I have to keep it to myself for another minute I shall expire. Such a dreadful thing, and you must all promise not to be too furious with the dear culprit.'

Elizabeth, had she not been so intent on Lucia's destruction, would have noticed that she did not have the full attention of her audience. All eyes were fixed on her (really quite magnificent) red-velvet costume, all minds were leaping to the same conclusion, and Diva secretly suspected the assistance of Janet's helpful nephew.

'Tell us, dear Mrs. Mapp-Flint,' said Mr. Wyse at last. 'What is it?'

'I'm afraid we have a black-marketeer in our midst,' said Elizabeth dramatically. Three people froze in horror, and Major Benjy took the opportunity to obtain a second glass of sherry. 'There! I sound like the detective in one of those dreadful penny-thrillers. I was doing my shopping in the High Street the other day, hunting for a little scrap of fish for my Benjy's dinner, when Lucia walked straight into me and dropped her basket. And what should fall out on to the cobbles but a dozen eggs, a leg of lamb, a pound of sugar and four oranges. Of course she pretended they were a parcel from America – such a childish lie – but I could plainly see that they were not legitimately come by. Poor Lucia! So sad, don't you think? She has to impress us by entertaining those soldiers, and then finds she must resort to breaking the law in order to do so. And to think that she was once the Mayor of our dear Tilling. What a comedown.'

These revelations, worthy of the messenger in a Greek tragedy, did not somehow seem to be having the desired effect of thrilling the listeners with pity and terror. The Wyses looked at each other. Diva grew red in the face until she was the precise colour of Elizabeth's gown, and then exclaimed, 'Well really, Elizabeth, I must say I don't think very much of that. There you go accusing poor Lucia behind her back of dreadful things, on very flimsy evidence, let me add, and you're dressed from head to toe in black-market velvet yourself. I'm sorry if my frankness offends you in any way, Elizabeth, but we have been friends for a long time, and I feel it's my duty to speak my mind. There!' she added.

Elizabeth tried to speak but no words came. Her

tongue had cleaved to the roof of her mouth, as if she had forgotten Zion.

'If Lucia is doing her bit by entertaining a few officers, good luck to her. I'm sure she's far too patriotic to stoop to such miserable depths as buying food to which she is not entitled,' continued Diva grandly. 'If she says she gets parcels from America I'm sure I believe her, even if you don't. There it is.'

Elizabeth really looked as if she was going to cry.

'But it's curtains,' she almost sobbed, 'a pair of velvet curtains I made into a dress. I would never dream. . . .'

'Of course not, Mrs. Mapp-Flint,' said Mr. Wyse icily, for all that his tone said the opposite. 'I am sure that we all believe that you are above such conduct. I must add, however, that I for my part believe that Mrs. Pillson is equally above suspicion.'

'Come on now, Liz,' said Major Benjy, 'what price that orange, eh? That Lord Tony caught you out last night, and now you've been caught out again.' The third glass of sherry burned within him, he mistook it for righteous indignation. 'Doesn't do to go calling the kettle black, old girl, not in front of company when the accused is not present to give her side of the story. Dashed fine orange it was, too. Anyway, all old friends together, and we shall say no more about it. Capital sherry, Wyse, prewar I'll be bound. Don't mind if I do.'

'It was one of Lucia's oranges,' protested Elizabeth.

'Very kind of her to give you one, I'm sure,' said Diva. 'Fine way you repay her generosity, I must say. Ah, dinner's ready, is it, Susan dear? Come on, Major Benjy.'

Throughout the meal Mr. and Mrs. Wyse seemed to run a commentary on the food, stressing the blamelessness of its origin. Whitebait was rare, of course, very much so, but they had been exceedingly fortunate . . . . Venison too, such a luxury, but some friends in Scotland had been kind enough to. . . . Such a good crop of elderflowers this year, and they make such an excellent jelly. Elizabeth hid most of these treats behind her knife and fork and was far too dispirited to prevent

54

Major Benjy from having several glasses of Mr. Wyse's excellent wine.

Once again Elizabeth felt that it was necessary to leave early in order to get back to Grebe before the cloudless sky began to send down torrents of rain. Once again Major Benjy was compelled, under loud protests, to do without his little cup of coffee and glass of port. . . As the door closed behind them a buzz of conversation started to rise and did not die down for quite some time.

Agamemnon, so the poet records, allowed some god to take away his wits when he snatched Briseis from doting Achilles, and this treacherous deity must have been active in Tilling the next morning, for he took away the wits of Elizabeth Mapp-Flint as she joined the queue in Worthington's the next day without looking carefully to see who was in front of her.

'Hello, Mapp,' said quaint Irene. 'Fancy seeing you here.'

'Why, quaint one?' asked Elizabeth, cursing her lack of prudence.

'Wouldn't have thought you needed to stand in line like us ordinary mortals to get your pound of flesh. Easier ways, if you don't mind breaking the law, eh, girlie?'

And she winked, almost as broadly as Major Benjy.

'What can you mean, Miss Coles?'

'I'd have thought you'd have got all your meat on the – now what is the new term for it? – the *marché noir*. I call that a bit greedy, Mapp. Not content with stuffing yourself with your ill-gotten gains, you've got to come and get your coupon's worth off King George. What do you do with it all? I'm sorry if my frankness offends you in any way, Elizabeth, but we have been friends for a long time and I feel it's my duty to speak my mind.'

This had gone far enough. 'Once and for all, Miss Coles, I have never engaged, nor do I ever intend to engage, in illicit trafficking in contraband food or clothing. Whatever nasty rumours you may have heard, that is all they are – rumours.'

The usual hum of conversation that hung over the butcher's queue like smoke had quite died away. Evie Bartlett, whose interest at this time would normally be in only the pound of liver and two pork chops that she had miraculously managed to convert to her own use, was trying to look over her shoulder while keeping her eyes fixed on the counter.

'Oh come on now, Liz,' said Irene, 'what about that orange?'

Evie nearly dropped the liver on to the sawdust-covered floor, and the Padre's faith in human nature took another deep but fascinating dive.

'Which orange?' said Elizabeth.

'I do call that a bit low, Mapp. Oranges are supposed to be for the children. Now, I know that you and Major Benjy have never been blessed in that respect, but. . . .'

'Irene Coles, you have gone too far!' shrieked Elizabeth, stung to the quick not by the appalling frankness of the remark but by the reference to one of her innumerable past deceits. 'Such a thoughtless creature, to rub salt into that old, old wound,' she added, retrieving something from the shambles.

'See if you can't get me a pair of silk stockings next time you meet your spiv,' called Irene after Elizabeth's retreating form. 'Some people!' she remarked to the world at large. 'No scruples. Still, what do you expect of someone who hoarded food during the coal-strike?' And, moving to the counter, she virtuously bought her four ounces of corned beef.

4

Although Elizabeth might well have thought that she had a monopoly of misery and unhappiness in Tilling that morning, Lucia also was undergoing a certain torment. Her cook, who had been with her for so many years in both Riseholme and Tilling, had seen a leaflet distributed by the Government encouraging civilians to leave areas of the country liable to be in the front line of invasion, and had taken it into her head that the Government meant what it printed. As if this was not enough, Grosvenor, the twin pillar of the house, had been directed to go and work at the Ordnance Factory. It had only been by the merest chance that Foljambe had been spared – she had an allergy to cordite, as it transpired – but the blow was horribly severe. Another cook was not to be had, and Grosvenor at least had been able to prepare food of a sort. But, as even Georgie was prepared to admit, and as her husband, the long-suffering Cadman, would be only too pleased to confirm, Foljambe was no cook, unrivalled though she undoubtedly was in the fields of endeavour to which she had devoted her life. Food had to be brought across the sea at the risk of brave men's lives; it would be sinful to expose it to Foljambe's culinary skills.

'Georgie,' said Lucia, collapsed in the garden-room, 'what shall we do? Lord Tony and Lieutenant Custard are bringing Prince Andrei and heaven knows who else to dinner on Thursday week. We must give them something to eat, if only corned beef and bottled plums.'

'I don't know,' admitted Georgie. 'This tar'some war is

going to spoil everything. I can't get my embroidery silk, however hard I try, and as for silver polish for cleaning my *bibelots*, why, they're likely to corrode away any day now. It's hopeless. And now this! And of course there's. . .'

He fell silent. He was going to say 'there's my hair-dye,' but even after all these years they still kept up the pretty fiction that nature, not the hairdresser in Hastings, maintained Georgie's hair and beard in their rich auburn colour. Even if the worry of losing Grosvenor and the cook could turn his hair white, surely it would not do it so very quickly. 'And of course we'll have to starve now, as well. Really, it's as bad as being occupied by the Hun.'

'Courage, Georgie. We cannot allow ourselves to become disheartened. One of us will have to learn to cook. I will try and learn.'

'Do you know anything about it?' asked Georgie.

'No,' admitted Lucia frankly.

'Neither do I, except that if you put cornflour in a sauce it thickens it, although what cornflour is, or whether it's good for a sauce to be thickened, I haven't a clue.'

'Never mind though, Georgie, it's a start,' said Lucia firmly, for she dreaded the thought of cooking. 'Think of all the great male *chefs* of the past. Escoffier! For a woman cookery is a chore, a drudge, but to a man it should be an art, a science! I have to entertain my guests, for no dinner party can be without a hostess even if it lacks a host. But you, Georgie, you learn things so quickly, and you're so nimble and delicate with your hands. I believe you'd learn it easily, and be very good at it too.'

The words of protest and refusal froze on Georgie's lips. For the thought of what he could achieve were he to apply himself to the art, combined with the mention of Escoffier, suddenly inspired him. He pictured himself, the loyal Foljambe at his side like the Sorcerer's apprentice (no, that was wrong), conjuring *soufflés* to rise by some necromantic power, or judging by skill and not by the cowardly use of a clock, exactly when the duck was ready. He would create soups out of scraps that would normally be cast out for the dogs, or build cakes that rivalled the mosques of Istanbul for their delicate geometric embellishments. . . . No one in Tilling could cook, not even Diva; the cakes that she had sold in the tea-shop she had once run in her house in the High Street had been made by her Janet. Surely the possession of such a fundamental skill, elevated into an art-form by his own artistic nature, would mark him out as a practical man, fitted to face a new sterner age, invested with all the dignity of labour. . . . Brimming with these socialistic ideas, he turned to Lucia.

'Very well, then,' said the nascent William Morris, 'how can I learn?'

'I'm sure that cook can give you a few lessons before she leaves,' replied Lucia, astonished by this ready capitulation. 'Can't be vewwy diffy for you big strong men if we silly women can do it. Oo vewwy clever Georgie, learn cooky so, so quickly.'

And so, his eyes blazing, Georgie retired to the kitchen to learn cooky. Cooky, however, proved to be rather harder than he had at first imagined, and an enormous amount of priceless food was destroyed before he had grasped the bare essentials. Lucia went often to the unpatriotic little man at the railway-station to obtain the raw materials for Georgie's pyrotechnics, while Georgie, who regarded a kitchen-range with the same awe as a Polynesian islander regards an aeroplane, vowed time and again that the tar'some thing was beyond him. But cook left, to seek the relative safety of a niece's house in Wolverhampton, and the household was forced to consume Georgie's burnt offerings at the shrine of the sainted Escoffier. When all seemed utterly lost and Georgie, having produced some omelettes as tough as *papier-mâché* trays, had retired to the garden-room in shame, Lucia remembered something. It was a book she had bought years ago, when there was a general feeling of approaching revolution, and a widespread fear that soon there would be no more cooks. The unprepossessing title of the volume was *Cooking for Gentle-folks*, and the author, a retired clergyman, explained in language that even Georgie could understand exactly what you had to do to dead animals and plants before they were fit for humans to eat. Quite remarkably soon Georgie had risen from the ashes of burnt herrings and carbonated toast, and from then on there was no stopping him. Amusing little snacks began to materialise at entirely unsuitable times of the day, pastry turned up all over the house, and sauces seemed to ooze up from the kitchen-table as from some subterranean well.

'There, you see,' said Georgie as they sat back in their chairs after consuming a remarkably fine Woolton Pie, 'I knew I could do it.'

'So palatable!' exclaimed Lucia. 'And the pastry so light. Georgie, you're an absolute marvel. And in so short a time, too.'

'It was that book,' admitted the *chef*. 'It had everything in it I needed, and then I sort of found an ability I never even guessed was there. Fancy that! There's me being able to cook all these years, and not knowing it. And weren't those potatoes good?'

'Exquisite. Why, I've eaten better in the last few days than ever before.' Georgie blushed. 'I can't think how we managed in the past. And so very clever of you to use things we can get to imitate things we can't.'

'I shall do lobster à *la Riseholme* for Lord Tony and Prince Andrei,' declared Georgie decisively. 'I've looked up the recipe, and it's quite straightforward really. A few things I shall have to work out substitutes for, but nothing terribly hard. And to think how dreadfully difficult I found it to begin with when it's really so simple. You could do it, or Evie Bartlett, or even dear Elizabeth. After the war I think I might open a restaurant.'

For a split second Lucia wondered whether she

should not have volunteered for this seemingly arduous but apparently pleasant duty. But she dismissed the thought, and decided that it was indeed a special talent of Georgie's that had lain hidden for so long.

'Lobster *à la Riseholme* it shall be then. And now I think I must go down to the High Street, and you must come with me, for you haven't left the house since you started to cook. A little fresh air after all those delicious fumes. Everyone will be wondering what has become of you.'

So, gathering shopping-baskets and ration-books, they set off down the narrow street, past quaint Irene's dewelling and round the corner. A quite remarkable spectacle greeted them. Major Benjy, in a tight, antiquated but undoubtedly authentic uniform, was leading a group of similarly antiquated but perhaps rather less genuine-looking soldiers, all armed to the teeth with an assortment of deadly weapons, in the middle of the street. Walking beside the Major, for all the world like a dangerous prisoner with a military escort, was Elizabeth with her shopping-basket over her arm.

'Platoon – halt!' commanded the Major, and the soldiers of Tilling performed an approximate manoeuvre to that effect. 'Good day to you, Pillson, and Mrs. Pillson.'

'Good morning, Major Benjy, such a lovely day it is too. Elizabeth dear, a new skirt surely? How you do stretch your coupons,' said Lucia, smiling graciously. 'Any nice things in the shops today?' And she peered into Elizabeth's basket as if searching it for black-market food.

'Very little, alas,' said Elizabeth, also smiling. 'And Mr. Georgie. Such a stranger these days. Haven't seen you for goodness knows how long. Not been unwell, I hope?'

Georgie had, up until now, been feeling remarkably healthy. Now he felt ever so slightly sick.

'A touch of this tar'some influenza, I'm afraid. All gone now,' he managed to say, although his eyes remained glued to the Major's uniform. Judicious work with the needle had not quite managed to undo the shrinking effect of time, but it had entirely repaired the moth-holes.

'Are you sure, Mr. Georgie? You look a trifle pale to me. And how are the dear officers, Lord Limpsfield, Captain Oldshaw? I did so much enjoy meeting them, dear Lucia – please send them my regards. Unfortunate that we had to leave so early, and it didn't rain after all. Now, Major Benjy – Lieutenant Benjy I should say – such a drop in rank but worth it to be able to do one's bit for Britain during these dark hours – I mustn't hold up the Army any longer, not even to chatter with such dear friends, or I shall be accused of sabotage. Good day to you, Lucia, Mr. Georgie.'

Still smiling, she led her troops (for so it seemed) towards the Landgate. A couple of small children fell in at the rear of the procession and mimicked the ungainly progress of the soilders, but Elizabeth did not notice. Her cup was running over.

As soon as they were out of earshot of the military, Lucia turned to Georgie, still smiling serenely.

'My dear,' she said, 'did you ever see such a spectacle? Much more tactful not to mention it. Did you notice that disreputable man at the back? I think it is the man who used to be the porter at the railway-staion until he was dismissed for drunkenness. No forage cap and his buckles so very tarnished. I fear I shall sleep no better in my bed tonight for the knowledge that Major Benjy has taken over the defence of Tilling. And poor Elizabeth, marching along at the head of the column. Chattering away at me as if she hadn't been doing her best to brand me a black-marketeer in the eyes of the entire town. I feel very sorry for her at times. Still, I am glad to know that she still feels she can show her face in public. I would hate her to be ostracised on my account. I wonder if there's any haddock? A dear little fish-pie for lunch tomorrow, Georgie?'

There was as little haddock in Mr. Hopkins's shop as there was peace in Georgie's soul, for the spectacle, as

Lucia had called it, had aroused quite different emotions in his heart. Sighing, he accompanied his wife to the butcher's, where Evie and the Padre were contemplating a rapidly diminishing pile of mince as fallen Lucifer must have gazed on the joys of heaven. Diva scurried across the road to join them

'Soldiers,' said Diva. 'Home Guard. Major Benjy in his old uniform, a bit tight round the waist and I think the moth's been at it, but still, a very dignified sight, nonetheless. Did you see them?'

'I saw Elizabeth, certainly,' replied Lucia with a faraway look in her eyes, 'and Major Benjy too in what I suppose was an old uniform of some sort, but the people with them looked like no soldiers I have ever come across. So untidy, dear Diva, so – so unsoldierly! What a contrast with the dear Staffordshires. Mince! What a treat. Oh dear, Evie's had most of it. I'm afraid you're not going to get any, dear.'

But Diva was not to be cheated.

'They looked quite like soldiers to me,' she said crossly, 'with their rifles and uniforms. And I think Major Benjy looked ten years younger.'

'Not knowing what Major Benjy looked like ten years ago, I cannot venture an opinion,' replied Lucia.

'Ho! Well, I think uniform has a marvellous effect on the male figure.' She looked meaningfully at Georgie.

'You can't expect them to look as smart as the Staffordshires already,' said Evie, joining the group. 'The Major's only had charge of them for a few days, and already they've improved tremendously. Mr. Phillipson, the bank manager, who commanded them before, let them get dreadfully sloppy, but now Major Benjy's in charge. . .'

'Aye, 'tis remarkable what the hand of authority can achieve,' added the Padre. 'They'll be needin' a chaplain, no doubt.'

'Such a comfort to have our own Home Guard, in case the Regular troops are posted elsewhere,' said Evie. 'All those brave men.' She too looked meaningfully at

Georgie, for all the world as if she were Kitchener on a poster.

Poor Georgie had not been oblivious to these significant glances, for his own thoughts had been tending in the same direction. How foolish and unmanly he had been, delighting in his cooking, when Major Benjy, whom he had regarded as a boozy old fraud, was preparing to do battle on the beaches. And it was true that he looked younger in his uniform – much younger and slimmer than in his civilian clothes. He had no need of scarce and shameful hair-dye to renew his lost youth, for the King's uniform achieved that so much more effectively. All of a sudden, Georgie was smitten with a longing that had been growing unnoticed in the back of his mind ever since the Staffordshires came. He wanted to be a soldier too, to wear gaiters and brass buckles and a cap set at a jaunty angle on his head, even if it meant calling Major Benjy 'sir' and standing to attention and shouldering arms (how tar'some that would be). Before, he had been convinced that if his country was so far gone as to need *him*, his country was probably done for; but compared to some of the decrepit old things who had been waddling along behind the Major, he was a mere boy. In fact, compared to the Major, he was a mere boy, at least as far as waistlines went. Were soldiers allowed to wear *toupées*? he wondered. And wouldn't Foljambe be impressed? She could never leave if he became a soldier. She would be his batman – no, batwoman – no, that didn't sound right either. . .

He was woken from this reverie by the sight of the platoon marching past the window, going back to the Institute, which was being used as their headquarters, for drill-practice, or unarmed combat, or a small whisky-and-soda before going home to Grebe. Only this time quaint Irene had joined the small boys, and was marching along with a saucepan on her head and a mop on her shoulder, while Elizabeth, still heading the parade, was looking absolutely furious, but trying to ignore her. Georgie's military ardour melted silently away.

Irene saluted, performed a balletic right turn and joined the queue in the butcher's.

'Just wait till I tell Henry about Fred Karno's army!' she said, removing the saucepan. 'He'll simply howl with laughter. Oh hello, Mr. Georgie. I thought Lucia had chopped you up and fed you to the officers, you're such a stranger these days. I'm so glad you haven't joined up with the rag-time infantry. Better stick to your *petit point*. Much more dignified. Oh damn, you'll get the last of the mince. Still, I don't begrudge you anything, Comrade Lucia. You take it all and make it into something nice; hang on though, your cook's left. How will you manage?'

'You'll see,' said Georgie enigmatically.

'Don't think you should refer to Major Benjy as Fred Karno,' said Diva, 'when he's doing his bit for King and Country. Not respectful.'

'It wasn't him I was referring to, it was Mapp. Don't you see? She'll take them over as her private army and stage a military coup in Tilling. Everyone who doesn't admire her new dress or who trumps her best heart will be shot at dawn. A soldier is better accommodated than with a wife, I read somewhere, especially one like old Mapp. I've got a good mind to do a picture of it, except that it wouldn't be patriotic. If only you'd lead the regiment, Lucia, like Boadicea on her scythed chariot. That would be much better, and you'd make an absolutely ripping *generalissima*.'

'Such things are better left to the Regular troops, dear one,' replied Lucia smugly, 'and I do think you're being a little hard on poor Major Benjy. I'm sure he's only doing his best. Nonetheless, I think it's just as well there really aren't any spies in Tilling. They would get quite the wrong impression.'

'Well, I don't agree,' said Diva. 'I think it's wrong to sneer at the Army, even if it is only Major Benjy in a patched uniform, and I'm sure I wish them every success.'

With which she swept her mince into her basket and

scuttled back to Wasters. Grebe had atoned for its black-market transgressions, while Mallards was getting a little above itself. The Padre and Evie, too, were cold in their goodbyes, and Evie left Irene to the rest of the mince (which was not much) with a pensive frown.

'We shall have to be careful,' said Lucia as they returned to Mallards. 'Clearly dear Diva and the Bartletts are quite taken in by Major Benjy's uniform. We must watch our step, Georgie, and use all our powers of tact and diplomacy.'

'Not in front of the officers, surely?'

'I'm not even sure about that, Georgie. Brothers-in-arms, you know, united by a common uniform. Now, put all such jarring thoughts from your mind and concentrate on lobster *à la Riseholme*. Oh yes, and we must practise our Polish phrases for Prince Andrei. Such an opportunity to learn accent and idiom from a native speaker, don't you think?'

Lobster *à la Riseholme* arrived in due course and rarely, if ever, had that culinary masterpiece been so well presented as on Georgie's public *début* as a *chef*. Although several quite important ingredients had been lacking, Georgie had devised alternatives that were as good as, if not better than, the orginals.

'I must congratulate you on your cook, Mrs. Pillson,' said Prince Andrei. 'Even in my own country, which has the best cooks in the world, I have never tasted lobster so exquisitely prepared. Even in my beloved Warsaw, which now squirms beneath the jackboot of a hated foe, I cannot remember to have consumed lobster of such extreme quality.'

'Dear Prince Andrei,' said Lucia, wishing more than ever that she had been the one to learn the mystic art, 'so kind of you, and I'm sure you'll never guess who cooked it.'

'Tell me, please – ah! I have it! You have a Polish cook.'

'No, it was me!' exclaimed Georgie, unable to contain his excitement any longer.

'Ah, Mr. Pillson,' replied the Prince, 'I see you follow the old Roman custom. For was it not the way of the gravest and most venerable senator of the Republic to entrust the preparation of the rarest dishes to none but his own hands? I think it is so – there is a passage in Athenaeus, although I cannot recall the exact reference. But it is true, Mr. Pillson. I applaud you. You are Renaissance Man.'

So taken aback was Georgie by this generous tribute that for a moment he thought that Renaissance Man was one of those tar'some fossils dug up in Africa that proved that Man was descended from the apes. No, that was Neanderthal Man. Renaissance Man was Leonardo da Vinci. He glowed with pleasure.

'All due respect to the fair sex, Mrs. Pillson,' said Captain Oldshaw gravely, 'but when it comes to the really difficult, dainty stuff, men cook just as well as women, if not better.'

'Oh fie, Captain Oldshaw,' said Prince Andrei.

'Well, you won't find many ladies cooking at the Savoy,' he replied. 'It's one of those things. What was that French chap's name? Escoffier. That's who you remind me of, Mr. Pillson.'

'And in wartime too,' concluded Lord Tony. 'How did you get all the ingredients? I'll swear that there was cinnamon in there somewhere.'

'You're far too clever to need cinnamon, aren't you, Georgie?' said Lucia. 'All those marvellous short cuts and substitutes. I believe you're an alchemist, turning powdered egg into gold.'

'This is very interesting,' said Lord Tony. 'I know a man in the Ministry of Food who's crying out for someone who can devise substitutes for unobtainable ingredients. I must mention your name to him, Pillson. I'm sure he'll be fascinated.'

Georgie blushed redder than any boiled lobster, as if angel voices were calling him towards a Higher Purpose.

'And now, *carissima* Lucia,' continued Lord Tony, 'I must tell you that we Staffordshires have rivals here in Tilling! As I was strolling in the town after lunch I saw a party of armed men up by the Norman Tower. At first I thought they were Germans dressed in civilian costume, for they looked remarkably unlike any British soldier past or present, and I was just about to rush to the church and ring all the bells when I saw your Major Benjy – the one who didn't get any coffee – strutting along in front of them, so I suppose they must be the Home Guard.'

'And was Elizabeth – Mrs. Mapp-Flint – also leading them?' asked Lucia excitedly. Condemnation of the Home Guard by the real Army should silence Diva and the Bartletts for ever.

'Yes, she was, and she was brandishing a ferocious-looking basket in her hand. I suppose they will use that for putting German tanks in. It's certainly big enough.'

'Come on now, Limpsfield,' said Captain Oldshaw. 'I'll admit they were a pretty unsoldierly lot, but at least it's something.'

'Ah yes, I'm afraid that we'll have to leave our beloved Tilling in their hands soon. We've been posted, you see, and we're leaving in a week and a bit. So this may be our first and last taste of Mr. Georgie's lobster.'

Lucia dropped her fork.

'Wicked Lord Tony,' she said, pulling herself together with an effort. 'What a way to break the news to us. Oh, how we shall all miss you.'

An idea formed itself in Lucia's mind. If she had to lose her officers and thereby lose the most effective hold she had had on Tilling for years, she would at least say farewell to them in as advantageous a manner as possible.

'And we shall miss you, my dear,' continued Lord Tony. 'Why, it's cheered me up no end to eat magnificent lobster, and hear all about the nefarious activities of Mapp, and meet the Birmingham-Scottish padre. We shall be quite as desolate as you, you may be certain of that.'

'We must have a farewell concert then,' said Lucia, 'for all the officers of the regiment, not just our little circle, so that your parting memory of Tilling will be of culture and sweet music.' Captain Oldshaw's face was observed to fall slightly. He had hoped that his parting memory of Tilling would be more lobster *à la Riseholme*. 'And of course a farewell dinner before our *broche musika*, as dear Prince Andrei would say,' she continued. Captain Oldshaw's smile returned. 'No more gloomy thoughts now. So, Georgie *kochany*, what else have you to delight us with? A meringue, is it not? *Piekna!*'

The meringue was certainly *piekna*, which was as far as Lucia's phrase-book got to *bella* in *Italiano*. It was a triumph, a towering ziggurat of a confection, and Lord Tony confessed that he would not have believed that only one egg could have been the foundation of such an edifice. He must certainly mention Georgie's name to Teddy Broome at the Ministry. What Britain needed, he maintained, more than tanks or Hurricanes, was a way of making such a meringue with only one egg. Count Andrei called down all the saints to witness that even in his native land, where the meringue had been invented and where all the most famous meringue-makers of antiquity had lived, he had never tasted so fine an example of the noblest of desserts. Even Captain Oldshaw, who was not given to passionate outbursts, declared that it was a jolly fine pudding, and he wished he had the recipe to send to his sister in Harrogate. The evening concluded with a little Chopin ('Ready, Georgie? *Jeden, due, TRIE!*') after which the Prince sang a very sad and beautiful folk-song from his native Poland, about a woodcutter who fell in love with a water-nymph, the tune of which sounded disconcertingly like 'For he's a jolly good fellow,' transferred to the minor key.

5

Lucia hired the Institute, and set about choosing her music. She would play a good deal of Chopin, and she and Georgie together would play a good deal more, as well as the Elgar and the madrigals and the Dowland. The Padre would sing some Scottish ballads, including 'Will ye no come back again?', and quaint Irene would, as a sop to the groundlings, do her celebrated impression of Hitler eating an orange – the orange, of course, to be mimed; real oranges were still a painful topic. As a grand finale she (Lucia) would take the leading *rôle* in a most ambitious and symbolic *tableau*: attired as Boadicea and representing the Spirit of England, she would chase the Teutonic dragon (Irene in her Hitler outfit and Diva in the tail section of the Christmas mummer's dragon) away from the South coast. This selection of delights would, she felt, not only give the troops a rousing send-off, but involve all Tilling except Elizabeth.

What with rehearsals and practising Chopin and limiting the Padre to only four ballads, at least two of which must be comprehensible to those unfamiliar with the Scottish dialect, and keeping Elizabeth from having anything to do with it, and encouraging Georgie to work out a rather complicated recipe for Stroganoff using almost none of the original ingredients, Lucia was kept very busy over the next few days. All Tilling buzzed with concert-fever. Diva spent hours in the dragon's tail, getting accustomed to the almost total darkness inside the costume, Irene strutted up and down in front of the

Wyses making violent gestures and spluttering (they were the only people with sufficient leisure to watch her rehearse, although they found the performance in highly doubtful taste), and anyone passing the Vicarage would have been startled by the bellowing of Caledonian folk-song that issued from within. On the eve of the concert Lucia returned, tired but content, from a final rehearsal at Starling Cottage, to find a letter from Lord Tony. She opened it eagerly, only to find that he had managed to persuade Teddy Broome from the Ministry of Food to come to dinner and the concert, and to meet Georgie. In a post-script, written in haste, he also said that Olga Bracely, who was entertaining the troops in Hastings on the same day, had heard of the concert, and had expressed an earnest wish to be present, although sadly she could not be in time for dinner.

This, not unnaturally, caused Lucia a moment's dismay. The presence of an important official from the Ministry of Food, come expressly to consult him about one-egg meringues and what not, combined with Olga, whom he undoubtedly still adored, might tend to make Georgie just a little above himself. Of course, she trusted him absolutely, but it was undeniably true that meeting Olga again always left him rather rebellious; and now that the officers were leaving she would have to find some other prestigious occupation for them both so that she might maintain her rightful position in Tilling. Olga alone she could have coped with by adhering to the two of them and hogging the conversation until Olga went away, but the man from the Ministry posed rather more serious problems.

Nevertheless, the triumph that she must surely enjoy with the concert would keep Elizabeth in check for the moment, and the preparations for that event continued to monopolise her thoughts. The Padre would insist on singing a very long and mournful ballad about an army of heroïc Scots warriors who went away to fight the marauding Norsemen and who, despite many deeds of notable prowess and impeccable valour all round, did not come back. That, she felt, was not quite what she had in mind.

Stroganoff and lemon *sorbet* (magically created with but one small lemon) came forth from Mallard's kitchen to astound and gratify the officers assembled around the Round Table of Lucia's Camelot for the last time, and Teddy Broome, seated in the Siege Perilous on Lucia's right, took but a small part in the sparkling conversation, for all his powers of concentration were devoted to the food. Try as he might he could not detect the substitutes and improvisations that he was assured had been employed in the Stroganoff and the *sorbet*. Once he lifted his solemn countenance and suggested 'Powdered egg?' in a hopeful voice, only to be informed that that deplorable substance had not entered into the process at all. Mystified and awash with imagination and *sorbet* he continued to munch and puzzle and analyse and wonder.

Then, when coffee (with an artificial cream of uncanny realism) had been hastily consumed, and when Lord Tony had thoughtfully suggested that a flask of coffee be taken out to Major Benjy, who might have had to miss his coffee again in order to take out the evening patrol, the assembled company departed, by Humber, on the short journey to the Institute. As it happened Major Benjy was indeed leading out his evening patrol from the Institute as they arrived, for the concert had forced them out of their cosy drill-hall into the cold night air. The Home Guard's rustic salutes were returned with professional precision by the Regulars, and Lord Tony said 'Qui-hi, Major Benjy' under his breath, though not sufficiently quietly for it not to be heard by the whole platoon. Lucia laughed shrilly, exclaimed 'Naughty Lord Tony,' and waved gaily to the furious Commander of the Tilling troop.

There was not a vacant seat in the Institute, for it was filled with officers of every shape and size, age and rank. In the front row was Henry Porteous, sitting next to quaint Irene, who was wearing a duffel-coat to conceal her Hitler costume. There seemed to be a coolness between them that Lucia would have investigated fully at any other time. . . And there was Olga, radiant and magnificent. Georgie blushed redder than the sunrise, and dropped his music. Gathering it hastily, he joined Lucia at the piano and prepared to turn the pages for her. There were, he noticed, a great many pages, and somehow the assembled officers struck him as being in not quite the mood for so much Chopin. When all was settled, Lucia seated herself at the piano, assumed her music face and began to play.

So deeply was her attention engaged in the glories (and difficulties) of the music that she did not at first notice the slight air of restlessness that followed the fifth piano solo. When her recital came to an end, the applause almost appeared to be as much relief as approval. When the Padre stepped on to the platform to sing his Scottish ballads in appropriate costume there were muffled cheers at the back of the hall, as if some uncultured minds were expecting a Harry Lauder routine. Their cheers turned to audible whispers as the Padre sang his first ballad (he had a loud voice, used mainly for plainsong). There seemed to be mounting speculation among the younger and less educated officers as to whether the 'turn' was meant to be funny or not. Lucia's lips were a thin white line as she played the first bars of 'Scots, wha hae wi' Wallace bled', but the whispers continued, and the clapping was surely somewhat slower than one heard at Covent Garden. With panic in his eyes the Padre turned and suggested that they should go straight on to the final ballad, and regrettably enough his rhetorical question 'Will ye no come back again?' was greeted by a few definite replies of 'No!'

After he had resumed his seat, followed by a few (doubtless good-humoured) suggestions as to how he should extend his repertoire, Georgie joined Lucia at the piano for the duets.

'I don't think they like it,' he whispered.

'Music hath charms to soothe the savage beast, Georgie,' she replied, but Georgie wasn't too sure. At times, he thought, music had exactly the opposite effect, and this was one of them. Surely the officers wouldn't throw things. . .

Lucia had determined to be entirely oblivious to the disturbances, but nonetheless the programme of madrigals was severely truncated, and Elgar wholly omitted. It seemd unlikely that the massed chivalry of Staffordshire would stand much more of Lucia's rousing send-off. The next item on the agenda was Irene's Hitler impersonation. She was dressed in knee-breeches, riding-boots and braces, her head topped by a cardboard cap and her upper lip daubed with boot-polish. Lucia shuddered slightly at the spectacle, but the audience roared with delight, and started demanding encores in advance, to get their orders in early, so to speak. When the storm of gesticulation and spluttering was over and the ovation had died away, Lucia rose to return to the piano. Chopin and Grieg. . . Georgie, seized with a sudden concern for his wife's safety, caught her arm and hissed 'Play the National Anthem' to her. As she hesitated, Lord Tony, who had been whispering with Olga, joined them and muttered something about Miss Bracely wanting to sing a few numbers, and could it be fitted in? Lucia was in two minds. She was unwilling to let dear Olga steal her show, but then, there was not much left of her show to steal. Besides, Olga was a professional and must by now be used to rowdies, while that world-famous voice might even save a situation rapidly becoming chaotic. Georgie joined in the discussion, declaring that he was willing to accompany Olga on the piano, and Lucia, glancing at the audience, assented. She too did not believe for a moment that British officers would throw things, but in case they did, the stains of over-ripe tomatoes would be easier to remove from Georgie's shirt than from her evening gown.

A decision having been reached, Lord Tony rose and announced a change in the programme. Miss Olga Bracely, the famous soprano, had consented to sing a few songs which would be familiar to them all. . . Lucia felt a pang of anxiety at these words, as almost simultaneously, Georgie began to play the tune (if it could be described as such) of 'Run, rabbit, run'.

And Olga sang.

Enormous, like a giant wave of the sea, was the applause that rocked the little hall. Never before had such applause, such clapping and cheering, been heard there, but never before had its roof re-echoed such a superb voice as that of the divine Olga. Like an alchemist who can make vile things precious she transmuted the vulgar melodies. Even 'Roll out the barrel', Lucia was forced to admit, seemed quite a jolly little tune when Olga sang it. Georgie, meanwhile, was playing as he had never played before, pounding the keys in an ecstasy of delight. Divine *Mozartino* it most certainly was not, but to accompany his Olga, even in 'There'll always be an England' and 'I'm going to get lit up when the lights go up in London', amid all this tumult of devotion, was the purest happiness. His eyes flitted from one unfamiliar page to the next, and he clouted the piano like a blacksmith. Finally, with 'Land of hope and glory' (which evidently was the only piece of Elgar's music that would be heard in Tilling that night) and a roaring crescendo of 'Rule Britannia', the concert came to an explosive end and Major Benjy, splashing along with his men through the puddles in the High Street, could hear the singing and the clapping in Malleson Street, and wondered how he was to break the news to Elizabeth that, in spite of all her predictions to the contrary, Lucia's concert appeared to have been a great success.

Dazed and shattered by his transcendent emotions, Georgie came away from the piano-stool, his ears ringing with the approbation of the soldiers. Although no husband could be as devotedly loyal as he, he knew that but for Olga the concert would have been a hopeless failure, and that Olga had turned it into a triumph for which Lucia would take the credit. As it was, the audience held no grudges, and officers of every rank were thanking Lucia for a highly entertaining evening, some perjuring their immortal souls by saying how much they had enjoyed her piano-playing. Admittedly they were also congratulating him, so that his blush became ever more crimson, and they were worshipping Olga, who was autographing a sea of programmes.

She broke away from the throng and joined him. With her were Teddy Broome and Lord Tony, and at the back of them, although Georgie did not see her, Lucia.

'Georgie, you were marvellous,' said Olga, and he could find no words with which to reply. 'I never knew you could play like that. It makes all the difference in the world to have a good accompaniment. I wish you could come and play for me on my tour. My usual accompanist isn't a patch on you. He never puts any feeling into the music – I imagine he thinks it's below his dignity to play popular songs.'

'You see,' said Lord Tony to Teddy Broome, 'not only can he create Stroganoff out of sawdust and brown paper, but he has the common touch, he can communicate. You'll have to sign him up now. He's better than all your stuffy professors.'

Teddy Broome nodded gravely, like a Prime Minister.

'Indeed, Mr. Pillson, I haven't yet had an opportunity to say how much I admired your skill and resourcefulness as a cook. I was deeply impressed.'

'Georgie,' cried Olga, 'don't tell me you can cook as well. You are a dark horse.'

'Cook!' exclaimed Lord Tony. 'He can do more than cook. Why, he created a perfect lemon *sorbet* tonight out of one little lemon the size of a golf-ball. So Teddy's going to sign him up to take part in a series of broadcasts he's getting up on hints to housewives on "Making the Most of Your Ration-Book".'

Georgie may have attempted to mumble a refusal, but it was not a very serious attempt. He was full of his own glory, and when Olga screamed 'Oh Georgie, you must!' at him, he said, 'Yes, please,' and turned from scarlet to mauve.

'That's settled, then,' said Teddy Broome. 'I'll write to you in a couple of days with details. You'll have to come up to London for a week or so.'

'That's all right, you can stay at my house,' said Olga. 'Brompton Square, Georgie, quite like old times. I won't be there because I'm on tour still, but Foljambe can look after you and I don't think you'll be needing a cook.'

Poor Georgie! In his hour of triumph he thought only of himself, broadcasting on the wireless, staying at Olga's house, doing his bit – more than his bit – towards the war-effort. He was useful at last after a half-century of being moderately ornamental, and the idea overwhelmed him. After all, as Lord Tony had said at dinner, designing a new vegetable pie for the Home Front was just as good as designing a new tank for the battlefront. And as for Lucia, well, she must make do without him for a while. For as long as he could remember he had supported her in her triumphs – now she must support him in his. It did not occur to him, of course, that with Grosvenor and the cook gone and Foljambe in London looking after him, Lucia would have to fend for herself, unless she could get a charwoman from the town. Oddly enough, this horrible thought did not occur to Lucia herself until the next morning. Her mind, up till then, had been far too busy with thoughts of betrayal and desertion.

Of course she had brought it on herself. She had overreached herself with the officers' concert, and Nemesis had been quick to strike her down. Of course, she should have been the one to man the abandoned tiller of the kitchen, then she would be going to London to broadcast on the B.B.C. while Georgie stayed behind and polished his *bibelots* (would he take them with him to London? No, he would be afraid of dropping them). It was simply the penalty of laziness. She had made a mistake – two mistakes – and she must rectify the situation as best she could. She must be realistic; Georgie could not be stopped from going to London, and so she must be all for it. As for herself, she would be in the same situation, she felt, as the wives of the fighting men at the front, for her husband would be away serving his country in the kitchen and the broadcasting studio, if not in the field of battle. Obviously while he was away she could not dream of entertaining, or taking part in the life of Tilling. Therefore she must have influenza (which with judicious management could be made to appear like pining for the departed) and do what she could to keep the house in order. Flight to the refuge of a hotel (even the Ambermere Arms in Riseholme) was not for her. That would be cowardice, and she was no coward. Besides, she could probably get a charwoman from the town through the agency, who might perhaps be persuaded with gold to do whatever was necessary to corned beef to make it edible, and as a last resort the tin-opener and the moderate stock of nutritious if simple provisions laid down in the cellar in case of emergencies (if this was not an emergency, what was?). Besides, she would have leisure enough to learn to cook herself, for if Georgie could do it so could she, and no doubt Mr. George Pillson, the radio expert, would be delighted to give her a few elementary lessons. The radio expert. . . She had hardly considered the glow of reflected glory that must inevitably surround her as she waited, influenza-ridden, in Mallards for his return.

'And to think,' she reflected cheerfully, 'that he's been frittering away his time with *gros point* and watercolours when he's really the Toscanini of the kitchen range! And if I learn to cook and can get a char to do the cleaning there's no reason why I shouldn't give tea parties, with Bridge to follow, and perhaps if Georgie's broadcasts are in the afternoon we can all gather round the radio and listen. That would be fun.'

* * *

Georgie, whose conscience was beginning to trouble him, eagerly agreed to introduce her to the freemasonry of the kitchen.

'My dear, it couldn't be simpler. So long as you follow the recipe you can't go wrong. You just put all the things together and heat them up. You'll be doing lobster *à la Riseholme* by the time I come back.'

So, armed with food and *Cooking for Gentlefolks*, they descended, like Dante and Virgil, into the kitchen, and Georgie, like the Roman poet, pointed out all the instruments of torture and described their dark purposes. That, he said, was a frying-pan; you put lard in it and it sizzled. That was a casserole; that was a baking-dish. These were the knives that you carved meat and vegetables with. This was a kettle, the source of boiling water without which tea could not be made.

'Oh Georgie,' she said, 'I shall never get used to all these different pans. What's this?'

'It's an omelette pan. You make omelettes in it, if you can get the eggs. And that's a whisk for beating eggs and making batter and things. The flour's kept in here, and this is for peeling potatoes. No, I'm not quite sure how you use it. Foljambe usually does that for me.'

Lucia proved a willing pupil, and after a day of concerted effort she produced her first cup of drinkable tea and her first slices of bread and butter that resembled food rather than masonry. The letter arrived from Teddy Broome with a week's notice for Georgie; and another from Prince Andrei – his mother the Princess and his younger brother the Count would be passing through Tilling in two days' time. Could she possibly spare them a few hours to make them welcome in the land of freedom? His mother had been particularly impressed, wrote the Prince, by his account of the miraculous Stroganoff that Georgie had cooked on the night of the wonderful concert, and had openly expressed her doubts that an Englishman could make a better Stroganoff than a Pole... Would it be possible for Mr. Pillson to vindicate his judgement and taste in the eyes of his beloved mother? He added that she spoke very little English, and the Count not much more, but since both Mr. and Mrs. Pillson seemed perfectly at home in the Polish tongue this would of course present no difficulty. Lucia wrote at once to say that they would be only too honoured. She was determined to have at least one other gaudy lunch, very little English or no, although it might be as well not to invite anyone else to the lunch party. *En famille*. The thought of the last two Chopin duets having been learnt in vain had angered her more than almost anything.

In the greater world of Tilling, marketing and news-gathering continued ignorant of the turmoil of Mallards. Diva had quite got over the disappointment of not being the hindquarters of Hitler in the *tableau*; she had been in the back-room most of the time, only emerging when her curiosity had overcome her discretion during Olga's singing, and therefore remained in ignorance of the less than entire success of the rest of the programme. Irene did nothing to correct her impression of overall triumph, merely stressing the excellent reception accorded to Hitler and the orange, so that for all that Diva knew the *tableau* had merely receded gracefully in favour of Olga's offer to sing, after which even her performance as the dragon's tail must have been an anti-climax.

' "Run, rabbit, run". Not quite my cup of tea, but certainly the stuff to give the troops,' she admitted to the Padre, whose lips were as sealed as Irene's, albeit from different motives. 'Jolly good for morale, all that singing. I know they enjoyed your ballads. Tell me, was Irene really such a big hit, or does she go round calling you Harry Lauder out of sheer jealously?'

Fortunately something distracted Diva's attention before he was called upon to give a truthful answer to her question, and Tilling was left with the impression that Lucia had been entirely responsible for giving the officers such a splendid farewell. Elizabeth, maddened by the news of Georgie's imminent fame, speculated endlessly that it had been otherwise, but there were too many witnesses and Irene (being loyal), Diva (being ignorant) and the Padre (being compromised) did nothing to confirm her suspicions. Meanwhile, all Tilling buzzed with excited anticipation, asking if a date had been set for Mr. Georgie's broadcasts, what he would say, would he betray the secret of lobster *à la Riseholme* that only Lucia and Elizabeth knew, and which Elizabeth had gone to sea on a kitchen-table to obtain. . . The sheer practicality of it astounded them, and aroused their jealous admiration. Diva, who had been compelled to close her tea-shop at the outbreak of war because she could not make head or tail of the endless official forms with which a concerned Government bombarded her, felt a certain reflected pride, for she could make pastry and pour tea. Nonetheless, Tilling shared Prince Andrei's view that Georgie was a Renaissance Man, equally at home with a palette or a skillet.

Elizabeth, for all her fury, was content to sit quietly and wait for the furore to die down. Her hour of glory was rapidly approaching, for now that Lucia's officers had evaporated she would be the sole purveyor of military personnel to Tilling. Major Benjy represented the native product, so to speak, and her cousin Herbert the imported commodity. He would be arriving soon, and there must be widespread tea and Bridge to welcome him. Besides, Major Benjy's troop of warriors was no longer followed about by hordes of ribald children, and she had written to the Red Cross, putting her name forward for a vacancy as its principal officer in Tilling. The post was largely honorary and, since there were no casualties yet, a sinecure anyway. She was eminently qualified for the job, for had she not taken a first-aid course in those first panic-stricken days of war and spent a number of seemingly wasted evenings bandaging the head of the draper's wife in the pretty fiction that she had burns?

As for dear Lulu, she reckoned that with Georgie and

Foljambe away and Grosvenor busy with her bombs at the factory, she would be reduced to eating grass and drinking rainwater unless the entire Mallards household had suddenly all become notable *chefs*. The thought of Lucia eating pilchards out of the tin with a fork, cold, gave Elizabeth a great deal of innocent amusement as she sat in the isolated splendour of Grebe and looked out over the unending marshes. Once, before that woman came out of Worcestershire like the Assyrian, before she had been ensnared by dear Lucia in reckless speculation and had lost so much money that she had been forced to sell her Mallards and retire to this desert spot like an Anatolian saint, she had had a garden-room to look out of from behind a curtain. She turned, choked with emotion, and listlessly counted her collection of Tilling china pigs, usually an infallible narcotic in time of stress. One of them was missing, however, and her vexation increaed, for she found its poor decimated corpse under the desk. She opened a drawer to hide the ruins from her sight and found a half-empty whisky flask. A chain of consequence involving Major Benjy, the flask, an erratic whisky-induced movement, a smash of china and frantic efforts to hide the debris, sprang complete into her mind. She ground her teeth and sat down at the desk to write the invitations for the tea and Bridge party that would introduce her cousin Herbert. She paused and wondered whether it might not be advisable to have him to lunch on his own the first time, just in case he turned out to be less than the paragon of virtue that she imagined him to be, but she dismissed the notion at once. She was impatient to regain her rightful crown, which she had surrendered, along with her house, to that interloper.

Having completed the last invitation, she set off down the long road that entered the town *via* the picturesque old stone archway. She intended to deliver the invitations by hand (for it was sinful, in such difficult times, to waste money on stamps, and the post was so erratic) and perhaps drop a few tantalising hints as she went. Her first call was on Diva, who was sitting in her favourite position at the front window of Wasters, from which she could overlook the High Street while getting on with whatever piece of needlework she was engaged in at the time. Just now she was trimming an old hat with the now familiar chintz roses.

'Diva dear,' called Elizabeth from the street, 'may I just pop in for a moment? An invitation to meet my cousin.'

Although eager to receive the invitation, Diva was rather put out by the unexpected visitation. Chintz roses were no longer a surprise to anyone, but on a hat they might take on a new lease of life, and she hoped that Elizabeth would not be sarcastic about them. Just to make sure, she hid the hat behind a cushion. Unfortunately Elizabeth saw it at once and drew it forth.

'Not another new hat already, dearest? No, it's the old straw one and, of course, chintz roses! Your trademark. Now, then, any news?'

'Not really,' replied Diva with a certain amount of reserve. Elizabeth's condescending tone demanded a slight coolness, but too much could precipitate a quarrel, which would mean that she would have to decline the invitation to meet Elizabeth's cousin. 'Except that Lucia has got a Polish Princess and Count going to lunch with her tomorrow, but she can't invite anyone else because they don't speak English. I suppose that means that Lucia and Georgie can speak Polish, and they haven't just been putting it on because they can't speak Italian any more. Fancy! And she's learning to cook from Mr. Georgie. Lucia, I mean, not the Princess.'

'No!' exclaimed Elizabeth in mock awe. 'Is there any limit to our dear Lucia's talents? A linguist and a *chef* as well. I suppose they really are Polish, and not just any old people?'

'Lucia showed me the letter,' replied Diva. 'She said it was to let me see how quaintly Prince Andrei wrote English, but I think it was documentary evidence to prove they were both real princesses and counts.'

'Such a relief to know that dear Lulu won't be entirely on her own now that the officers have gone, and Mr. Georgie about to go away as well. She will have the comfort of knowing that the aristocracy of half of Europe may drop by at any time and share a tin of sardines with her. Otherwise she should be quite on her own in that great big house. I remember how lonely I used to be there before my Benjy-boy and I were married.'

Nonsense, thought Diva, you were too busy spying on everyone from the garden-room to be lonely for a moment.

'Don't suppose she'll have time to be lonely,' replied Diva. 'You know how busy she always is even though she's not Mayor any more. She's still chairman of the governors of the hospital, and now she'll be cooking as well – she'll be busier than ever.'

'Yes, dear,' said Elizabeth sweetly, 'so brave to be embarking on something new at her time of life. Of course, we're never too old to learn.' (Elizabeth was believed by the charitably minded to be a year or two younger than Lucia and since, in fact, she was, their charity was rather superfluous.) 'Nevertheless, it must be a dreadful worry to her, with Mallard to look after and no servants. I hope it doesn't go to rack and ruin while Foljambe is away. A disagreeable woman I have always found, but no doubt very capable at her job. I should hate to think that I had parted with dear Aunt Caroline's house only to see it crumble away before my very eyes.'

'Really, Elizabeth,' said Diva crossly (Elizabeth was being intolerable today) 'compared to what it was like when you had it, it's a different house altogether. Painted. Re-wired. Doors close properly.'

That was an unfortunate thing to say, for who could forget a certain cupboard door that had failed to close properly during a certain coal-strike? Diva thought of her invitation and tried to be more pleasant.

'Anyway,' she said, 'I'm looking forward to meeting your cousin. Great respect for the Air Force. Brave men. Admirable.'

'I always think they are the cream of the armed forces,' replied Elizabeth, ignoring the unfortunate reference to ill-closing doors, 'and with so much responsibility on their young shoulders. Major Benjy – so well informed on military matters – was saying only yesterday that unless we make sure of winning the war in the air, we cannot hope to win the war on the ground.'

In fact this piece of wisdom had been said by Mr. Churchill on the wireless, but Major Benjy had repeated it, if only to disagree violently with it, and so he might be supposed to have said it too.

'Have you met him before? Herbert I mean,' asked Diva, eagerly.

'No alas, he is from a collateral branch of the family, the Lancashire branch you know. Dear Herbert is the grandson of my aunt Elizabeth, for whom I was named. So appropriate, don't you think, that we should meet at last. I don't know what he actually does in the Air Force – I expect he flies Hurricanes and shoots down lots of Germans. Or do you think his work is so secret that he is not at liberty to talk about it? Wouldn't that be marvellous! And now I must press on and go and deliver the rest of these invitations. Such a long way back to Grebe, and I fear it may rain later on.'

Elizabeth did not stop and chat at the Vicarage for fear of the rain and of hearing more nice things about Lucia, but simply delivered the invitation and hastened away past beloved Mallards (poor Aunt Caroline!) towards Porpoise Street. She had been in two minds as to whether or not she should invite the Wyses, for Starling Cottage was still counted in the collective mind of Tilling as part of Italy. But the need to deprive Lucia of any potential allies, and the demands of the Bridge-table had decided her, for without the Wyses there would not be eight people, unless she invited Irene and the Curate. After all, they were not entirely ostracised, for she herself had been to dinner there only recently (although that particular dinner party was not one of her happiest memories). Even in wartime, it was Elizabeth's principle always to think the best of people.

6

The visit of the Polish Princess was not such a great triumph as Lucia had hoped it would be. Despite Lucia's study of the Polish tongue, conversation had been difficult, for the pronunciation of those curious words without vowels in them turned out to be very confusing, and the phrase-book's range of phrases was by no means comprehensive. After the Princess had (apparently) asked her the time, and Lucia had replied that it was a quarter-past one, and the Princess's son had said in very broken English that his mother had asked how old the house was, she dispensed with linguistics entirely and relied on the son's doubtful abilities as a translator. Again, although Georgie's Stroganoff was beyond reproach, it caused the Princess to burst into tears, the young Count explaining that the excellence of the dish reminded his mother of her childhood home and the good old days before the war. Georgie was rather flattered, but Lucia was inclined to be embarrassed and changed the subject to Polish music, about which the Count knew nothing, so that the rest of the meal was eaten in almost complete silence. The Princess fell asleep during the specially prepared Chopin duets, and left at half-past three.

And that, said Lucia to herself, is the last bit of entertaining that I shall be able to do until Georgie gets back. This reflection did not please her and it was with a heavy heart that she opened the afternoon post. That scarcely cheered her up, for all it said was that the salvage men were coming to remove her railings, to be made, no doubt, into tanks and cannons and battleships. She comforted herself with the thought that part of Mallards would be safeguarding merchant shipping in the turbulent Atlantic (all those dear dried apricots) or driving the foe in headlong flight across the plains of North Africa. Would it be possible, she wondered, to find out which battleship or which tank her railings had gone to? Then she could name it after its former location: His Majesty's Tank Mallards, or the Star of Tilling. Perhaps a small brass plaque: 'This howitzer once comprised the front railings of Mallards House, Tilling', with perhaps a quotation from an appropriate psalm. More likely, she thought, her beautiful railings would be jumbled up with a lot of manhole covers and cast-iron baths. That was a depressing notion in itself.

Georgie had departed, catching that same early train that in happier days had rescued the duellists of Tilling from mutual destruction. Lucia had waved a little handkerchief and Georgie had promised to write, and a cinder from the engine had caught in his beard and almost set it alight before the stately locomotive had started on its way, wrapped in clouds of unwholesome steam. She walked back up Malleson Street with her eyes slightly red (although that may have been an effect of the steam); their redness could certainly be encouraged into a more effective show of grief with a little gentle rubbing by the time she reached the High Street. But it was too early in the morning for there to be anyone about to see her, and so she returned to the station twenty minutes before the start of the usual marketing hour (to consult the timetables) and came back with her eyes unmistakably red and tastefully anointed with water from the tap in the ladies' waiting-room.

'Just been seeing off Mr. Georgie,' she remarked to the sympathetic Padre. 'So wonderful to know that he is serving his country, and so sad for us poor women to be able to do nothing but sit and wait.' She attempted a stifled sob, but it went wrong and she turned it into a cough before hurrying away to Mallards, clearly overcome by emotion.

Outside Mallards was a lorry, and two workmen were busily engaged in pulling up the railings. She was about to go into the house when she saw Elizabeth coming round the corner by the crooked chimney, so she stopped and pulled out her handkerchief again, to remove a particle of grit from her eye (although Elizabeth was not to know that).

'What are you doing to my railings? demanded Elizabeth furiously.

'Alas, dear Elizabeth, they're not your railings and they're not my railings any more,' said Lucia sweetly. 'They belong to King George now, and he's going to turn them into battleships.'

'How could you!' screeched Elizabeth. 'It's hardly two minutes since you forced me out of dear Aunt Caroline's house, and already you're tearing it down. I knew I should never have sold it to you. What would poor Auntie think?'

'Auntie would be delighted to know that her charming railings were going to help fight the Germans. Solid metal. Enough for a whole cannon. Oh, and by the way, I noticed that that handsome wrought-iron gate is still in position outside Grebe. I'm sure these gentlemen would be able to find time to collect it. Just think! Your front gate and my railings, fused together to fight Hitler. That's how it should be, of course. The whole community welded together to resist the enemy.'

With a snort of fury Elizabeth stalked off down the street. The morning had been a melancholy one, thought Lucia, as she let herself into the house, but not without its redeeming features.

Elizabeth, as it happened, was on her way back from a little quiet sketching in Church Square, as a prelude to the excitement of the day. For today, this very lunchtime, her cousin Herbert would arrive, resplendent in his Air Force uniform, his neck no doubt adorned with a white silk scarf, to have lunch and tea and play Bridge with all the most noteworthy citizens of Tilling except Lucia. Lucia, of course, would not feel up to visiting and celebrating on the day of Georgie's departure, and besides, she should not be called upon to betray her allegiance to the Staffordshires. In the High Street Elizabeth bought a number of inexpensive delicacies to supplement the simple but traditional fare that would be prepared for her heroic cousin. There would also be a bottle of burgundy, drawn out of long hibernation in the kitchen, almost the last survivor of the magnificent cellar that Major Benjy had collected under the false impression that Elizabeth had been drowned and left him all her money. . . It was a pity that Mr. Georgie had not yet begun his series of broadcasts, for without question (she reflected sourly) he knew of excellent methods for making cakes without eggs or fruit, and then they could have had cake with their tea. As it was, bread and marrow-jam must serve their turn, and hot water lightly stained with tea. If nothing else good came out of this war, it gave tremendous scope for imaginative frugality.

Woolton Pie and a sort of bread-and-butter pudding, however, would surely satisfy the palate of Nero himself, especially if rounded off with a few preserved plums (for the plum-trees of Grebe had done their share in defying the Hun). As a special mark of festivity, equivalent to a general amnesty, Major Benjy would be allowed a whisky-and-soda before lunch (although the affair of the broken pig and the hip-flask was by no means forgotten); it would not be fair to provide her cousin with whisky and soda (should he request it) and withhold it from her husband. A very small whisky-and-soda, from time to time, helped to keep one's morale up in the dark days of war.

The chubby gilded cherubs on the top of the church-tower hammered out half-past twelve on their little bells as Elizabeth hurried down the High Street towards Grebe. She was an energetic walker, and the journey never took her much more than a quarter-of-an-hour. Herbert would not be arriving before twelve-thirty; nonetheless it would be as well to be at home in plenty of time. As she walked through the Landgate she was nearly knocked down by a powerful motor-bicycle which was travelling far too fast. The rider of the offending machine sounded his horn and exclaimed 'Mind out, pet!' in an uncouth voice as he roared away, causing the ancient gate to re-echo with clamorous noise. Elizabeth muttered something about louts, and continued her journey on the pavement.

As she arrived at Grebe she saw to her horror the same motor-bicycle that had come so close to terminating her existence standing outside the house. Her mind was filled with horrible forebodings as she let herself in at the front-door. She heard the sound of joyous male laughter and the clink of glasses coming from her drawing-room.

A large stout man with a thick moustache and a countenance of the kind usually described as florid was sitting in her most comfortable chair holding a glass amply filled with whisky and soda. Lounging opposite was Major Benjy, also holding a brimming tumbler and smoking a cigar.

'Hello, Auntie Betty,' said the stout man, rising (rather unsteadily perhaps?) to his feet and extending an enormous hand. 'I'm your cousin Herbert. Very pleased to meet you.'

Elizabeth smiled and took the massive paw as if it had been dead for three days. Her lower lip was trembling; nor was it the emotion of meeting her cousin for the first time that had so shaken her composure.

'Hang on though,' said Cousin Herbert, his broad face developing a huge grin, 'you're the lady who stepped out in front of me when I was coming through that arch affair in town. You ought to look where you're going, Auntie Betty. Gave me a fright, you did. Why, folks might jump to all sorts of conclusions if they saw you wandering about all over the place. Might think you were a little bit tipsy, eh?' And he roared with laughter at this horrible joke.

Elizabeth shot a glance of fury mixed with terror at her husband, who, failing to interpret it, also laughed loudly and cried, 'Very good, yes, upon my soul,' then helped himself to more whisky. 'He's got a point there, Liz, you know,' he continued. 'Mustn't give people ideas, 'specially in Tilling. Very fond of gossip in Tilling, liable to jump to conclusions, two an' two make five, misunderstand the simplest thing. Like going' out at ten-o'clock at night to post a letter with no address on it.'

With this pointed reference to past dishonours, he winked hugely so that Elizabeth, unable to speak, collapsed into a chair.

'We've been getting on like a house on fire, Major Flint an' me,' continued the appalling Herbert. 'A man's man, I don't mind saying, and not stingy with his whisky. And that reminds me, I've got a little present for both of you. A bottle of Scotch for you, Major, and this is for you, Auntie. Go on, open it.'

He thrust something like a flat plate wrapped in newspaper at his stunned cousin, who opened it with numb fingers. It was a gramophone recording of Mr. George Formby singing 'I'm leaning on a lamp-post at the corner of the street'. Never, thought Elizabeth, have I suffered so much in such a short time.

'I like a nice tune myself,' said Herbert, 'and that's all the rage up in Sefton Park. We can put it on after our lunch, if you're not familiar with the tune. Ah, thank you, Major, I don't mind if I do. Will you join us, Auntie?'

Too aghast to utter a sound, Elizabeth shook her head. Her lips were as if welded together. All Tilling would be arriving at four-o'clock.

'I hear from the Major that we're going to have a little game of Bridge later on,' continued Herbert, his glass refilled. 'That's grand, I must say, though I'd just as soon play a nice game of Whist or Pontoon. We often go to Whist drives at home. Well, this is very pleasant, I must say.'

'Privilege to be able to entertain one of our knights of the air at our humble home,' said the perfidious Major.

Wedged behind him in the recesses of the chair was the bottle of whisky that Herbert had brought. No doubt it would be spirited away and referred back to in the future, to bring about further smashing of china and disruption in the home.

'Greatest respect for our brave boys, protectin' hearth and home from the Hun. I say, Lizbeth, aren't you proud of your cousin, my cousin by marriage, God bless him, flyin' those damn' great Hurricanes up an' down the sky all day an' shootin' down the Messerschmitts, pop-pop-pop, eh? Pop-pop-pop.' He sniggered into his glass.

'Me fly Hurricanes? No fear!' exclaimed Herbert. 'You wouldn't get me up in one of those things, not for all the tea in China, nor all the Scotch in Scotchland, I mean Scotland. No, it's *terra firma* and me own two feet for old Bertie Mapp. Officer Commanding Transport Pool. The quiet life and plenty of dodges for them that know them, eh?'

'Damn' useful work it is too,' said the Major admiringly. 'Can't fight a war without a transport pool, as Mr. Churchill was sayin' on the wireless the other night. Sinews of war. An army marchin' on its stomach. Never could understand that, by the way.'

Withers, like an angel of deliverance, made her appearance at the door to announce that lunch was ready. It was not a successful meal. The bottle of burgundy evaporated all too quickly, for Bertie declared that he liked a drop o' wine, especially at Christmas, and the Major said it wasn't long to Christmas so why not, and soon Withers had been despatched to bring in another bottle. Herbert ate hugely of Woolton Pie and bread-and-butter pudding, remarking that it reminded him of home (this made Elizabeth shudder). After lunch the Major suggested a drop of port, enabling Elizabeth to slip away, 'leaving you men to your port', to the garden where she cooled her burning face and tried to think of

93

some way out of this disaster. It was too late to call off the Bridge party now, and besides, Herbert had been promised Bridge. If he were to be deprived of it, God alone knew what he might say. What was more, Major Benjy was in such a dangerously rebellious mood than he might broadcast throughout Tilling the news that Elizabeth had cancelled her Bridge party because she didn't think her cousin was good enough to meet her friends. . . On all sides she was hedged in by disaster.

'How was I to know?' she demanded of her sweet flowers; the sweet flowers nodded their heads in tacit agreement.

Major Benjy, oblivious of his wife's torment, helped his cousin by marriage, with whom he was well pleased, to some more port. 'Nothin' too good for our brave lads,' he exclaimed, lifting his full glass to his lips, 'not even Lizbeth's best port, eh Herbert?'

'The fellows in the Mess all call me Bertie.'

'Here's health, then, Bertie old man,' replied the Major.

'That was a grand meal, Major, and a grand drop of port to wash it down,' continued Bertie Mapp. 'She's a good sort, is Auntie Betty. Not at all stuck up or anything. A real brick.'

'Fine woman, Lizbeth Mapp-Flint,' agreed the Major. 'Greatest esteem for the li'l woman. Won' hear a word said against her, not even if the King himself were to say it, not that he would, God bless him. Challenge any man who says a word against my Liz to a duel. Two duels. Fact is, I once challenged a fellow to a duel for saying a word 'gainst my Liz. Lizbeth Mapp as she was then.'

'Go on!' said Bertie, much impresed. 'A duel? Who won?'

'Oh, duel never got fought. Padre stopped it.' The Major sighed, as if reflecting on missed opportunities. 'But the feller did die shortly after, so I s'pose I did.'

'You're a character and no mistake,' said the admiring Bertie. 'I'm too fond of my health to go getting involved in duels, and there might not be a Padre handy to stop it.'

'Mind you,' continued the Major, 'and don't go repeating this to all an' sundry, but Lizbeth can be a li'l bit hard on a feller at times. A marvellous woman, but a man likes a li'l drink from time to time. A li'l drink before lunch, perhaps, and a glass o' wine with his lunch, and a spot o' port after, an' pr'aps a whisky-an'-soda around five-o'clock and so on. But Lizbeth – Lizbeth Mapp-Flint, God bless her, and so say all of us – she don't hold wi' li'l drinks. Fine woman nonetheless. Wouldn't dream o' criticisin' her. Fight any man that says a word against her, as I said just now. But there it is. The ladies!' He drank a toast.

'Come on now, Major,' said Bertie when they had refilled their glasses, 'all respect where respect's due, and don't you go challenging me to a duel, but things have come to a pretty poor pass when a chap can't have a spot of whisky or a glass of wine in his own home. A spot of whisky is a man's birthright when the lights are low and the little birdies are singing in the hedgerows. A spot of whisky and a glass of wine with your lunch, or a glass of ale, or a drop of brandy, that's what we're fighting this war for. Won't be any small glasses of whisky or drops of wine if Hitler has his way. Not that I'm saying Auntie Betty's like Hitler. Not the ame thing at all. What I mean is, here you've got an old soldier, autumn of his days, served his country under the burning Indian sun, shot tigers to protect cowering villagers, needs a bit of the right stuff to cheer the evening-tide of life. Hello, Auntie,' he cried as Elizabeth entered the room, 'bad show this, not letting the Major here have a small glass of whisky now and again. Not British.'

Elizabeth, who had been doing deep breathing exercises in the garden, was able to smile broadly at this outrageous remark.

'What nonsense! Dear Benjy-boy's always welcome to drink spirits if he feels in need of them. There you go, nuisance, telling all sorts of lies about me when my back is turned. Naughty boy! But I'm sure you'd rather come and look at my lovely flowers instead of frowsting indoors on such a glorious day!'

'Not a glorious day,' grumbled the Major, 'going to rain any minute.'

But Cousin Bertie was only too pleased to look at the lovely flowers and, as Elizabeth had hoped, the fresh air did something to clear his addled head, for he talked authoritatively about early potatoes and pruning fruit-trees, and managed to smell the lovely flowers without falling over, rather more than Elizabeth had dared to expect. Major Benjy, anxious to appear knowledgeable in front of his new friend, suddenly became a great authority on horticulture, and with a great sweep of the arm towards the onions, exclaimed that the carrots were shaping up well for the time of year.

'Or is it tomatoes?' he wondered.

By taking a leisurely tour of both front and back gardens, examining every living thing as if it were some unique specimen from the greenhouses of Kew Gardens (and discussing its future prospects with grave concern), Elizabeth managed to keep the inebriates out in the fresh air and away from fermented liquor until four-o'clock. At that point Bertie offered to take the Major for a spin on the back of his motor-bicycle, and although the prospect of becoming a widow had appeared to be not without its advantages during the last few hours, Elizabeth came down on the side of married bliss and expressed playful horror at such a proposal. So the Major and Cousin Bertie went to look at the Major's tiger-skins, while Elizabeth hastened to make preparations for the tea party. All might conceivably not be lost if the tea was short and the Bridge so engrossing that her guests did not notice the condition her menfolk were in. Thank God that Lucia would not be there to see. Or (perish the thought) quaint Irene. But Bridge at a shilling a hundred instead of the usual sixpence would induce a greater absorption in the game and a corresponding lack of attention to the honoured guest, ruinous though the financial outcome might be.

Diva, Evie and the Padre (on foot) and the Wyses (on

tricycles) struggled up the Military Road, finding refuge in Grebe just as the clouds began to burst.

'So fortunate!' exclaimed Mr. Wyse when introductions had been made. 'I would be greatly distressed were Susan's sables to be exposed to rainwater. Such a pity that we can no longer use the Royce.'

'A Rolls-Royce!' exclaimed Bertie. 'You don't say. I'm rather keen on motor-cars, as a matter o' fact. Always wanted to have a look under the bonnet of a Rolls-Royce. Broke down, is it?'

'Not at all,' replied Mr. Wyse coldly. 'But alas! Petroleum is so hard to obtain in the present national emergency and we must forgo our frivolous pleasures in the interests of the war-effort.'

'Get away!' exclaimed Bertie. 'Now as it happens I'm in charge of the transport pool at the base, which is how I get juice for my Rudge. You just say the word, Algy old man, and I can get you all the coupons you want. Any pal of Auntie's is a pal of mine, as they say, and it's sinful to leave a Rolls-Royce motor-car gathering dust in a garage.'

Elizabeth shuddered. That she should live to see the day when a cousin of hers should address Mr. Wyse as 'Algy old man' in her house. Why, it was as bad as calling the King 'Georgie'. Or, she could not help but think, *Georgino*. Even without the damnable familiarity, the offer was bad enough, and Elizabeth's guests were dumbfounded by it.

'My deepest thanks for your most unselfish offer,' replied Mr. Wyse, 'but I could not expose you to the risk of the displeasure of your superiors by allowing me unauthorised access to petroleum coupons. I would never forgive myself if, through your generosity, you were to incur the wrath of the authorities.'

A muffled gasp arose from the assembled Tillingites. Never had the courteous Mr. Wyse been heard to utter such a violent rebuke.

'That's very considerate of you, Algy old chap,' replied Bertie, on whom this fulminating blast appeared

97

to have no effect, 'though I can't say as I think there's any risk o' being caught out. Why, half the chaps in the camp are on the fiddle in one way or other, and the brass-hats too, I'll be bound. Still, there it is, and I won't twist your arm. If you change your mind just mention it to Auntie Betty, and she'll pass on the message, I'm sure. How about you, Reverend, or you, Mrs. Plaistow? No? Well, there we go.'

Evie uttered a shrill squeak and the Padre explained that neither he nor Mrs. Plaistow kept a motor.

'Don't you now?' replied Bertie. 'Well, that's odd, folks of your standing. I suppose you wouldn't bother in a little place like this, with the narrow streets and the cobblestones. All very inconvenient if you ask me. The town council should pull up those cobbles and put down tarmac. Much easier on tyres.'

If the odious Bertie's offer of illicit petroleum had not already condemned him in the eyes of Elizabeth's guests, such blatant criticism of the town would surely have done so. Those who were fortunate enough to be of Tilling needless to say looked with scorn and pity on those who lived elsewhere; that a person from Liverpool (Diva was not quite sure where Liverpool was, but that in no way diminished her condemnation of the place) should take it upon himself to disparage the narrow cobbled streets that were such a feature of the town was a crime against God. Evie looked at Diva, and Diva looked at the Padre. If cobbled streets and pneumatic tyres were incompatible, then clearly it was the pneumatic tyres that were at fault.

'Aye, 'twud be a sair matter to a body to justify a motor in our wee town,' said the Padre stiffly, 'it being as a city compactly builded together, as the Psalmist says. And I dinna ken that we feel the lack o' such things, eh, Mistress Plaistow?'

'Absolutely,' said Diva. 'No need. Do perfectly well without.' This of course was by way of being an unintentional criticism of the Wyses who, before the war and petroleum shortage, had been known to order the Royce to travel the fifty yards from Starling Cottage to Mallards on a warm sunny day. 'So much easier to go by tricycle,' Diva added, trying to conciliate.

'You wouldn't catch me on one of those potty little things,' said Bertie. 'Give me my old Rudge every day. Eighty-five it'll do on the straight with a slight downhill, gradient.'

'Now, I hate to interrupt your sweet chatter, but how about a nice game of Bridge?' demanded Elizabeth grimly.

It was a malign Fate that had made Elizabeth invite all her friends to meet this beastly man before she had the chance to see what he was like, and a malign Fate followed her relentlessly throughout the day. The cut for tables matched Mr. Wyse, Evie, Bertie and Elizabeth, and the cut for partners completed the disaster. Bertie was to partner Mr. Wyse while Evie partnered Elizabeth. Diva, Susan and the Padre, at the other table with Major Benjy, seemed uninterested in their game despite the monumental stakes, for all the attention that they would normally have directed towards the rubber was given to eavesdropping on the prodigal cousin. The result was that Major Benjy was able to revoke without detection, and his normal errors passed without criticism and, on one occasion, earned absent-minded praise from his partner. The monster meanwhile assured his table that he enjoyed a little flutter on a game of cards, although Pontoon was his game really; his Bridge was certainly after the school of Sefton Park, and the conventions of that barbarous place were entirely foreign to Mr. Wyse, for all his knowledge of the conventions of Tilling, Whitchurch and Capri. As a result the men were hopelessly overbid, and only monstrous mismanagement of her hand prevented Elizabeth from acquiring untold wealth from Mr. Wyse. This was all the more heartrending as Elizabeth's cards were invariably excellent, and she who had so frequently declared that she was liable to forget what an ace looked like, so rarely did she see one, was fully enabled on this occasion to refresh her memory. As a result of Bertie's recklessness and Elizabeth's desperate attempts to protect Mr. Wyse from financial ruin, total confusion reigned, and Elizabeth began to wonder whether Mr. Wyse might not suspect that he had been lured there to be fleeced of his money, as card-sharpers fleece unsuspecting travellers on race-trains. Meanwhile, Evie was continually reviling her for her incompetence, and she could do nothing but apologise meekly.

'Well now, Algy,' said Bertie as the cards were gathered in, 'we don't seem to be doing very well. We'll have to pull our socks up if we don't want to lose our shirts, eh?'

Mr Wyse admitted that his partner had been a trifle unfortunate in getting such poor cards.

'Never mind,' replied Bertie. 'Let's just keep awake, shall we? My bid? Three hearts.'

This time Elizabeth's hand was laden with hearts – when spades had been trumps her hand had been as black as coal, and when diamonds had been turned up her hand was a positive Kimberley – and in a desperate attempt to avert disaster she overbid to such an extent that she could not conceivably win. Unfortunately, she did, and by doing so won the rubber.

'Well, blow me,' said the odious one, 'you're a sly one, Auntie Betty. That was a cracking good game, anyhow, even though it's cost us dear. Still, easy come, easy go, eh Algy? What a game!'

'Allow me to pay our joint debts, partner,' said Mr. Wyse icily. 'It was entirely due to my inability to respond properly to your bidding that we suffered this calamity.'

'That's very decent of you,' said Bertie, 'a very gentlemanly thing to do. Not that it was entirely your fault, but you did get in rather a tangle. Never mind though, it's only a bit of fun, isn't it?'

It had proved an expensive bit of fun for Mr. Wyse, and Elizabeth's hand shook as she received the mountain of silver – not quite thirty pieces but very nearly – and divided it with her partner. In the next rubber, however, she was her cousin's partner, and as he strove to better his fortune by still more adventurous bidding she was left after its conclusion not only with the shame of having sponsored this barbarian's entry into Tilling society but with a heavily depleted purse as well, so that Mr. Wyse got his shillings back and Evie positively clanked as she rose from the table. Since Major Benjy had also been a heavy loser, it did not seem improbable that the Bartletts would now be able to afford a motor, probably a Royce.

'Many thanks for a most enjoyable afternoon, Mrs. Mapp-Flint,' said Mr. Wyse, and Elizabeth felt a wave of sympathy for the *Titanic*: collison with an iceberg was a horrible thing. She knew all too well what chatterings and whisperings and cries of 'No!' there would be in the High Street tomorrow, the little groups that would form outside the shops to disperse like flocks of peewits at her approach, for had not she so often thrilled such gatherings with tales of other people's failings and disasters, heartless woman that she was! Worst of all, she could see Lucia in her mind's eye, smiling sweetly and refusing to rejoice in her rival's downfall, angelic in her mercy and magnanimity, while Irene pranced about, turning the full force of her diabolic power of mimicry towards Sefton Park.

'Such a pleasure to meet your cousin,' squeaked Evie, as she scuttled away through the overcast evening; and such a pleasure it would be, reflected Elizabeth, to rend the characters of the Mapp-Flints (and especially the Mapps) over dinner. As the Wyses followed on in a cloud of tricycles and sables, Elizabeth heard the clink of glasses and the whoosh of the siphon. Bertie and Benjy were having another little drink.

Lucia dined that evening at the Vicarage, in reply to a somewhat incoherent summons from wee wifie. Pausing only to change and collect some sugar for her coffee (for only at Starling Cottage and Mallards was that priceless commodity issued free to guests) she sped into the night, her senses racing with pleasurable anticipation. She knew that today Elizabeth had unveiled her cousin, the dashing young fighter-pilot, and it was one of the ancient customs of Tilling, of an antiquity comparable only with the beating of the bounds and the decoration of the church at Harvest Festival, that tea at someone else's house meant just a bit of something on a tray for dinner. If the Padre and Evie had decided to organise a last-minute party, they must have news that could not wait for marketing time tomorrow, and this news, unless it was that Hitler had surrendered, must concern Elizabeth's cousin and, in addition, must mean disaster. A triumph could have waited until morning.

7

One of the most melancholy tasks imposed upon the good people of Tilling by the war was firewatching from the church-tower. What was so pleasant and vital during the day (namely looking down from high places at what was going on) was a dreary business by night, with no one about and no news, and the miserable possibility of seeing something catch fire (although mercifully such events were rare). Even the ladies of Tilling, who would generally find enough topics of conversation in the doings of their neighbours to last for ever, generally fell silent after a few hours of this unpleasant duty. Yet none shirked their turn, and Mr. Rice the poulterer, who was now the A.R.P. warden, had no gaps in his roster. Susan Wyse in her sables, Lucia with one of her first husband's telescopes, even Diva, whose short, round shape was ill designed for scrambling up spiral staircases, all took their places at the appointed time. By a monstrous error on Mr. Rice's part, it was Elizabeth and quaint Irene who kept watch on the evening of the day after the disastrous tea party.

'Qui-hi, Auntie Betty!' exclaimed the quaint one, in accents redolent of Sefton Park. 'I like a spot o' firewatching meself, though this tower's a bit too high off the ground for an airman like me.'

Elizabeth bit her tongue. Although she was tempted to say something rather acid in reply to this childish taunt, her wit was alkaline compared with that of Irene Coles. If the two of them were to be marooned on a church-tower for any length of time, a state of armed neutrality should be arrived at.

'Naughty girl!' laughed Elizabeth tolerantly. 'How wicked of you to tease me with that affectionate nickname. So sorry you couldn't have come to meet my dear Herbert. I feel you and he would have had so much in common.'

'Common sounds about right, from what I've heard. Still, we Socialists are above such things, aren't we, Comrade Mapp?'

'So few young people in Tilling these days,' ground on Elizabeth. 'Only the old fogies left. And no doubt you feel a little lonely, now that a certain rather special person has gone away.'

'Who?' asked Irene. 'Mr. Georgie?'

'No, dear, a certain officer in the Staffordshire Regiment,' said Elizabeth, grimly coy. Attack, the best form of defence.

'What, old Henry? Come off it, Mapp!' The quaint one hooted with laughter that echoed off the roofs of the ancient town. 'Glad to see the back of him in the end. I don't know. Men!'

Elizabeth glowed so red in the dark that she was in danger of being taken for a fire herself.

'A trifle too blasted familiar, old Henry was becoming,' continued Irene, 'so I sent him away with a flea in his ear. He only tried to kiss me in the street. Me! But you know what these soldiers are like, eh, Mapp old girl?' And she winked and nudged Elizabeth viciously with her elbow.

Elizabeth winced, and her blush threatened to illuminate all Sussex. Attack, it seemed, was a particularly weak form of defence. 'Oh look,' she said quickly, and pointed.

'Where?'

'Such a pretty full moon, I mean,' replied Elizabeth. 'Almost like daylight.'

'So much easier for those dear little bombers to see their way,' cooed Irene. 'Sounds suspiciously like you *want* them to be able to navigate accurately.'

'What a wicked thing to say!'

'I'm not so sure about you, Mapp. On the face of it you're respectable enough, but you never can tell. And what are these reports I've been hearing of lights down on the sand-dunes late at night? Have you been signalling to the U-boats? No wonder you were so keen to scrape acquaintance with Lucia's officers.'

This level of quaintness would usually be answered by a slammed door and retreating footsteps; sadly, there was no escape. Elizabeth stood up and walked across to the other side of the tower, from which she could look out over the Norman Tower and the ornamental cannon. Thence her beloved Benjy-boy would soon be making his way, on patrol with the Home Guard. Indeed, at that very moment she heard footsteps, albeit more staggering than marching, and the sound of singing. To her disgust she recognised the voice, and recalled that there was an unsavoury little public-house down just below the tower. She stood up again and as Major Benjy, faintly but definitely audible, assured the darkling town that beside the old Moulmein Pagoda, looking eastwards to the sea, there was a Burmah girl a-setting, and that he was sure that she thought of him, she returned to the other side of the tower.

'For the wind is in the palm-trees,' warbled Irene in her pleasant contralto, 'and the temple bells do say. . . . Oh hello, Mapp. Back already?' She, like Elizabeth, was blessed with acute hearing. 'Someone singing in Lion Street. Pretty song. Here, do you think it's a spy passing coded messages? Or just a drunk?' Elizabeth set her jaw and did not answer. 'Rather romantic, I think. As if the boring old church of Tilling was a Buddhist pagoda, and you some saffron-skinned enchantress waiting for his return from the wars. Very touching, I call it, being serenaded like that. Will you join me in a chorus of "Pale hands I loved beside the Shalimar"?'

Another corner of the church-tower directly overlooked Mallards, and Elizabeth transferred her scowl and her self to it. Perhaps, she thought, a German bomber on its way somewhere might accidentally drop a stick of bombs on her ancestral home. She would, of course be heartbroken, but then again, Lucia might be at home tonight playing her piano or reading Aristophanes in the study. That would be something. . . .

Irene, as was her custom on these occasions, had set up her easel and begun to paint. She had begun a series of studies of Tilling by night, all of which were almost completely black.

'It might interest you to know that I got my call-up papers today,' she shouted.

'No!' cried Elizabeth. Within her, her heart sang as loudly as Major Benjy and much more tunefully. 'How cruel! What a terrible loss to us all! Is there no way of avoiding it? When will you be going?'

' 'Fraid it won't be for some time yet, Mapp. I've volunteered to go and work on the canals. They'll let me know when they want me. I've fixed it up with some pals of mine in London, artists and so on. We'll be taking a canal boat from . . . but I'd better not tell you. Careless talk, you know, and I'm still not sure you aren't passing messages to Adolf. Only joking. In fact, you ought to come with us, make up a four for Bridge. I like a little flutter meself, don't I, Auntie Betty?'

'Alas, I fear that my advanced years would not permit me to be of any use. I leave it all to·you young things. So strenuous, hauling those picturesque barges along the towpath. How brave you are!'

'It ought to be a bit of a lark, I suppose. There, how do you like the effect of that?'

'Delightful. So full of colour and movement,' said Elizabeth distractedly, without looking at the pitch-black canvas. 'Approximately how long before you leave?'

'Can't say I'm sure. Not like Mr. Georgie, dashing off to London at a moment's notice. Have you ever thought of having the inside of Grebe done all in black? Very colourful colour, black. Full of movement. Black walls, black ceilings, black carpets on the floor. Very effective, and keeps the A.R.P. out of your hair. Say the word and I'll be round in my overalls.'

*　　*　　*

106

The war had certainly had an inflationary effect on the value of news in Tilling. The minor incidents of life – Benjy getting tipsy or Diva resurrecting the chintz roses – no longer provided material for two or three days of intense discussion and speculation as they would once have done, for greater and more momentous events were now so plentiful, what with officers and black markets and wireless broadcasts, that there were simply not enough hours in the day to do them justice. Next morning the High Street buzzed with two enormous issues – Irene was going away to lug barges with a lot of painters, and Elizabeth had been appointed head of the Tilling Red Cross, no other candidate having been found to oppose her. In the draper's queue, Diva imparted these tidings to Evie, who had already heard them from Elizabeth.

'Head of the Red Cross!' said Diva. 'She's going to be measured for her uniform on Monday. Grey serge with a velour hat to match. Quite a monopoly of uniforms. Major Benjy in his and Elizabeth in hers,' she concluded enviously, thinking of the grey serge.

Evie gasped. 'Just like Florence Nightingale! Do you suppose she'll have a watch pinned on the front, or is that just nurses?'

'And Irene going to work on the barges with two artists from London. They'll have lots of time for painting, when they're not pulling the barges along.'

'Don't the boats have engines nowadays? I must ask her. Fancy that!' For a moment Evie wished that she was going away on a barge, or had joined the Red Cross, or was going to broadcast on the B.B.C. or something. 'Do you suppose Elizabeth will actually tend the sick? How exciting.'

'Doubt it, even if there were any wounded to tend, which there aren't, thank God. Hate to think what would happen if the Hun did invade. Major Benjy doing the fighting and Elizabeth looking after the casualties. Not that I don't think it's very good of them both. Still, I could have sworn I heard the Major singing in the High Street last night.'

'No! What?'

' "Road to Mandalay". Almost as if he were tipsy or

something. Still, I suppose it was a marching song, though if his men march like that they must get out of step a lot.'

'They probably do,' said Evie.

Lucia, hermit-like in Mallards, crunched a piece of carbonised toast topped with some rather unpleasant corned beef from the emergency store, and fought off the despairing thoughts that crowded in on her from every side of the empty house. In front of her was a letter from Georgie.

> ... will be broadcast on Monday, with me talking about Things To Do With Corned Beef [was there anything, she mused, that anyone could do with corned beef?] and Tasty Ways with Parsnips. Teddy Broome says that that will do to start with, because not everybody can get the ingredients for lobster à la Riseholme, even doing it my way without the lobster. And Lord Tony's left the Staffordshires and is working here in London, and he says he can't tell me what he's doing in case I'm a German. How horrid of him! But he did say that he's mentioned my cooking to Mr. Churchill. Apparently they were having dinner somewhere and the boiled potatoes had gone all floury. Anyway, there're all so impressed with my recipes that they want me to do even more broadcasts if the first one is a success, so I don't know when I shall be back. Foljambe has bought herself a new pair of shoes for the broadcasts – she's assisting me in the kitchen. Oh, you know that of course. Anyway, take care of yourself. Remember, a pinch of salt makes all the difference to a packet of custard.

> Your devoted husband,
Georgie.

She folded the letter and replaced it in its envelope. Diva had called earlier to tell her the news – the devastating bomb-shell about the Red Cross appointment and the grey serge, and the depressing news that Irene was going away. Quaint she most undoubtedly was, embarrassingly so at times, but she was the only person in Tilling capable of keeping Elizabeth in order. The whole disastrous Bertie incident would be drowned in the flood of grey serge and glory. Why, oh why, had she not thought of it herself? Too wrapped up in officers and cooking and her own unfortunate plight. . .

'It's too unkind,' she exclaimed. 'If only Georgie were here! We would put our heads together and I would be sure to think of something.'

The doorbell rang – so preoccupied had she been that she had not kept her eye on the street – and she remembered that she would have to answer it herself. She slid the piece of toast and corned beef into a drawer, for it would scarcely do for anyone to see her eating such rubbish when her husband was the country's leading authority on corned beef, and tripped out into the hall. Elizabeth was standing on the doorstep, clad in a uniform that made her look like an enormous grey tent. She'll be doing her shopping with a lamp in her hand instead of a basket, Lucia thought sourly, for the sight of her rival surrounded by so much grey serge was more distasteful than even toast and corned beef.

'And how is our dear anchorite today? May I just pop in for a moment? A brief chat about medical matters, since you are still chairman of the hospital board.' The word 'still' stressed a little bit too heavily perhaps. 'Such a long time since we had one of our little tête-à-têtes.'

'Dear Elizabeth, how thoughtful of you to come and see me. I feel so very lonely with my dear Georgie away. A letter from him this morning. Doing such good work in London – the first broadcast is on Monday, and already his fame has reached the ears of Mr. Churchill himself. I am inviting everyone to come and listen. It's at four-o'clock, so we can have tea and perhaps a little Bridge afterwards. And do be sure to get your cook to listen, dear. Such useful ideas! Corned beef and parsnips he promises us, and Foljambe will be helping him in the studio kitchen, handing him his instruments like a nurse assisting a surgeon. Let us go to the garden-room.'

Elizabeth licked her lips. Would Lucia offer her a cup of tea? And if so, would she make it herself? And if so, how horrible could it taste?

'So sorry you did not drop by earlier,' drawled Lucia, 'for then we could have lunched together. Carrot pie and bottled plums – Georgie's recipe, of course, and there was plenty for two. And to think that, had cook not taken into her head to fly off to Wolverhampton, neither of us could have learnt to cook, and the nation would have lost the use of an invaluable talent.'

'What a comfort it is to us to know that our menfolk are doing their bit,' replied Elizabeth raggedly. 'I see nothing, positively nothing, of my Benjy these days.'

No, thought Lucia, but you hear enough of him, by all accounts, 'Indeed,' she drawled, 'and how good for him to be able to feel he can still contribute something, however small, towards the war-effort. Not everyone can have a special talent, like my Georgie for instance, but – how does Karl Marx put it? – from each according to his ability. And the Major does have a wealth of military experience, albeit that little of it is likely to be applicable to modern conditions. Whereas – just think! who would have thought Georgie had that priceless gift locked away in his head, like a Gutenberg bible gathering dust in some junk shop, waiting to be discovered. Or,' she added, for the junk-shop analogy could have been better expressed, 'even like Sir Francis Drake, poised to return should England ever need him again.'

'Such a quaint legend!' said Elizabeth.

The battle-lines were drawn. Lucia clearly would talk of nothing but Georgie, while Elizabeth had determined to speak of nothing but the Red Cross and the Home Guard. Would sheer lung-power decide the issue, or was timing the key to victory?.

'And even little, insignificant me. I am so pleased, so honoured that the Red Cross saw fit to ask me to join them in their essential work,' Elizabeth almost shouted,

110

for she had opted for volume against finesse. 'The care of the sick, so important in wartime.'

'Oh my dear Elizabeth, it is vital, vital. That is why I bless heaven that I was inspired – it must have been inspiration – to endow the Emmeline Lucas Operating Theatre when I did. Involved as I have been ever since in the running of the hospital, I have been able to reassure myself that in the event – *absit omen!* – of its being required to do so, the hospital will be able to provide the most up-to-date facilities. . . .'

'But surely you will agree that what counts is dedicated and compassionate nursing. . . .' howled Elizabeth.

'Naturally. You have put your finger on the hub of the matter.' Lucia's drawl was becoming softer and more relaxed the shriller Elizabeth became. 'What is the use of the most advanced equipment if the doctors and nurses are not of an equally high standard? And, as chairman of the board of governors, I hope that I have made my small contribution towards setting that excellent standard that now prevails.'

'Such a blessing,' snarled her companion, 'but how valuable is the work of the voluntary services, taking pressure off the overworked. . .'

'Fortunately over half our beds are empty at the moment. But it is such a relief to know that there would be so many willing helpers should they ever be required. What a hive of patriotic endeavour our blessed little town is! I feel it is a legacy of my – of our joint term of public office, this spirit of community, this willingness to devote oneself to the welfare of others.'

'Major Benjy's troop is to get an anti-tank projector,' said Elizabeth desperately.

'Just the one?' replied Lucia sweetly. 'Then let us hope there will be only one tank. Better still, let us hope there will be none at all. So wretched that our dear Home Guard should be in such want of proper equipment. How they can be expected to face the German hordes with inadequate or antiquated weapons I fail to understand.

Indeed, I should say that they need better equipment than the Regular forces, so that what they lack in youth, experience and fitness might be somewhat compensated for in superior armament. But enough of these gloomy thoughts. Look! The sun is shining again. How blue the sky is.'

'And while we yet command that sky,' ventured Elizabeth, 'the enemy cannot touch us, thanks to our brave men of the R.A.F.'

Elizabeth realised at once that this was a mistake. She should not have introduced that of all topics. Lucia smiled. 'Ah yes, an admirable body of young men,' she said, 'drawn from all parts of the country and all walks of life, all classes of society, all united in the common cause of freedom. The rank is, after all, but the penny-stamp; that is one thing that the war has taught me. To think that before these dark days, I would not have cared to know some of the fearless airmen who now risk their lives daily both in the air and,' she added mercilessly, 'on the ground. Simply because their appetites are material, not spiritual, because they would rather expend their energies on motor-bicycles and whisky than on poetry and music! How blind we are to the good in our fellow-man, until Circumstance fairly takes us by the scruff of the neck and shakes us! I shall never again laugh at anyone because they appear uncouth in their behaviour or commonplace in their speech. Never!'

This eloquent apologia seemed to affect Elizabeth deeply, for she rose as if to leave. 'Don't bother to show me out,' she said, 'I know how difficult it must be for you without any servants.'

'Servants!' cried Lucia. 'Why, I hardly miss them at all. You see, dear, another disguised blessing of the war. When I had people at my beck and call, to open doors for me and cook my food, I hardly did anything for myself at all. I was not properly alive. I was cushioned from all the hard realities of the world. How out of touch I was! Now I cook, I clean, I do my share of the work; I don't think I could bring myself to become reliant on the service of

112

others ever again. Domestic service, I believe, is an institution which should not survive the war. It is demeaning both to the servant and the served. Why, it makes one like a little baby again, who must be washed and fed and clothed by others. So demoralising!'

'Such a pretty cobweb!' exclaimed Elizabeth. 'How beautifully its silken threads catch the light. So sensitive of you to have left it there when you last dusted. So nice to have had such a pleasant chat.'

'Monday, four-o'clock, Georgie's broadcast,' Lucia called after her retreating form, and retired to finish her toast and corned beef. She must mention that cobweb to the cleaning woman when she came in later on that afternoon.

It was pleasant, she reflected, as she forced her teeth to meet through the slate-like toast, to crush Elizabeth in private, to ignore her uniform (she hadn't referred to it once) and to drown her in Georgie and Socialism. She was flexing her dialectic muscles, performing intellectual callisthenics. In public, of course, it would not be so easy. Uniforms, and Red Crosses, and soon no doubt anti-tank projectors, fascinated the easily led citizens of the town, and she knew that they would be impatient to see battle joined between herself and the pretender to her throne. As if there were not enough conflict in the world. . . But the thought of Georgie's broadcast, and the tea and Bridge to follow, inspired her. She pushed away her plate (the char could see to it later) and went forth into the street, eager to know what quaint Irene had said about Elizabeth as grey-serge-clad comforter of the sick, and whether Major Benjy had really sung 'The Road to Mandalay' in a drunken voice all over the town the other night.

The Padre was coming out of the church as she walked around the charming square, with its timbered houses and low windows.

'Guid morrow to ye, Mistress Pillson. And have ye heard from that guid man o' yourn that's awa in t' city o'

113

Lunnon?' The Padre had added Captain Oldshaw's Yorkshire and Bertie Mapp's Sefton Park to the Woolton Pie of language that he spoke. 'Happen he'll be ready soon to gi' us his first wee talk on mekkin' t' most of our ration-books.'

'A letter only this morning. Monday, at four-o'clock. So you and dear Evie must come and listen with me, and a little tea and Bridge to follow. He says the first talk will be on corned beef and parsnips.'

'No!' exclaimed the Padre, fascinated. 'And what will he find tae say about sich puir fare? 'Twud be like to our Lord turning t'water into wine, an he ken a way o' turning corned beef into victuals.'

'Oh fie, Padre, such blasphemy! I shall stop up my ears,' replied Lucia, delighted to find that Georgie's glorious deeds were the subject of such interest. 'And now you must tell me what's been happening, for I have been so isolated in my little house of late that I hardly know whether the town is still here or not. How is dear Elizabeth? And the Major?'

'So ye've no heard about Mistress Elizabeth's glorious new appointment?' declared the Padre, and went on to reveal that Elizabeth and the Major were in especial favour at the moment. He waxed almost lyrical about the Red Cross, and the anti-tank projector was clearly a gift from the Almighty. The projector, it appeared, was a sort of device that hurled bombs at an approaching tank, and although no one could work it and there were no bombs to go with it at present, could clearly turn the tide of a battle, should such an unfortunate situation arise. The Padre had therefore chosen as the text of Sunday's sermon 'He breaketh the bow, and knappeth the spear in sunder, and burneth the chariots in the fire.' A tank, after all, was a sort of modern chariot, and the projector would doubtless have a similarly devastating effect on bows and spears were it to encounter them.

Thoughtfully Lucia made her way down the narrow street overlooked by the magnificent tower of the church, and knocked at the door of Wasters. She issued her invitation to Diva, and was quizzed about the broadcast, which was pleasant, but was also briefed on Elizabeth's saintliness, which was not. Vexed by this, she took herself off to Taormina, to imbibe some venom from Irene, who obliged with a fine imitation of Elizabeth tending a sick airman from Sefton Park. This pleasure was muted by an encounter with the Wyses, who praised Elizabeth but did not ask about Georgie until she prompted them to it. As she returned to Mallards, she felt that the contest was evenly balanced, neither side having the advantage. One notable success, or one disaster, would settle it. If she failed to provide drinkable tea and edible toast on Monday, or if Major Benjy's new projector went wrong or blew up a cow, then Tilling would desert the failure and adhere to the other. But if Georgie's parsnips were a success, or if Elizabeth contrived to tend a sick person before the cessation of hostilities, then the successful candidate would enjoy the adulation of the masses, and her rival must be forgotten.

Sunday was a tense, anxious time, and the usual assembly at the church-door brief and unusually tactful. The Padre's sermon had praised the anti-tank projector, but the second lesson had been the miracle of loaves and fishes, which must remind everyone of the forthcoming miracle of the parsnips and corned beef. Scriptural references to the healing of the sick had endorsed Elizabeth, but the Lord's Prayer itself, with its reference to daily bread, had favoured Lucia. The heavenly powers, then, were undecided. Lucia spent the evening at the piano; Elizabeth bandaged Withers until that worthy soul protested that she must go and make the dinner.

Monday morning passed slowly, and in the High Street the queues in the shops hissed with whispered speculation. Corned beef was in unusually great demand, and parsnips, which were as a rule easily obtainable, suddenly became as scarce as truffles. Lucia noticeably

115

bought both, while Elizabeth examined everyone minutely for the slightest signs of ill health. Lunch was hurriedly consumed, and Patience cards laid out to beguile the impatience of expectation. A light shower began at half-past two. Would someone slip on the wet cobbles in West Street and twist their ankle, so that Elizabeth could render medical assistance?

The wireless had been installed in the garden-room ever since the outbreak of war, and the chairs were arranged around it as for a concert or recital. Elizabeth sat in the front row, wearing more grey serge than ever and smiling sweetly, beside Lucia, who was also smiling, and who gripped a notebook with which to take down Georgie's every word in case anyone missed anything. The room filled up, and the apparatus was switched on. There was the usual humming, as of countless bees busy about a honeypot, a few sharp crackles, and a faint sound, growing more distinct. There were a few minutes to go before the appointed time for the broadcast and the previous programme, a collection of popular songs sung by some female or other, was not yet finished. Lucia assumed the pained expression usually reserved for the gramophone, and waited. The voice, albeit cacophonous, was somehow familiar. . . .

'That was Miss Olga Bracely,' crackled the wireless, 'singing for us some of the numbers that she will be performing before an invited audience Somewhere in London tomorrow night.'

The gramophone face was replaced by a look of shock and horror. If Olga was going to sing in London tomorrow, if she was in the studio this afternoon broadcasting, then she must *be* in London, and staying at her house in Brompton Square with Georgie. And no mention of it in his letter! What on earth was she supposed to think about that? Or, for that matter, what could she do about it? She must go to London first thing tomorrow morning.

'The time is now four-o'clock,' enunciated the wireless, oblivious of Lucia's suffering. 'Mr. George Pillson

116

will now address us on "Making the Most of Your Ration-Book".'

A pause, interrupted by a crackle from the apparatus, and then Georgie's voice, sounding sheepish but marvellously clear.

'Hello everybody,' said Georgie. 'I'm going to talk to you today about "Making the Most of Your Ration-Book". Oh, he's just said that, how tar'some. As you may know, corned beef is a highly nutritious form of preserved meat, and can, with a little care, be transformed into a tasty and appetising dish. Here, then, is my recipe for corned beef à la Riseholme, to feed a family of two adults and two children. This is very economical and simple to make, and requires two ounces of corned beef. First, we weigh out the corned beef – hand me the scales, Miss Foljambe. . . .'

Mouths watered and imaginations ran riot as Georgie went through the recipe for corned beef à la Riseholme. Elizabeth alone remained stonily smiling, except when Georgie appeared to have knocked something over, probably a cup of milk, and said 'Drat the thing!' quite audibly, whereupon she permitted one of her eyebrows to rise slightly. The other guests, meanwhile, were as if transfixed, and the Padre licked his lips loudly several times. Corned beef à la Riseholme was followed by parsnip-and-potato pie, the mere assonance of which was enough to conjure up visions of replete and satisfied gourmets pushing back their chairs and voicing their praise of the cook.

'Next week,' concluded Georgie, 'we shall be making the best of rabbit and seeking substitutes for the artichoke. Goodbye, everyone. Are we off the air now? Oh!'

Victory was Lucia's, and such a victory! Yet she paid as much attention to the chatter of her guests as she would to idle talk of the weather. She could see only unpleasant conspiracy and distasteful intrigue. Georgie and Olga. Of course, they would dine together and congratulate each other on their cleverness, and perhaps Georgie might be persuaded to produce his celebrated

117

parsnip-and-potato pie, or even corned beef à la
Riseholme. The fact that all over the country, from Truro
to Thurso, her Georgie's recipe would undoubtedly be
followed to the letter was no consolation to her; rather
the reverse. The ovation he had received in Tilling Institute had been enough to make him abandon his wife and
home for the glamour of London. What effect would the
praise and respect of the entire nation, the eloquent
praise of the epicure who could once again enjoy artichoke where no antichokes were, the grunted thanks of
the coal-miner whose evening was illuminated by a glorious carrot pie, have upon his weak and vacillating
mind? He would probably never come back now; he
would tour the country with Olga, she singing vulgar
songs, he giving cookery demonstrations, the length and
breadth of Britain and the Empire, unless she went to
London tomorrow by the first train and stopped him. As
she made the tea and brought in the toast and apricot-
jam she resolved to do it, and having made the resolu-
tion, dismissed the unpleasant matter from her mind, for
there was work to be done here. Oh dear, she thought, I
hope I've made the tea strong enough.

There was comfort at least in the obvious discom-
fiture of Elizabeth, who was now so cast down that she
drank her tea and ate her toast without the slightest
grimace.

' 'Twud be a bonny thing if a' the menfolk o' Tilling
would do so much tae help their country,' she heard the
Padre remark to Diva. 'Sich a canny way wi' t'corned
beef, and the disguising o' t'malice in t'wee parsnips.'

'Dear Padre,' cooed Lucia, 'I am so glad you thought
so. And such reflected glory on our dear Tilling.'

'You must put up a plaque, dear,' said Elizabeth iron-
ically, 'to record the fact. "It was in this house that Mr.
George Pillson first discovered parsnip pie", or words to
that effect.'

'I don't think so, dear,' replied Lucia in her very best
drawl. 'It would look so much out of place, and besides,
one doesn't like to appear conspicuous or self-

advertising. Service is its own reward, after all.'

'Never would have thought so much could be done with parsnips,' wondered Diva. 'Such imagination. I've always been a bit wary of the beastly things, but now I shall have them at least once a week. I wonder what he'll do with turnips?'

'Just fancy, Kenneth,' squeaked Evie, 'and you always said that parsnips weren't fit for human beings to eat, not if they were starving in the desert, and it was a waste of valuable land growing them.'

'That was before yon master *chef* created sich a fine recipe. Why, I'll warrant he could conjure toothsome viands out o'firewood.'

'I too must confess that parsnips have never been greatly to my taste in the past,' added Mr. Wyse solemnly, 'but thanks to your talented husband, Mrs. Pillson, I feel that I am now much more aware of the potential of the vegetable. Susan, my dear, we must persuade our cook to make us parsnip pie this evening, and corned beef *à la Riseholme* tomorrow. And as soon as the recipe has been mastered – and so lucidly expressed was it by Mr. Pillson that I feel confident that the process will take no great time – it would be a signal honour, Mrs. Pillson, if you would dine with us and give, so to speak, your endorsement to our cook's interpretation of the recipe.'

'Delighted, Mr. Wyse,' said Lucia. 'Now then, a little rubber of Bridge? Excellent.'

But before the tables could be ordered and partners chosen, there was a furious knocking and ringing at the front-door. Lucia rose swiftly and answered it. On the step stood Major Benjy in his uniform, looking pale and haggard.

'Is my wife here, Mrs. Pillson? I'm afraid I have some rather bad news for her. In the garden-room? Thank you.'

The Major fairly raced through and leapt up the steps in a manner that belied his years. Elizabeth was in the process of trying to understand Diva's bid, and the unexpected intrusion of her husband caused her to drop her hand, which was heavy with aces.

'I've got something to tell you, Liz,' said the Major. 'Only just heard it myself. I had a message from the officer commanding the new garrison. They're carrying out manoeuvres near the river and the fact of the matter is, we're going to have to get out of Grebe for a while. Well, to cut a long story short, they want us out by tomorrow lunchtime, so we'd better start packing now.'

8

Lucia departed to London to keep an eye on Georgie. Unable to get a taxi at Waterloo, she was compelled to travel by omnibus to Brompton Square and, carrying her own suitcase, she struggled wearily up to the doorstep of Olga's house, just across the street from the rather more attractive dwelling where she herself had briefly held court as pretender to the social throne of the capital. But that interlude seemed to her now no more than a dream, an improbable fantasy. She put down her heavy load and rang the bell. The door was opened by Foljambe, imperturbable as ever. Georgie, it transpired, was having his bath and would be down shortly, so Lucia had an opportunity to inspect Miss Bracely's property. A small house, as she remembered, very expensively furnished yet managing at every turn to strike exactly the wrong note.

'Lucia!' exclaimed Georgie. 'How unexpected! What are you doing here?'

That, like everything else in the house, seemed to strike exactly the wrong note, but she put it down to the confusion of joyous reunion.

'Oh Georgie,' she gushed, 'the broadcast! When I heard it I simply had to drop everything and rush to your side.'

'Was it as bad as all that?'

'Georgie, it was a triumph! Magnificent! Tremendous! Not a parsnip to be had in the whole of Tilling. The only topic of conversation. How proud I felt. And yet, hearing your voice, distorted by that dwefful wireless but

121

unmistakably you, how lonely and how sad I felt, Georgie. As sweet Ovid so felicitously phrases it, *surgit amar'aliquid*, and I felt that I must congratulate you in person. So I caught the duellists' train and hurried up to London at once. I had to take an omnibus at Waterloo – what an adventure – and you'll never guess what all the cockney wives were talking about. Your broadcast, of course. I heard one of them say "parsnips" distinctly three times, another discoursed of corned beef, a third told her companions how she would look forward to Monday afternoons in future. And now, do you think I might have a cup of tea?'

Georgie, had he been able, like Lucia, to make classical references at this awful hour of the morning, would have reflected on the power of Orpheus to cause trees and rocks to follow him by the power of his poetry; as it was, he could only think of the Pied Piper of Hamelin, and that did not seem polite somehow.

'Fancy!' he said. 'You came all this way just because of my broadcast. How flattering. Will you be staying long?'

'Staying?' replied his wife, slipping her coat over her suitcases. 'The thought had not crossed my mind. Let me see; I've got so much to do in Tilling. And would dear Olga be able to put me up? Such a charming house, but so small.'

'Olga isn't staying here,' said Georgie firmly. 'Just me and Foljambe.'

'But she's singing in London tonight,' said Lucia, rather too much in the style of counsel for the prosecution for Georgie's liking.

'Yes, but she's singing in Lincoln this morning, and as soon as the concert is over tonight she's catching the night train to Edinburgh for a concert tomorrow. So she won't be coming here at all.'

A flood of relief came over Lucia's heart, and such was its force that she found herself able to praise Olga without apparent effort.

'What a marvellous woman she is, Georgie, so unsparing of herself. Lincoln! Edinburgh! She is an example to all of us. Such constant movement. Are you going to the concert tonight?'

'No, I'm not,' moped Georgie. 'I've got to rehearse my next broadcast. Too tar'some. The Ministry has sent me a whole sackful of carrots, and I'm to make up a recipe for carrot casserole. Nothing but carrots wherever I turn these days. Why, I'm beginning to look like a carrot.'

In Lucia's opinion he already did, especially in moments of stress, but she thought it inadvisable to tell him this. He had paused, as if preparing to face some momentous decision, and then burst out, 'I'm getting terribly bored with all this cooking. It was great fun to do in Tilling, preparing ingenious things for the officers and our friends, but doing it all day with no music or sketching or Bridge, and no company, and Olga hurtling around the country like the Flying Scotsman – it's so very tedious, and I don't want to do it any more. I'm not used to doing the same thing all day. I like doing different things, and when I'm bored with doing one thing, I want to stop doing that and start doing something else. Imagine how tar'some it would be to play croquet all day from seven in the morning to seven at night, even if you particularly enjoyed croquet or were terribly good at it. It's as bad as working in a factory. And then there's these broadcasts – why, I'm terrified in case something goes wrong, and there's nobody about to reassure me and say they liked it except Foljambe, and she's doing it too, so she can't really tell and besides, she's far too polite to tell me if I sounded really awful.'

'You poor dear,' said Lucia.

'Teddy Broome says they're bound to be very popular,' he went on, 'but I'm getting to the stage now where I can't think of another thing to do with parsnips and carrots and tripe and so forth. I've already written them a booklet, which they say they're going to distribute right across the country. I do think that that's enough to be going on with, without being stuck here in London like a slave. I've decided that after I've finished this series of broadcasts – two more – I shall go back to Tilling and

123

invent recipes there. They can get someone else to broadcast them, or else I can come up to London for the day. Then they can send all those sacks of onions and potatoes and things to Mallards, and we can eat them rather than letting them all go to waste. I've had to eat my way through mountains of cold parsnips before I got the recipe exactly right, and Foljambe says that if she has to eat any more corned beef she'll give up her position and go and live with her married sister in Worcester until the war is over. I couldn't face that. So there it is.' And, although as a rule he never smoked in the morning, he lit a cigarette and got bits of tobacco all over his tongue.

'Georgie, what a wonderful idea!' exclaimed Lucia. 'No, not Foljambe going to Worcester, you coming back to Tilling. Then we can have proper dinner parties, with lots of food, and you can try out your recipes on all our friends, which will be much more rewarding. And even Elizabeth couldn't pretend that the food was black market if she saw it being delivered at Mallards in big sacks with Government arrows printed on them. I'll tell you what, Georgie; if you don't think Olga will be coming back here for a while, I'll stay here for the next fortnight – Tilling can look after itself for a change – and we can have games of *piquet* and duets, and visits to the theatre and the galleries, unless they've sent all the pictures away by now, I can't remember, and you'll do far more work that way than if you're stuck in a gloomy kitchen from sunrise to sunset, and I can read to you when you're cooking, and eat up all the corned beef so that Foljambe won't run away to Worcester. Much more agreeable than being stuck here on your own with nothing but carrots to keep you company, and much nicer for me than being all alone at Mallards.'

So depressed had Georgie become, practically buried alive in peeled vegetables and constantly badgered by Teddy Broome and the B.B.C., that the prospect seemed quite appealing.

'That's settled then,' he cried joyously, 'and now tell me all about Tilling. What has Elizabeth been getting up to, and what did they all think of my broadcast? Was she furious?'

No need to ask who 'she' was. 'Absolutely livid, Georgie, and she and Major Benjy have been turned out of Grebe by the Army, because they're doing manoeuvres up by the river. And Elizabeth has been made head of the Red Cross, would you believe it, although the only thing she knows about medicine is that it comes from the chemist. She's only doing it to interfere with my hospital.'

'And swank around in her uniform, I'll bet.'

'Grey serge with a grey velour hat, although we don't know yet whether she'll get a watch that pins on the front.'

'Goodness!' said Georgie, somewhat taken aback by the thought. 'But this is perfectly dreadful. What are you going to do?'

'I shall co-operate fully, of course, while letting it be known, gently but firmly, that the hospital is fully capable of dealing with all emergencies. But this is why you're needed so badly, Georgie. You must help me put Elizabeth firmly in her place again.'

As Ulysses longed for Ithaca, even on Calypso's enchanted island, so Georgie's soul longed for Tilling. He had had enough of Brompton Square and vegetables; he wanted to see once more the clash of personalities in the High Street, and hear again the clamour of voices as equal battle was joined.

'And where are they both living,' he asked, 'if they've been thrown out of Grebe? In a tent on the beach? Or have they gone into one of the alms-houses?'

'I'm letting them stay at Mallards, naturally, at least while I'm in London,' she replied, thereby betraying the fact that she had planned to make a long stay, but Georgie, who had seen the suitcases, knew that anyway. 'It was the least I could do. Magnanimity to those less fortunate than ourselves is a form of patriotism too. Not that I expect the slightest display of gratitude from Elizabeth. I'm sure she's prowling round my house at this very moment, saying how much it's changed since her time, and how *pauvre tante* Caroline must be spinning in her grave.'

In this, Lucia was perfectly right.

'What a relief that poor Aunt Caroline is not alive to see it, Benjy,' were Elizabeth's actual words as she ran her finger over the oak panels of the hallway in the vain hope of finding some dust. 'Such memories, and all violated by that woman's criminal lack of discernment.'

'Much more cheerful than it was in our day, if you ask me,' replied the Major. 'Bright colours, smart furniture, all as good as new.'

'Certainly there are no moth-eaten tigers-skin or mouldy native spears hanging on the walls, as there are at Grebe,' retorted Elizabeth sharply, 'but as for the rest of it, I repeat that the *décor* displays a complete lack of understanding for a house of this age and character.'

She opened a cupboard, no doubt to observe what errors of taste had been perpetrated in the decoration of its interior. She had already discovered much that was of intrest in the cupboards of Mallards; but they were not the sort of feature that would be mentioned in a guide-book, unless it were a guide to a grocer's shop. One of the first things she had done, after taking off her hat, was to inspect the secret cupboard in the garden-room, which Lucia had, in her haste, omitted to lock securely. There, as she had suspected, was Lucia's hoard of illegal provisions, concrete evidence for all those foolish people who still refused to believe in Lucia's black-market traffickings.

None of the other usual hiding-places had revealed much, however, and as soon as the inspection was complete, Elizabeth telephoned to the Bartletts to invite them for tea and Bridge that afternoon. Lucia had, after all, invited her before all Tilling to make herself at home while she was away in London. There could be no possible objection to her entertaining two mutual friends, especially since she had brought her own tea and sugar from Grebe. In fact, she planned to do quite a bit of entertaining, given the wealth of luxuries that the house contained. If Lucia cared to come to her afterwards and demand 'Where are the three tins of South African peaches I had hidden away in the cellar?' she would simply be confessing her own guilt. Today, however, she must expend her own stores; and tea would, as ever, be in the garden-room. Now, should the door of the secret cupboard negligently be left ajar, allowing those doubting Thomases to see the contents of it. . . She slipped out to the garden-room and adjusted the cupboard door to give maximum field of view, then returned to the house. The post had arrived, and dutifully she looked through it in case there was anything that seemed as if it should be forwarded to London without delay. With astonishment she saw that one envelope bore the Royal crest and the words 'Windsor Castle' on the back. She threw the other letters on to a table and retired to the drawing-room to study this extraordinary article.

For a long while she sat in silence, wrapt in thought, with the letter upon her knees. Clearly a communication from Windsor Castle was of the utmost importance, so important in fact that to re-address it and forward it to London might waste valuable time, especially with the post the way it was. Suppose Their Majesties meant to visit Tilling (although why they should write to Lucia in such an event was a mystery; surely *they* would not require Lucia's permission), and suppose Elizabeth dutifully sent on the letter to London. While it was tumbling about in the Royal Mail, there they would be in their ermine robes, kicking their heels on the station platform with no one to receive them. . . . Surely it was up to Elizabeth to open it and convey its contents to London at once by telephone. Her fingers ached to open it, and soon the ache became unbearable. Finally, with a prayer that the honour it must inevitably bestow upon her hostess be not too great, she sliced it open and drew out a broad white card. She read it, re-read it, and hurled it to the ground.

It was an invitation to a garden party to be held at

Windsor Castle, in honour of the governors and benefactors of certain hospitals in the South of England, and Lucia, being chairman of the governors and chief benefactor of Tilling Hospital, was cordially invited to attend. Rage filled Elizabeth, and, had Lucia been standing nearby, Elizabeth would undoubtedly have put her in need of the excellent medical facilities provided by her own operating theatre. For a moment she contemplated casting the hideous object on the fire and swearing, if questioned, that she had never seen it. Then a brilliant idea occured to her, and she looked at the date for which the party had been arranged. It was three weeks hence. Now although Lucia had said that she would be gone for a week at most, who was to say that she might not be gone for even longer – a fortnight, say, or three weeks, even a month? In which case she could, in all honesty, write to the Castle saying that Mrs. Pillson was away at the moment, she had no idea when she would be back, but she was willing, as head of the Read Cross in Tilling and as such her second-in-command, to represent Mrs. Pillson and Tilling at the party.

The telephone rang and she answered it herself, for it might be the Castle and she wanted no independent witnesses. But it was Lucia, to say that she would be in London for another fortnight. Elizabeth was aware of that tide in the affairs of men which, taken at the flood, leads on to Fortune; indeed, that tide was fairly washing about her ankles. She thanked Lucia for letting her know, and bade her stay on longer if she wished; all was under control, there seemed to be no urgent messages. She replaced the receiver quickly in case Lucia should say anything else, then sat down at the desk in Lucia's study and took out a sheet of Tilling Hospital writing-paper (of which Lucia kept a plentiful supply). She wrote a note to the Castle, telling her tale and suggesting that a new invitation should be issued in her name, addressed the envelope (her fingers trembled as she wrote the words 'Windsor Castle'), stamped it and darted across the road to the post-box. In her excitement she had forgotten the original invitation, lying on the sofa, which, as is the way of letters and other objects of value, unostentatiously made its way down between the cushions at the back.

The stirring events of the morning – moving into Mallards again, seeking out and finding the illicit hoard, and now the execution of the twin crimes of deceit and interference with the Royal Mail – left her feeling buoyant and exhilarated, and she returned to the house to put on her uniform and collect her market-basket. As she passed the pillar-box on her way to the High Street and thought of the letter that lay inside it, she could not help but shudder apprehensively at the thought of what might happen if the truth ever leaked out. But the fear passed by, and she entered the poulterer's with uplifted heart. The Romans were wont to seek omens in the behaviour of birds, and it was surely a good omen that there should be three fat woodpigeons hanging there – exactly what she wanted for dinner tonight. With a basket full of pigeons and a mind full of strategy, she returned to Mallards for lunch. She had ordered corned beef *à la Riseholme* (humble pie *à la Riseholme* would soon be a recipe for the Pillsons to savour) and was grudgingly forced to admit that it was exceedingly palatable. Certainly Major Benjy found it so, and waxed eloquent concerning its inventor's ingenuity. Hearing this praise of Georgie's cunning, she longed to reveal her own, but decided after a struggle to keep the secret to herself. He, and indeed the whole town, would, after all, see the invitation that should arrive by tomorrow's post. Patience and discretion must be her watchwords, and there would be plenty to occupy her mind until tomorrow, with the disclosure of the hideous secret of the garden-room cupboard.

'Three pigeons in Mr. Rice's shop today, Benjy-boy,' she said. 'How pitiful they looked hanging by their feet from that cruel hook. So I rescued them and brought them home for dinner.'

'Better in a pie than eating the farmer's corn, eh Liz? I wonder if Pillson has a recipe for pigeon pie – tell Withers to look for one in his recipe book. Marvellously talented man, Pillson, now that he's stopped frittering away his time on embroidery and sketches and such like fiddle-faddle. Not man's work, strictly speaking of course, but fair's fair, and we must all help our country in whatever way we can.' He helped himself to more corned beef.

'How like you, dear, to see the best in everyone. And I suppose Mr. Georgie is doing his bit in the only way he is able. Still, I would not compare his contribution to the war-effort to yours, for instance. He merely makes palatable food that our tireless farmers produce for us, or that our gallant merchant seamen convey across the ocean in the teeth of the Atlantic gales. You, on the other hand, are actively participating in our nation's defence, thereby freeing men more able-bodied than yourself for active service abroad. Not that I wish in any way to demean Mr. Georgie's achievements – they are very considerable within a rather limited field of endeavour – but I cannot help thinking that he would be better occupied in patrolling the Harbour with the Home Guard.'

'Haw, that's a good joke, Liz. Don't honestly think your Mr. Georgie is Home Guard material. He could darn our uniforms for us, I suppose, or paint the camouflage, ha! But the Tilling troop is a fairly decent body of fighting men, though I say it myself, and an army marches at the pace of the slowest man. Let Mr. Georgie stick to his pots and his pans and his cushy billet in London. That's where his talents lie, just as yours lie in tending the sick, or would do if there were any sick to tend, which there aren't, thank God. Anyway, each man to his own is what I think.'

'Thank you, dear,' said Elizabeth.

No sooner had lunch been cleared away than it was time to prepare for tea and Bridge, so it was indeed just as well that there were no sick to tend or Germans to fight, for they would have had to wait until the morrow. Elizabeth made a final adjustment to the angle of the cupboard door, and placed a tin of pineapple where none but a blind man would fail to observe it, then went to await her guests, who soon arrived along the cobbled street clutching the paper bags that held their sugar and powdered milk.

'Tea in the garden-room,' cooed Elizabeth. 'Just like old times, isn't it?'

'Aye, 'tis fair reminiscent o' when ye were the mistress o' Mallards, Mistress Mapp-Flint. How accustomed we are grown tae our beloved Lucia, and how sair we miss her, for a' that she's been awa' but a day.'

This was scarcely tactful, but Evie squeaked her characteristic squeak to mark the gaffe. 'How long do you think it will be before you return to Grebe?' she asked Elizabeth.

'Alas, we have not been informed, but I should think those manoeuvres will take ever so long. My Benjy-boy knows all about such things, of course, and he thinks it will be a week at least before we can return to our own little home. Such a wrench, of course; but then, Mallards is so much like home to us that we won't notice until it's time to go back, even if it is so completely different now.'

'Aye, there's been a few improvements,' declared the Padre, and he would have elaborated the point further had he not observed the open door of the cupboard and the tin of pineapple. Evie had seen it too, and her searching gaze had passed by the pineapple to the other treasures at the back. After a moment of tongue-tied silence, the Padre strode over to the cupboard and closed the door firmly. The catch clicked shut. The Padre bestowed on Elizabeth a glance filled with contempt mixed with compassion, such as one might give to a person hopelessly addicted to some narcotic.

'Well,' he said wearily, 'I see you had time tae bring a few wee provisions with ye from Grebe, some of those little luxuries that make life worthwhile, do what ye must to obtain them. And still the same auld hiding-place, Mistress Mapp-Flint. I ken that some things dinna change. Ah, here is the tea.'

9

A second invitation, suitably amended, arrived at Mallards the very next day, and Elizabeth read its contents aloud to her husband over the breakfast-table.

''Pon my soul, girlie, that's handsome tribute. Makes it all worthwhile, and one in the eye for Mrs. Pillson.'

For a fraction of a second the Major wondered why the King should write to Elizabeth at Mallards, but the brilliance of his wife's achievement evaporated this doubt.

'Being able to make my own contribution, however small, to the war-effort is reward enough, dear. I regard this not as a personal meed of honour, but as a decoration for the men and women of Tilling Red Cross. I shall simply be their representative, their spokeswoman, their ambassador.' The ambassador graciously poured herself another cup of tea.

'Will you – ah – be away for long?' asked the Major, attempting to sound disinterested, but unable to stop himself thinking of the small glass of whisky and soda with which he would console himself while he pined for his absent spouse.

'Just for the day of the party, and I shall stay overnight in Windsor. I cannot allow myself to neglect my duties for any longer.'

'Why not take the opportunity to have a little holiday, like Mrs. Pillson?' urged the Major. 'You work too hard. A little holiday would do you the world of good.'

'I would scarcely describe a week in an air-raid shelter listening to the sound of explosions as a holiday,' she replied frostily, suspecting that her husband was eager to find new sorrows to drown. 'Besides, I owe it to Tilling not to desert my post. We must be on constant alert, you and I. Eternal vigilance day and night.'

Just now, her post was clearly in the High Street, whither the shoppers of Tilling must come and be informed of the great honour bestowed (vicariously) upon them by His Gracious Majesty. 'We do not hunger and thirst after recognition,' she explained to the Padre, 'but when we have recognition thrust upon us, so to speak, we accept it gratefully. We set an example to the rest of Britain, and for that example to have the greatest effect it must be made as visible as possible.'

The Padre was naturally thrilled and proud, but he could not help noticing that the queue in the butcher's was growing steadily, and he was not in it. He did not hunger and thirst after mutton, but he did not mind having it thrust upon him. Also, he had a suspicion that when Elizabeth spoke of 'we' and 'us' she was using the pronouns in the manner favoured by the late Queen Victoria.

' 'Twas a lucky day for our wee toun that ye conde-scended to head the physicians and the bonny nurses, Mistress Mapp-Flint,' he said as Elizabeth paused for breath. 'And noo I mun gang forth and see if I canna get me a fragment of sheep.'

Elizabeth turned away and headed for Wasters, where Diva would be sitting at her customary window, like a stout and red-faced Juliet.

'May I pop in for a moment?' Elizabeth called up to her, before she could disappear and hide behind the cur-tain.

'Come on up,' cried Diva, who was bored with her game of Patience, and therefore did not object to any company so long as it brought news and interest, even if it was only Elizabeth chattering interminably about the Red Cross and the Home Guard.

'Any news?' was her first question. She had become

used to a very rich diet of news these days, and what she saw from her window, once so exhilarating, seemed somewhat dull. With Lucia and Georgie away life was undoubtedly flat.

'Just the teeniest snippet, love. Just that a certain person has been honoured with an invitation to a garden party at Windsor Castle.'

'Lucia?'

'No, not Lucia.'

'Susan Wyse?'

'Not this time.'

'The Padre? Major Benjy? Who is it?'

'Me!' cried Elizabeth irritably. 'Just fancy that. Little me among all those noble and exalted people. I declare I'm quite terrified, and I don't think I shall go.'

'But why you?' Diva could be infuriating at times.

'His Majesty has seen fit to honour the representatives of the Red Cross with a modest reception. A great honour. I regard it not as a compliment to myself but. . .'

'How wonderful! And when is it to be? And what will you wear?'

'Three weeks. And I think my uniform will be splendour enough, even for Windsor Castle. It is, after all, His Majesty's uniform. Especially since I am going not as Mrs. Mapp-Flint of Grebe, near Tilling, Sussex, but as. . . .'

'Is it fancy dress then?'

'But as Mrs. Mapp-Flint, representative of Tilling Red Cross and the medical services of the town. I shall therefore be a sort of ambassador. . . .'

'Oh well,' said Diva brightly, 'never mind. In your place I'd have splashed out on something rather grand, but if you've got to wear your uniform, that'll have to do. Grey serge. Rather becoming, in fact.'

'Thank you, dear. And now, what else has been happening? Anything interesting?'

'Nothing at all. Everything as dreary as death without Lucia and Mr. Georgie. Susan Wyse brought a new hat, and her sables were splashed by the delivery boy from Twemlow's going past on his bicycle, but who cares? Oh yes, and Janet tried to make corned beef *à la Riseholme*, but it stuck. Who else is going to be there?'

'Other representatives of the Red Cross and various hospitals, I suppose. But I don't want to talk about it. We had corned beef *à la Riseholme*, too. I must say I didn't think very much of it, although Withers may have made some error in following the recipe. Not too clearly expressed in places.'

A small missile clattered against the window, causing Diva to jump and upset the Patience cards all over the floor. The perpetrator of the attack proved to be Irene, who was standing under the window, her hand drawn back as if to throw again.

'Hello, Diva!' she called. 'Any chance of a cup of tea? I've heard some horrible rumours about Mapp being made a Dame or a General or something, and I want to know if they're true. Can I come up?'

'Yes,' cried Diva, and she shut the window with a bang. 'Stupid child!' she muttered. 'Could have broken the glass.'

'Dear Irene,' said Elizabeth. 'Quite like a child in some respects, although perhaps she is getting a little bit too old for her pranks to be so readily passed off. Still, a sweet nature, underneath it all.'

'Hello, Diva. Qui-hi, Mapp!' exclaimed the sweet-natured child, bursting in through the door and settling in a chair like a small hurricane. 'They're spreading extraordinary rumours about you in the High Street.'

'And what, pray, might they be saying?' said Elizabeth, through a luminous smile.

'Well, they say that you're going off to the Tower of London to have your head chopped off, or something,' replied Irene, lighting a cigarette and daintily hurling the spent match into the waste-paper basket.

'Dear one!' cooed Elizabeth, as if to a small, wilful infant. 'I suppose you mean that you have heard that I am to go to Windsor Castle and meet the King.'

'Well, a cat can look at a King,' said Irene, blowing a cloud of smoke at her, 'and I suppose that what a cat can do, a Mapp can do just as well. Nor does the resemblance stop there. But aren't you a bit old to be presented at court, Mapp? And will you invite me to your coming-out ball?'

Eizabeth's smile, like the cliffs against which the sea pounds with frustrated fury, remained fixed. Irene was never more fanciful than when she was baffled.

'No dear, I'm not going for any frivolous reasons, but to represent the Red Cross. I see myself as a sort of ambassador. . . .'

'So I should jolly well think! All you've done is strut around in your uniform, looking like a blessed wedding-cake, while the nurses do all the work!' fulminated Irene. 'Just like you, Mapp, filching all the credit for other people's efforts. And anyway, it shouldn't be you going to this rout, but Lucia. Why, she virtually built the hospital single-handed – well, she paid for the operating theatre, which I expect you will one day honour with your presence when you eventually burst with pride – and she's chairman of the governing board. I think the invitation was for her, and you crossed out her name and scrawled "Elizabeth Mapp" over the top.'

This was an awkward moment for Elizabeth, but she found that she could say, 'I did nothing of the sort, you rude darling,' without apparent effort, for of course she hadn't. She had been much more clever. 'I can see that you won't be satisfied until you've seen the actual invitation.' So saying, she produced that magical document.

'So it's true, is it?' exclaimed Irene. 'Oh well, there it is. Fair play's a jewel, as Benjy-boy says in his cups. I'd better say how pleased and proud I am, although I'm not. Remember, you'll be there as a sort of ambassador, so behave yourself. I don't want to be shown up by you. I must see if I've got any pumpkins or white mice I could let you have. But you must promise to be back by midnight, and don't go losing your shoes.'

And she swept out and pedalled back to Taormina on

her racing-bicycle to begin a new canvas. It was to be Elizabeth, crowned and seated upon a throne, with Major Benjy seated beside her with a whisky bottle in his hand, receiving the homage of all nations, while behind her, crammed with every conceivable luxury, stood open a hidden cupboard as big as the Albert Hall.

Despite the miseries, petty discomforts and constant worries that attended it, war was an exhilarating business for the inhabitants of Tilling. Life's tempo was quickened, and the people of the town found tremendous scope for doing what they had always done, on a bigger and more tremendous scale. Scarcely had Lucia and Georgie returned from their three weeks' exile in London, riding in a lorry laden with Government-issued provisions for Georgie's culinary researches, than Elizabeth departed for Windsor, resembling nothing so much as a monarch departing for an official visit to another monarch of slightly inferior status – the King of England, for instance, visiting the King of Swaziland.

As it turned out, she did not enjoy herself very much at the party; she handed her gas-mask case to a man who looked like a footman, but who turned out to be an equerry, a peer of the realm with several thousand acres in Lincolnshire, and, while attempting to scriggle through a knot of people, spilt a cup of tea over the dress of the Duchess of Kent, who smiled charmingly and said, 'So sorry!' In full flight from this disaster, she collided with the King, who apologised in similarly gracious terms and asked her who she was. Panicking, and thinking of headlines announcing 'Disgraceful scenes at Windsor', she said she was Lucia Pillson of Tilling, and was about to run away when His Majesty said, 'Ah yes, Mrs. Pillson, I have heard of your generosity to the town. A new operating theatre for the hospital. So public-spirited.' As far she could remember, Elizabeth had smiled and thanked His Majesty, and then retired to a corner where she spent the rest of the afternoon counting biscuits. As she left, she heard someone saying,

137

'Who was that large woman?', and although there had been many large women present, she was sure that the description was of herself. She had never felt so large and conspicuous in all her life.

Nevertheless, the newspapers had made no mention of what had verged upon two incidents of attempted High Treason, but instead had named Mrs. Elizabeth Mapp-Flint as among those present; Tilling would know only that she had been there, had met the King and the Duchess of Kent, and had rubbed shoulders with Royalty; the extent of the physical contact need never be known. She returned to Tilling on the train (where a soldier mistook her for a nurse and asked her to take a look at his feet) and emerged from the station fully prepared to recount the history of her triumph.

At the very moment of Elizabeth's arrival, Lucia was sitting on the sofa in her drawing-room. She was thinking free and patient thoughts (as recommended by Edgar in *King Lear*), but in spite of this something troubled her. To a certain extent her discomfort was due to the fact that Elizabeth had been staying in her house; that woman seemed to leave a miasma behind her, rather like the feeling that hangs about a house that has recently been burgled: a sense of unwarranted intrusion. But there was something more to it than that. Lucia realised that she, and not Elizabeth, should have been invited to the Castle. She, not Elizabeth, was the senior representative of the Aesculapian fraternity in Tilling. Yet His Majesty had chosen Elizabeth for the honour. Why?

Naturally this sudden elevation to Royal circles was not to be regarded as any sort of victory for Elizabeth. A clear precedent had been set by Susan Wyse's M.B.E. The people of Tilling naturally regarded anything that happened outside the parish boundaries as unimportant, and in such a way might Elizabeth's jaunt be regarded. 'Did you have a nice holiday, dear? So glad,' would prove to be a satisfactory gambit if the distasteful subject should ever need to be referred to. On the other hand, if such strict principles were to be applied, how could Georgie expect to be lionised for triumphs that had been enacted in London, even further away than Windsor? Here was a difficulty; it might, of course, be argued that since Georgie's voice had been heard within the boundaries of Tilling (by means of the wireless) the event was a Tilling event and thus legitimate. Such fine reasoning might, however, be beyond the capacity of the majority of Tilling folk. They had applauded Georgie's London adventures, and so they must applaud Elizabeth's achievements in Windsor too. Both parties had brought glory on the town and, in truth, Georgie's were individual honours, whereas Elizabeth had been, as she herself pointed out, a sort of ambassador. To belittle her was to belittle Tilling – disaster. Once again it struck her that by rights she, not Elizabeth, should have gone to Windsor.

She looked at her watch. The London train would be arriving now, and Elizabeth would be alighting from it, smiling as broadly as ever, pretending no doubt that nothing out of the ordinary had happened, waiting impatiently for the events of the trip to be dragged out of her by eager enquirers.

Lucia squirmed involuntarily at this thought and as she did so, something seemed to dig into the small of her back. She turned round, and noticed an envelope that had worked its way up from the depths of the sofa, addressed to herself and – goodness! – bearing the crest of Windsor Castle. It was already open and from it she drew an invitation card summoning Mrs. Emmeline Pillson to a party at the Castle in honour of the representatives of the medical services. The day appointed for the party was yesterday.

'*Hoc habet!*' exclaimed the Roman gladiator who struck down his opponent and turned to see whether the wretch should live or die. Doubtless Lucia was familiar with the phrase, and might have used it had she not been taken by another thought that expelled the joy of discovery from her mind. Had they both been invited to the Castle? In that case Elizabeth was guilty simply of concealment. Or had she alone been invited, and had Elizabeth opened this letter, resolved on treachery, and written back saying that Mrs. Pillson could not attend and offering to come in her stead? In that case, Elizabeth was guilty of nothing less than fraud. If Elizabeth had committed the former crime, surely she would have taken more care over destroying the evidence. The card would have gone on the fire rather than down the back of a sofa. Sofas, unlike dead men, do tell tales. If it were the latter (and more serious) offence, then the criminal might easily forget about the first invitation in the excitement of procuring the second.

She seemed to see directly into Elizabeth's soul, and was amazed by the blackness of it. The brilliance of the Machiavellian mind, the courage and ingenuity of the felon also astonished her; the malefactor was worthy of some respect, even a sort of dubious admiration. Certainly the punishment must be fittingly severe. But how was that to be? Simply to display the invitation and broadcast her reconstruction of the act, like one of Mrs. Agatha Christie's detectives, would not satisfy her sense of poetic justice. Better still – forego the exposure of the criminal and keep the evidence. With this deadliest of weapons she could subdue Elizabeth to her will for ever, leaving her attentions and powers free for worthier, more uplifting purposes than petty social conflict.

With a decisive action she slipped the card back into the envelope and the envelope into her pocket. Elizabeth would be confronted *tête à tête* as soon as she got back ('Longing to hear about your wonderful trip to Sandringham – no, Windsor wasn't it?') and on the mantelpiece would be displayed that silent witness to her corruption. Elizabeth would at once perceive the full horror of her situation, and would find herself with no alternative but to behave submissively for the rest of her life. Punishment indeed!

'Georgie!' she called, and then remembered that these days her husband spent most of his time underground, like a cave-dweller. So she tripped lightly down the stairs and found him studying a carrot.

'If only one could disguise the beastly colour of it,' he reflected.

Swiftly and accurately she told him of her discovery and rehearsed her hypothesis, concluding with a summary of her plan of campaign.

'Monstrous!' he exclaimed, thumping the carrot, which disappeared on to the floor. 'I never would have thought she could have stooped so low.'

'Never mind, Georgie, it's turned out all right in the end. Think of dear Elizabeth having to be pleasant for the rest of time, or else we show everyone the invitation. Isn't it a fitting punishment?'

'It's like the Sword of Demosthenes – no, Damocles – hanging over her,' said Georgie. 'I do think that's clever. But I don't think I could resist telling everyone if I were in your shoes. Just imagine their faces!'

'Such a waste of this gift from heaven, Georgie, and rather petty too. We should not seek to destroy the poor woman, however misguided she may have been. Instead we shall take this opportunity to compel her to change her ways – for her own good as much as anything. Besides, if we were to smite her down with this thunderbolt, she would be sure to attempt some terrible revenge upon us, and that would be too tedious for words. I tire of these annoying little plots and counterplots, Georgie – they are out of place in wartime. We have other, more important, matters to attend to.'

That seemed to settle the matter, and Lucia returned to the garden-room to wait for Elizabeth. Before she could sit down, however, she saw her victim trotting gaily down from Church Square. She tapped on the window and waved to indicate her presence, and Elizabeth went to the front-door and rang the bell. There was just enough time to place the invitation on the mantelpiece and take her stand in front of it before the doomed woman was shown in by Foljambe.

'Elizabeth dear, how nice to see you. Now I won't keep you from your reunion with Major Benjy, but you must quickly tell me all about it. Did you see the King?'

'Oh yes,' she replied, 'we had a nice little chat. He knew all about Tilling, would you believe it, and congratulated us on our work here.'

That means my operating theatre, thought Lucia, but she can't bring herself to say it. How typical! 'And did you see anyone else?' she asked.

'Oh yes, the Duchess of Kent was there – such a sweet woman. She spilt a little drop of tea on my uniform – there, such a little speck, but she apologised most prettily, and so I forgave her. Withers will be able to get rid of the mark,but I'm almost tempted to leave it there as a memento.'

'Better not, dear. People might think it was soup.' Lucia moved away from the mantelpiece and sat down. At once Elizabeth saw the invitation: at once she recognised it. Her first instinct was to leap up and fling it on the fire, where it should have gone in the first place, but although she was larger, Lucia was nimbler than she and would prevent her. She stared at the hideous thing, and waited for the tirade of vituperation that must now follow.

'And were there many people there?' continued Lucia calmly, fixing her with a piercing gaze.

'Yes, lots,' mumbled Elizabeth. 'Packed.'

'How exciting for you! I do wish I could have gone, but then, many are called but few are chosen, as the Bible so succinctly puts it.' She rose and put the invitation in her pocket. 'As I believe you pointed out to everyone, you went not as Mrs. Elizabeth Mapp-Flint, but as a sort of ambassador for us all. As a citizen of Tilling, therefore, I feel that I too have been to Windsor. I too have met the King and the Duchess of Kent, albeit vicariously. Do sit down, dear, make yourself at home, although I could not recommend the sofa. Things do tend to fall down the back of it, which can lead to some discomfort. Take one of the chairs, that's better. Now, I expect you would like to hear all about Mr. Georgie's broadcasts and my trip to London.'

A little later, the two celebrities issued forth, almost but not quite arm-in-arm, for one was fractionally behind the other as if giving due deference to a superior, and they made their statuesque way to the High Street. Those who encountered them questioned them eagerly about their adventures, but found that whereas Lucia was only too pleased to relate every detail of her comparatively mundane experience in London, the sort of ambassador was somewhat reticent about her mission to Windsor; in fact, she seemed somewhat put out if anyone mentioned it at all.

'Oh dear,' said Evie to Diva after an inconclusive interview with the august pair, 'that means it can't have been a success. I wonder what could have happened?'

'Perhaps she spilt something over the King or broke a vase,' replied Diva, not knowing that she grazed the truth with her words. 'Don't think much of that. Before she went off she was telling us all that she was going as – how did she put it? – our ambassador representing the whole town, in which case she really ought in all fairness to tell us something about it instead of keeping it all to herself. But isn't it wonderful about Mr. Georgie! And a whole lorry full of vegetables!'

She looked at Evie meaningfully.

'I expect they'll do a lot of entertaining now that they're both back again,' said Evie.

'I hope so,' replied Diva.

10

The Mapp-Flints returned to Grebe. There they found a certain amount of disorder; a military vehicle had used their garden as a short cut, squashing a number of sweet flowers flat, and a nest of cigarette-ends came to light under the plum-tree. Elizabeth moaned when she saw these desecrations, while the Major, who had never completely shared his wife's love of flowers, said that he supposed things were worse in occupied France and the best thing would be to turn the wrecked flower-bed into another vegetable patch. Elizabeth gave a strangled sob at this insensitivity and fled into the house to count her Tilling pigs.

Evie's forecast of lavish entertainment at Mallards proved to be correct. Feasts exceeding even the quantity and quality of peacetime were staged there once or twice a week. Georgie insisted on conducting what he called 'consumer research', and his assistants in this vital work were only too pleased to co-operate. All thoughts of reciprocal hospitality were quickly abandoned, for no one could hope to match the Homeric opulence of Mallards, and besides, it was their patriotic duty to eat the delicacies that Mr. Georgie's talented hands prepared for them. Rarely in the political history of the world have citizens been so quick to answer their country's call as the folk of Tilling. To round off the pleasure, there was the thrill of hearing the recipes they had eaten on Fridays (in the development of which they had all played their parts) broadcast by the B.B.C. on the following Mondays. An actor had been found who could reproduce Georgie's voice exactly (he also did Mr. Churchill when the need arose) and so Georgie simply wrote the scripts and sent them to Teddy Broome in London. What with eating out and listening in, most Tillingites spent a large proportion of their lives at Mallards, with a corresponding saving in fuel and electricity. As a result, Lucia's authority over the town was to all intents and purposes absolute, for Elizabeth had capitulated entirely.

This was, perhaps, the most fascinating part of it. When Georgie started to give courses in elementary domestic science, Elizabeth and Major Benjy were among the first to enrol. They listened with apparently insatiable curiosity to Chopin, Elgar, even Berlioz, and were always insistent on 'Just one more delightful air, sweet Lucia'. Although Elizabeth wore her uniform during the day, she never wore it at Mallards, and the civilian clothes she wore were deliberatly dowdy, so that Lucia was undisputed arbiter of elegance in matters of apparel. Only at the Bridge-table were traces of the old Eve to be distinguished, and even these seemed to vanish at the slightest mention of Royalty. The more percipient of the spectators in this curious drama soon observed that a reference to court cards or speculation as to the conventions of Bridge employed at Balmoral or Sandringham quickly rendered Elizabeth as meek as a lamb.

'I see, Lucia, I should have played the eight of clubs there. So sorry.'

Even when out of the presence of her sovereign, Elizabeth could not be induced to utter a word of treason, so that the Padre speculated openly whether she was afflicted with some sort of nervous strain.

So drastic was the change in Elizabeth's character that even Major Benjy became aware of it. On one of the rare evenings when he and his wife dined at home, he decided to explore (tactfully, of course) this unexpected change of character. All in all he was in favour of it, for

145

he ate better now and had more access to wine than before the war.

'May I say something, Liz?' he ventured.

'By all means,' she replied.

'Don't quite know how to put this,' he continued. 'I am only an old soldier, although I hope, by God, a gentleman, but I feel I must say how pleased I am with the reconciliation between yourself and Lucia – Mrs. Pillson,' he added quickly, in case there hadn't been one. 'It always struck me as a shame that the two ornaments of Tilling should always be at each other's throats like that.' He paused. Talking of throats, his was dry and he felt distinctly uncomfortable. 'I'm glad you seem to see eye to eye more these days. Twin flowers entwined in harmony, don't you know.'

He stopped and peered anxiously at his wife. She seemed in the grip of strong, conflicting emotions, like a pool of water blown by two powerful winds.

'Yes, isn't it nice?' she said at length. 'So harmonious. All quarrels put aside in the face of the common enemy.'

'Ah,' said the Major. But something still troubled him. He drank some soup in silence, but he still felt vaguely dissatisfied. 'It's odd, though,' he said. 'A few weeks ago, you two didn't seem to be getting on at all. Then, after you got back from Windsor. . . . Perhaps I'm wrong, but that's how it struck me, anyhow.'

There was another long pause. Elizabeth laid down her soup-spoon and was staring at her plate as if the soup was full of vipers.

'Oh Benjy!' she exclaimed at last. 'It's too cruel! And it's all my own fault. A moment's weakness, that's all. And it wasn't really a lie. She *was* unavailable at the time, and we didn't really know when she was coming back. Oh what shall I do?'

'What on earth's the matter?' asked Major Benjy.

'I see I must confess everything,' said Elizabeth, her hands moving imaginary beads. 'The invitation to Windsor Castle was for Lucia. She was away so I opened the letter to see if it was important and because I

146

thought she would be unavailable for the party I wrote back, as deputy head of Tilling medical services, to inform them. I know I should have telephoned Lucia, but I couldn't find the number in London. I did look. Then the people at Windsor sent another invitation for me to go in Lucia's place. When at last I did hear from Lucia, she said she would be away for at least another fortnight – poor Mr. Georgie. Well, I couldn't face telling her how I had opened her letter – you know how she finds wickedness in the most innocent actions – and so I went to Windsor in her place. I went as a sort of ... well, you know. And while I was away, she found the original invitation and jumped to the most outrageous conclusions, and now she's threatening to show it to all our friends in Tilling if I do anything to cross her or contradict her. It's too wretched and life isn't worth living.'

There was hardly a word of this story that was not, at least to a certain extent, literally true. Admittedly the order of some of the events had got jumbled up a little and some minor details had been omitted altogether, but any historian, from Thucydides to Lord Macaulay, would testify that all historical narrative must of necessity incorporate a certain degree of interpretation.

'Damnable!' cried Major Benjy, unaware that he was echoing the very sentiments that Mr. Georgie had expressed on hearing the tale. 'Blackmail, that's what I call it. Why, you were simply acting in the best interests of the town. How dare she hold you to ransom like this? When all you were doing was acting as her ambass – ... as her representative while she was off gallivanting in London. Scandalous!'

Elizabeth doubted whether everyone would see it in this light, although this was evidently the light that favoured it most. Could Lucia's blackmail cancel out her crime? Dare she?

'Everything I have ever done I have done in the public interest,' she said solemnly. '*Pro bono publico*. Oh what a wretched life a politican must lead! I expect this sort of thing is daily bread to them. But I can't cope with it,

Benjy, not poor, innocent I. She will tell you that I deliberately took advantage of her hospitality to get myself invited to Windsor Castle. But think how it would have looked to His Majesty if I had written to say that Mrs. Pillson cannot attend the reception because she is on holiday!'

'I thought you did,' said Benjy.

'Of course I did not phrase it like that,' said Elizabeth quickly. 'Imagine His Majesty's feelings if he had thought that no one here was prepared to accept his invitation. "Very well, then", he would have said, "if Tilling is too busy to attend my party, I shall not ask them again." But that's so like Lucia. She takes it upon herself to secure the most illustrious public offices and then leaves all the work to her deputies. As her Mayoress, I was continually called upon to perform her duties for her.' (Lucia had once asked Elizabeth to present the prizes at the school's speech-day, since she herself was in bed with a temperature of a hundred and four.) 'And now, I suppose, I must see myself made a laughing-stock, with the threat of total humiliation hanging over me.'

'There must be something we can do.'

'What? Am I to ask you to break into Mallards at dead of night to abstract the document?' The thought had crossed her mind.

'If she were a man,' said the Major, 'I would challenge her to a duel.'

'Oh Benjy, how chivalrous! You are a brave, kind man and I don't deserve such a husband, I truly don't. But she isn't and you can't. It's tantamount to obtaining money by menaces,' she continued, warming to her theme, 'for every time I play Bridge against her, I feel obliged to lose on purpose, and so she fills her purse with my sixpences. What a tragedy it was when that woman first came to Tilling. First my house, now my reputation.'

'Cheer up, old girl,' said Benjy, 'we'll think of something, mark my words. Let her show everyone the invitation! Publish and be – blowed to her. You tell everyone the truth, just as you've told it to me, and then they'll know just what sort of woman she is. That'll stop her mouth for her.'

Elizabeth toyed with this attractive notion. Nobody could tell the truth like she could. But the stakes were too high.

'No, Benjy. Your courageous heart prompts you to direct and straightforward action, but I am only a weak woman' (with an effort she prevented herself from adding that she had the heart of a prince) 'and I fear that I must capitulate. And now we'll say no more about this horrible business. Tell me some good news. How about the Home Guard? You told me it would not be long before they were ready to face any soldiers in the world.'

'Bad news on that front, I'm afraid. My sergeant, who was the only man in the whole bunch worth tuppence, got his calling-up papers this week. Without him, the whole lot of them will go to pot. Must have a good sergeant, you know. Backbone of the military unit, the non-commissioned officer.'

'And is there no one to take his place?'

'No. Well, there's Hopkins the fishmonger. Early fifties, fine figure of a man. He could do it standing on his head.'

'There you are, then,' cried Elizabeth. 'Hopkins it shall be.'

'Unfortunately he won't join up. Says he's far too busy to fool about playing at soldiers when he's a shop to run. Treason, that's what I call it. Sabotage. In fact, I have my doubts about Hopkins. Spends all his time down by the Harbour, claims to be buying fish, but you can never tell.'

'I shall buy my fish from the other fish-shop,' said Elizabeth firmly, 'even though he rarely has anything worth eating. We must show Hopkins what we think about his behaviour.'

'The other chap won't join up either. Pity. If one of them joined up we'd be sure of a decent bit of fish from time to time, instead of the muck we usually have to put up with.'

Gloomily he returned to his soup, which was cold. His mind moved upon the problems that beset him, Lucia's malignity and the intransigence of fishmongers. As he turned them over in his mind, a quite brilliant idea struck him. What if he were to offer the sergeant's stripes to Pillson? The man would jump at the chance – any man whose soul had not been poisoned by prolonged contact with fish must surely do – and then he would have no time for cooking and arranging dinner parties. If there were no more dinner parties, Lucia could no longer oppress Elizabeth at them, would no longer be able to entertain in magnificent style. That would jolly well serve her right. It was an ingenious idea, although it would involve him in considerable inconvenience. He would lose all those excellent dinners at Mallards, unless, of course, the new sergeant could be prevailed upon to throw together a little supper for his comrades-in-arms after a night's patrol. But imagine trying to make a soldier out of Miss Milliner Michael-Angelo Courvoisier. He could scarcely bring himself to be civil to the fellow at the best of times. Civility, however, was not normally a part of the intercourse between sergeant and commanding officer; once Pillson had signed on the dotted line, he had better watch his step. All in all, it was a good plan. It would make Liz happy, and a happy Liz was a damn' sight easier to live with than the other sort. Best not tell her, though. Let it be a surprise for her.

Having thus resolved upon independent action, Benjy prepared to seize the first opportunity to confront Georgie and force the King's shilling into his hand. But how to do it? He weighed up the various alternatives. He could go to Mallards, demand an audience and, backing him into a corner of the garden-room, of which there was only one door, point a military finger at him and exclaim, 'Your country needs you!' Such a manoeuvre could not fail to make an immediate impact, but it seemed to lack the finesse necessary when dealing with a slippery customer like Pillson. He could send for him; a

Home Guard private sent to Mallards, an urgent summons, a situation had arisen, best man for the job, special talents. Try as he might, Major Benjy could think of no special talents that Georgie possessed bar one, and that was not obviously relevant to the field of battle. Perhaps a gentle hint dropped over the port. But would Pillson take such a hint? Difficulties everywhere.

Gloomily the Major walked through the Landgate on his way to the Institute, where his soldiers were waiting for him. There was Pillson, sitting on a camp-stool sketching the arch, as had been his habit in more tranquil times. Georgie's heart was not in it, however. It seemed a frivolous thing to be doing, and at the sight of the Major in his khaki Georgie's conscience pricked him. Rain or shine, he thought, there's old Benjy, out on patrol with the Home Guard, while I fritter away my spare time making sketches. Olga wouldn't approve. Wouldn't she be impressed by me in a uniform? Probably not, he concluded, for he was a realist.

Major Benjy was a firm believer in Destiny and he decided to speak his piece.

'Afternoon, Pillson!' he cried.

'Good afternoon, Major' replied Georgie. 'Such a good light for sketching, don't you think?'

'Sketching,' snorted the Major. 'Don't know how you can think of sketching at a time like this. Still, you carry on.'

Guiltily, Georgie sharpened his pencil. The voice of Duty was growing ever louder inside him, and this seemed uncommonly like an omen.

'Pardon my bluntness, Pillson, but shouldn't you be – ah – cooking something for the Government?'

A picture rose up in Georgie's mind of the Cabinet, rattling their spoons on the table. He dismissed it.

'Not today. Very glad, really. So tar'some, being cooped up all day in the kitchen. They tell me I've invented so many useful recipes that I mustn't send them any more for at least a month, because it will take that long to use up the ones they've already got. Isn't that exciting?'

The Major paused and summoned up his powers of eloquence.

'Excellent, excellent, but you know, we can't really do too much for our country, can we? We've come to expect a lot from you, Pillson,' he said, feeling his soul blacken within him at this perjury. 'Greatly respected in Tilling, if I might make so bold to say so. A civic leader. A setter of examples. If you do something everybody's bound to follow. A little more shading there, perhaps? No, maybe not.'

Georgie sat spellbound. He a civic leader! A setter of examples! Admittedly Mr. Wyse had said that he had always wanted a dinner-suit like his, but that was scarcely the same thing.

'Magnificent arch, what?' said the Major, who felt badly in need of a whisky-and-soda. 'Military in origin, of course. A last line of defence against the Spanish. Or the Dutch. Or was it the French? Of course the art of warfare has progressed a great deal since this was erected. Gunpowder, you know, and bombs and machine-guns.'

'Yes, I suppose so,' said the civic leader. What was Major Benjy getting at?

'No use relying on old stones these days,' said the Major. 'We need men, not old stones. Good men and true. Trouble is, all the good men are away at the front, and only the old crocks like myself are left. We do our best of course, but I don't think we'd have much of a chance if the Hun decided to have a go. Old fossils like myself,' he added significantly.

'That's being rather defeatist, isn't it?'

'What we need is some young blood,' continued the Major. What he needed was a strong whisky-and-soda. 'Able-bodied men, not so young that they're needed at the front, but men in the prime of life. Men like yourself. To be frank with you, Pillson, I must admit to being a little bit disappointed in you. Considering what a high opinion of you I have, I mean, a very high opinion, but disappointed nonetheless.'

'Oh,' said Georgie. What did the Major want him to do? Cook the Home Guard Annual Dinner, perhaps?

'I mean, invaluable work, yes. Army marches on its stomach, as Hannibal said to Alexander the Great, and the same goes for civilians. But you yourself said that you don't spend all your time cooking, dammit. No, you fritter away your energies on sketching and Bridge with a lot of old cats. Dinner parties. Tea parties. Pshaw! That's all right for the ladies, God bless 'em. Takes their minds off the war. But we men shouldn't let our minds be taken off the war. We should think about it day and night.'

'How unpleasant,' said Georgie, but the guilt throbbed in his breast.

'We must face facts. Jerry's out there,' Benjy cried, waving his hand in the general direction of Hastings. 'He's biding his time, waiting to pounce. And to make matters worse, my sergeant's been called up. Terrible! Ah well, there it is. It's here he'll attack, you mark my words. Think of William the Conqueror,' he added darkly.

'He was French,' said Georgie.

'Ah, but the French were our enemies then. Puts a whole new complexion on the matter. Now, if I had a good man as my sergeant, a man in his – his late forties, let us say, in the prime of life, a man of intelligence as well as a fine physical specimen, a man of parts, well, I should feel much happier about it all. But there it is. You can see why I lie awake at nights. And now I find you. Instead of devoting your talents to the well-being of our little town, you are frittering away your time – pardon my strong language, old fellow, but I feel this deeply – in sketching and idleness. Why you're just the sort of chap. . . . But there it is.'

Major Benjy turned and faced the arch. He felt satisfied that he had combined all his possible approaches – the gentle hint, the direct appeal, tact

153

and bluntness – in one powerful address. Oh, for a whisky-and-soda!

'You mean me?' said Georgie, suspiciously. This was most unlike the Major. Perhaps he was drunk.

Major Benjy closed his eyes and prayed to heaven for patience. He turned on his heel and faced Georgie.

'Your country needs you, Pillson!' he thundered, shooting out a massive forefinger that punched a neat hole through Georgie's sketch. 'Oh, sorry about that. Yes, I mean you. The only man in Tilling, apart from those dratted fishmongers. And they haven't an ounce of brain between them. You have. More than an ounce. Pounds.'

Georgie looked at his ruined sketch and then at the Major. Now there was an omen if ever he saw one. The vision of himself in uniform, which had haunted his mind sporadically ever since he had first seen the Home Guard, returned to him now, with no saucepan-clad Irene or jeering children to mar it. His heart had yearned for many things in his life; he had wanted to be a talented pianist, a celebrated singer, a famous artist, a romantic lover – he was none of these, and never would be. Instead he was a talented and useful cook, and although that was very pleasant as far as it went, it was a little humiliating to have won his place in history as the man who could disguise the chemical taste of powdered egg. Inside George Pillson, he knew there lurked a man of steel, and although this man of steel had hitherto been too timid to venture out into the light of day, he knew the hour would come. Aeschylus, he recalled, had fought at the Battle of Marathon.

'Well?' said Major Benjy. He looked hard at the vacillating Georgie and wondered if his monumental efforts had gone to waste. He was generally a man of few words and, except when tipsy, he preferred to express himself in terse, military language. But the thought of what Elizabeth would say when she heard that he had subverted the mainspring of Lucia's dinner parties, cut the supply-lines of her table and thereby

154

silenced for ever the batteries of her wrath, filled him with hope. He planned a little deal; Lucia would get Georgie back three nights a week in return for the document. He puffed up his chest and prepared to drive the point home. Silver-Tongued Benjy, they had called him in Rangoon.

'What I'm getting at,' he said, 'is this. We need a sergeant for the Home Guard. The chap we've got at the moment has been called up. Will you take his place?'

'Me?' said Georgie. 'Well, I don't know.'

The man of steel clanked within him and he forced his face into a stern expression.

'I don't know about that, Major Flint. I do have rather a lot on my plate at the moment. Cooking,' he said gruffly. 'Preparing recipes. The war cannot be won at the front if the back – the Home Front is – neglected. Morale.'

This ponderous statement silenced them both for a while. The Major thought it might be a refusal, while Georgie was waiting to be wooed further. What if the Major said, 'Oh very well, then,' and went off to enrol the newsagent or someone?

'And besides,' Georgie added, 'I couldn't just become a sergeant straightaway. I would have to be a private first, then a corporal, then a lance-corporal. Too tar'some.'

'Nonsense, man, you'd go straight to the sergeant's stripes. Sergeant-major, even. Your dear wife, for instance. Think how she'd admire you in the King's uniform.'

The thought of Lucia sent the man of steel scuttling away like a crab.

'I'll have to think about it,' he said, grabbing his easel and camp-stool. 'Such a decision! Goodbye!'

'Damn' the man,' muttered the Major, as the potential sergeant dashed away up the High Street. 'Now, he's run off and I've put myself through all that for nothing. I'm going to go and have a drink.'

Which he did.

*   *   *

Georgie let himself into Mallards and collapsed into a chair.

'Oh dear!' he exclaimed to the empty room. 'What shall I do? Major Benjy's right, of course. And if I'm expected to set an example... But what will Lucia say?'

And then it occured to him that what Lucia said did not matter at all. He had had one moment of glory, as cook and broadcaster. But somehow, he was not sure how, Lucia had brought him home and an actor now broadcast the recipes that he wrote with such an effort. Now he spent all his time at home, like a prisoner, cooking not for Mr. Churchill and Teddy Broome, but for Lucia's guests and Lucia's dinner parties. It was wonderful to be good at something; but there was no reason why he should do it all the time. Ever since Lucia had found that invitation, he thought, she's been insufferable, worse than when she was Mayor. There's no one to keep her in check now, and she thinks of nothing but humiliating Elizabeth. Elizabeth may be a nuisance at times, but it's sheer cruelty. And there's no fun in life any more, and it's all because Lucia's defeated Elizabeth. Why, what with tormenting her at tea parties and ticking her off at Bridge, Lucia's forgotten all about the war, because of my food, which I should be using for recipes. She'll turn everyone against her if she goes on like this. She objected to me having an afternoon off today. It's like being her servant. Well then, if that's what she thinks, there are others who think otherwise. Even Major Benjy! I'm a civic leader, it seems, a setter of examples. Then I might as well be a teacher of lessons, too. She'll find she can't impose upon the pride of Tilling. That makes me sound like a steam-engine – but so I am, drawing the whole town behind me and I do think I'll look well in uniform.

'Damn', damn', damn'!' he said aloud, and leapt to his feet. Then he caught sight of his reflection in a mirror and stood awhile contemplating it. He was getting very pale, and no wonder, seeing that he spent all day in the kitchen.

'Sergeant Pillson,' he announced grandly and stood motionless, almost, but not quite, to attention.

Lucia had been shopping in the High Street. Although she scarcely needed to buy provisions these days, it was pleasant to join the queues in the shops and exchange news with her fellow-citizens. Elizabeth would be there, of course; today she had given up her place in the queue, so that Lucia had managed to get the last of the sausages. That was delightful in itself. With Elizabeth's malice stopped up at source, life had become most enjoyable.

'Georgie,' she said, as she laid down her market-basket when she got home, 'I've come to a decision. We play too much Bridge in Tilling.'

'What do you mean?' cried Georgie, startled. He turned away from the mirror and looked at her.

'Gambling is all very well,' she went on, 'though, personally, I play for the interest of the game, the skill, the mental exercise, not for the shillings or sixpences, which for Elizabeth, for example, are the gauge of success or failure. But it is frivolous to be forever filling our minds with kings and aces and trumps and revokes when we should be thinking of bigger things. Yet it is all that the town cares about. They have Bridge at teatime, then they dress for dinner and play Bridge all night. It's only a card-game, designed to while away an empty hour, yet they all work at it like a profession. They are devoted to it, as to a religion.'

'You enjoy a game of Bridge,' said Georgie. 'When you are winning.'

Lucia took no notice.

'I think we shall have less Bridge from now on. Let us reserve it for the afternoons and leave our evenings free for music, poetry and philosophical discussion. We had no Bridge at Riseholme, and yet I fancy we were able to amuse ourselves fairly well. Now that Elizabeth no longer opposes every little change that I attempt to make in our daily routine, I feel I ought to use my influence – I can say, in all modesty, that my example is generally followed in Tilling – to do some good in the community.'

Georgie felt he ought to interrupt this torrent of words, but he decided not to bother. There was no telling her anything when she was in this sort of mood.

'We are in Plato's cave, Georgie,' Lucia continued in her most infuriating, speaking-to-Elizabeth drawl. 'We should not be playing silly games of chance, but contemplating the Forms of Beauty, Philosophy and Art. There, I knew that you would agree with me, for you and I are of one mind in everything. Think how few of our friends play a musical instrument! I see now that I shall have to teach them. Piano-lessons, Georgie, and you must help me. You shall instruct them in the basics – scales and such – while I shall teach them to interpret, to make music. I feel that some of our friends will make fine musicians – Mr. Wyse, for instance. Others will never rise to great heights – dear Diva, and just think of Elizabeth! But we shall teach them at least the rudiments of music; that must be our task. And *that* ought to fill up the long evenings when we are not playing Bridge.'

Georgie had been waiting for this awful speech to stop, as a soldier in a trench awaits the end of the enemy barrage. When he was satisfied that it was safe to come out, he made one last attempt to reason with her.

'But Lucia,' he pleaded, 'are you sure? No more Bridge, and compulsory piano-lessons? They're all very set in their ways, you know. I think Diva and Evie Bartlett and even Elizabeth might object if you took away their Bridge. In fact, I think they would object very much. I'm sure of it.'

'Elizabeth will do what she's told,' replied Lucia coolly, 'and all the others will fall into line. Just mark my words. They will come to see the sense of it for themselves, with no Elizabeth to cause trouble.'

Georgie knew that she was right. His fellow-citizens were as weak as he when confronted by Lucia in purposeful mood.

'You must do what you think is best!' he said enigmatically, and left the room.

In his bedroom, with the door locked, he took out his embroidery things, so long neglected. He cut out a chevron of black felt and took some mellow gold silk, of the sort he usually reserved for cornfields. As he stitched, the design of a sergeant's stripes slowly began to take recognised shape.

11

Lucia's views on Bridge were soon known all over Tilling and were greeted with dismay. All eyes were turned to Elizabeth, as the natural leader of the resistance movement, but she declared that the same thoughts had been running through her mind for several weeks, and that she entirely agreed with dear Lucia, in this as in everything. How clever of her sweet friend to lead the way! How grateful she was!

'But Elizabeth,' said Evie, as they stood in Twistevant's queue, 'no more Bridge! It's appalling. What shall we do?'

Elizabeth smiled broadly.

'What a sweet Philistine you are, Evie dear. Why, I welcome this initiative. I applaud it. What would we do without our Lucia? And her kind, kind offer to teach us all to play the piano, although I'll warrant that none of us will ever be able to play as daintily as she. I dare say that I have little enough talent in that direction, yet I have already begged Lucia to take me on as a pupil. I am delighted to say that she has agreed to it. Such music. Evie dear, all day, every day. And poetry too, so she says. Now won't that be fun!'

'Ho!' said Diva, who was standing behind her. 'Poetry as well! If it wasn't for Mr. Georgie's cooking, I wouldn't set foot in Mallards again. And I'm not sure that I will, anyway. Surely you aren't in favour of this, Elizabeth?'

She gazed up at Elizabeth pleadingly.

'I think it would do you the world of good, Diva,' replied Elizabeth. 'We have been friends now for a long time, and I feel it my duty to speak plainly to you. You have been vegetating for too long. Your soul is rusty. Your mind is a closed room, a smoke-filled tap-room where men eat, drink and play cards, and never consider Art and Music. What has become of your painting, you darling reprobate, your delicious watercolours? No, it is high time we all took stock of ourselves. This terrible war is an opportunity for us all to reflect on what matters most in life. We are not fighting for Bridge and boiled cabbage, but for Beauty and Truth. Don't you agree?'

'No,' said Diva, who thought it all nonsense, 'but I suppose if everyone else is going to give up, I shall have to follow suit. Can't play Bridge on my own. This is too bad of you, Elizabeth. I don't know what's come over you lately.'

Elizabeth's smile was as luminous as ever, but in her heart there was bitterness. As she handed over her ration-book, she mused on whether it might be possible, without running undue risks of detection and retribution, to murder Lucia and hide her body in the secret cupboard in the garden-room.

Just then, out of the corner of her eye, she saw Major Benjy in the High Street, with Georgie, hurrying in the direction of Malleson Street. She wondered what this could mean, but her spirit was so heavily laden with her own misery that her usual analytical powers failed her, and she dismissed the incident from her mind. Had she been less dispirited, she might have guessed the truth and so been in time to stop them. For Georgie was on his way to try on his uniform (he had insisted on this before taking the drastic step of inscribing his name on the Nominal Roll), and Major Benjy, his teeth gritted and his jaw set, was quietly confident that he had found his new sergeant.

Georgie examined himself in the cracked mirror of the Institute, and positioned the beautifully embroidered stripes on his arm. They completed the entirely favourable impression.

'Will I have to shave off my beard?' he enquired, suddenly struck by this horrible thought. It was some time now since he had seen his chin, and he was afraid lest it had declined somewhat.

'Well, you would usually have to,' replied the Major. Georgie's face fell. 'But it is at the – ah – discretion of the commanding officer to make exceptions. I'm sure we can overlook it, just this once.'

'Well, that's all right then,' said Georgie. 'I do think that's smart. Can I see a rifle now?' he asked with the air of a customer in a Bond Street shop.

'Let's not rush things,' said the Major, afraid that all his work might be undone were Georgie to come into contact prematurely with one of the instruments of destruction. 'There'll be plenty of time for that sort of thing later.' He searched his mind for something to say. 'Nice shade of brown, the rifle we use here. It'll go nicely with your beard.'

'Very well, then. I'll do it. Where do I sign?'

'Just a moment,' said the Major. 'I'll get the Roll. Damn' it, it doesn't seem to be here. It must be in my desk over at Grebe. Tell you what, I'll just nip up home and fetch it. You go back and sew on those stripes.'

'I'd better change first,' said Georgie, embarrassed by the thought of walking through the streets in uniform. 'I'm not really entitled to wear these clothes yet.'

'Nonsense, my boy, you go right ahead. Take a pride in the uniform. Think of the admiring glances of the ladies, bless 'em.' He guffawed.

Nevertheless, Georgie put his cape over the uniform of which he was so proud, and took a long détour to avoid the High Street. He slipped into Mallards and removed the cape, only to find himself face to face with Lucia.

She had been taking a cup of coffee out to the garden-room, where she had planned a quiet hour at the piano. Seeing a strange man in uniform, possibly a German in disguise, standing in her hall, she screamed and dropped the cup.

'Lucia!' exclaimed Georgie. 'Don't be alarmed. It's me! Georgie!' he added to remove all further uncertainty.

162

'Georgie?' she repeated feebly. 'What are you doing in those clothes?'

'It's my unform,' he said proudly. 'I'm the new Home Guard sergeant.'

Lucia stared at him as if he had changed into a frog.

'Your're joking,' she said at last.

'No, I'm not. I've decided to do my bit. It's high time I did something other than cook and write scripts for broadcasts. Besides, Major Benjy said that everyone in Tilling expected it of me. And don't you go saying that I can't because I've made up my mind. Here, what do you think of these stripes? I did them myself. Aren't the colours nice?'

Lucia continued to stare at him, so that he wondered if she was about to have some sort of fit.

'It's no use looking at me like that,' he went on, feeling more and more sheepish by the minute. 'And I think I look very well in the uniform. And Major Benjy says I can keep my beard, because it goes well with the rifles. I haven't seen any rifles yet, of course. I don't think you see them until you've actually signed up.'

'So you haven't signed anything yet?'

'No, not yet. But I will,' he added defiantly.

Lucia paused and counted from one to five in her head. Sometimes she wanted to hit Georgie.

'Darling,' she said sweetly, 'why on earth should you want to join the Home Guard? You'd hate it. Why, I remember that when I wanted you to be an A.R.P. warden you were full of reasons against it. Very cogent reasons they were, too,' she added quickly, 'as I recall. And that was before you discovered your true calling, your real vocation. Everyone says so – think of Lord Tony, think of Teddy Broome. Think of Olga,' she added for good measure, and then wished she hadn't. 'Think of me. Think how disappointed we'd all be if you laid aside this wonderful talent, this national resource of yours.'

'You make me sound like a coal-mine,' said Georgie crossly.

'It is from the mines of our talented men that we draw

the ore that makes the sinews of war,' said Lucia grandly. 'Indeed it's a very apt parallel. Think of all those brave coal-miners, cutting the coal that feeds the furnaces that smelt the steel. . . .'

She stopped. This was turning into a nursery rhyme.

'I'm sure they'd all like to join up, but the Government makes them stay at home.'

'But I needn't give up my work for the Government. I'd only be needed in the evening most of the time. Major Benjy assured me of that. I'd have plenty of time to do recipes and write scripts. Think how grand it would sound: "Making the Most of Your Ration-Book", with *Sergeant* Pillson!'

Something seemed to fall into place in Lucia's mind. Of course! How could she have been so blind!

'You realise what's going on, Georgie?' she said. 'You realise why Major Benjy is so keen to make you his sergeant – I take it he's been nagging away at you, wheedling you into accepting?'

Georgie nodded. How had she guessed?

'Elizabeth's behind this, you mark my words. She just wants to stop me holding my dinner parties. So she's made poor Major Benjy trick you into joining his Home Guard.'

'What on earth has it all got to do with Elizabeth?' demanded Georgie, but with a failing heart. Dimly he perceived her meaning.

'Why, it's obvious, dear. If you're out every evening, stomping up and down the Harbour with all those old men and catching your death of cold, you won't be able to cook dinner for my guests. It's pure spite, that's what it is. I think you'll find she's trying to lure you away, just to stop me.'

'She wouldn't!' wailed Georgie. 'She wouldn't be so devious!'

'She would!' cried Lucia vehemently, and Georgie agreed with her in his heart.

'She's furious because she can't get at me any more, and she's trying to find a way to do it without it seeming to be her. So she's got poor Major Benjy to do her dirty work for her. How I pity that man!'

The bottom had suddenly fallen out of Georgie's world. All the bright visions, the cheering crowds, the renewal of youth, all gone, leaving only an echo of mockery behind. He wasn't a civic leader after all.

Lucia saw that she was having some effect.

'You wouldn't want to be used like that, not by Elizabeth? Too shaming, and everyone laughing behind your back. Of course, you would make an excellent sergeant under other circumstances.' (What other circumstances? God alone knew.) 'Your bearing, your manly features. Why, you are the very image of one or other of King Charles's Generals. Prince Rupert, even. But you couldn't possibly accept office under such conditions. Your pride would not permit it.'

'No, of course not,' said Georgie stiffly. 'I wouldn't dream of doing such a thing. And how dare Elizabeth try and use me against you! It's too bad. I've got a good mind to – to punch Major Benjy on the nose!'

'No need,' said Lucia soothingly. 'Ickle Lucia not want big strong men fighting over her. Besides, he might hit you back, and that would be too distressing. No, me got a plan of my vewwy own. Me teach naughty Elizabeth a lesson she not forget. Oh yes,' she added with relish.

'My dear, what are you going to do?' demanded Georgie fascinated. This was more like the old Lucia; not the haughty, superior, Bridge-suppressing dictator, but the prime mover of Tilling life, the bringer of excitement.

'I think we might have a little dinner party, Georgie. All our friends, including, of course, Elizabeth. And what do you think they'll see on the mantelpiece as they sip their sherry? I'll wager you'll never guess.'

'No!' gasped Georgie. 'The invitation! Oh how glorious! That'll show her.'

'Not a word from you or me, of course. Let it be a silent indictment of that woman's evil nature. And now, please go and take off those dreadful clothes.'

'Oh Lord, I'd completely forgotten!' said Georgie. 'Major Benjy's waiting for me to sign his dratted register. And my second-best fawn trousers are at the Institute.'

Major Benjy walked briskly back to Grebe, anxious to fetch the vital documents quickly and bring his subtle stratagem to fruition. Not bad at all for an old soldier, he reflected, a man like himself, used to simple and straightforward dealings. But Benjy Flint could be as ingenious as any of the old cats of Tilling on his day. And wouldn't Elizabeth be pleased!

The Roll was not in its accustomed place. He seached in the whisky-flask desk, on the bookshelves, even behind the sofa. No sign of it.

'Liz,' he called, 'have you seen the Nominal Roll?'

'The what, dear?' she called back from the garden. 'And please don't bellow like that. I'm not deaf, although I'm sure I shall be soon if you keep on shouting like that.'

'Sorry, old girl,' he said, 'but I'm looking for the Nominal Roll. The Home Guard Register, don't you know. I think I've found us a new sergeant.'

'How exciting,' said his wife, bustling in from the kitchen. 'Who is it?'

'Guess!' chuckled the Major. He had planned to keep it a surprise, but now seemed as good a time as any to be congratulated for his cleverness.

'Hopkins?' asked Elizabeth.

'No.'

'The Padre? Algernon Wyse?'

'Wrong and wrong again. I didn't think you'd guess. Not the likeliest person to be a leader of men, I'll admit, nor the best suited for the job, not by a long chalk. But it's not Hitler that this particular sergeant's going to be putting in his place. It's the other dictator we were talking about.'

'Mussolini?' hazarded Elizabeth vaguely.

'No, no, old girl. It's a certain wretch whom we once thought of as a friend of sorts, but who betrayed our

166

friendship in a most foul and despicable way.'

'You mean Marshal Pétain?'

'No. Lucia, Lucia Pillson. I've got Mr. Georgie Pillson to be the new sergeant. Sergeant Milliner Michael-Angelo. Ha!'

'But why should Mr. Georgie want to be in the Home Guard?' demanded Elizabeth. Something was wrong here, she thought.

'Because I persuaded him, that's why. Dickens of a job it was, too. But nothing to old Silver-Tongued Benjy, as they used to call me. So that'll put a stop to our Lucia's jolly dinner parties, unless she's prepared to put on an apron and peel the carrots herself. When Georgie-boy should be down in the kitchen cooking dinner, he'll be out with me, marching up and down the Military Road, and may God help him if his belt-buckles are tarnished! Revenge is sweet, eh? I knew you'd be pleased.'

'Fool!' cried Elizabeth hoarsely. 'Fool, fool, fool!' She began to sob.

'Steady on, old thing,' urged the flabbergasted Manjor. This was not the reaction he had expected.

'You wretch!' she screamed. 'How could you do this to me after all the work I've done, the agonies I've suffered, abasing myself before that creature! Silver-Tongued Benjy, was it? Idiot Benjy it must be from now on. I suppose you must have been drunk at the time, but that is no excuse. I shall never, never speak to you again.'

At this juncture, that seemed a very agreeable prospect. Unfortunately it was not to be, for she continued:

'You know what she'll do, as soon as she's seen through your infantile scheme, which will take her precisely three seconds? She'll show that invitation to everyone and start telling them – the most terrible lies about me. Oh how cruel!'

'Hang on, Liz. I said she won't be able to see through it.'

'She'll see through it all right. She'll think I put you up to it. It's bad enough that Lucia should think me capable of such a puerile stratagem.'

The full injustice of this aspect of the disaster seemed to go through Elizabeth like a knife. She struggled to contain her emotions, like an overheating engine, and then seized one of her china pigs and dashed it to the ground.

'Now look what you've done!' she howled.

'Well, I'm sorry, I'm sure,' said the Major, trying to sound offended but making a poor job of it. 'I only did what I thought was for the best, as an old soldier and a gentleman. I apologise for my thoughtless conduct, which was unworthy of one of His Majesty's officers, unworthy indeed,' he added, 'of any Englishman. Dashed silly thing to do.'

Elizabeth picked up a copy of the *Daily Mirror* and began to tear it to pieces. This seemed to calm her down, for she spoke in level tones.

'Tell me exactly what happened,' she said, as she crumpled a picture of Mr. Anthony Eden into a tight ball. 'What did you say to him?'

'I suggested that he might like to be our sergeant,' Major Benjy almost whispered. 'Said it was his duty, and all that. He seemed very keen.'

'Well, the damage is done. Or is it, Benjy? The Roll, has he signed it?'

'Of course not. I was just looking for it.'

A faint glimmer of hope dawned in Elizabeth's mind.

'And where is he now?'

'He went back to Mallards to sew on his sergeant's stripes, while I came back here to get the Roll. Chances are that Lucia hasn't seen him yet. She may not know anything about it.'

'Thank God he didn't sign,' said Elizabeth. 'Well, don't stand there. Run back to town and tell him it's all been a ghastly mistake. Say that his cooking must come first. Say anything! Run!'

And Major Benjy ran.

Exhausted and perspiring heavily, almost dehydrated by the lack of whisky and soda, the Major burst through the door of the Institute, only to find Georgie, attired in civilian dress, collecting his second-best fawn trousers, with an air of utter disdain.

'Pillson,my dear feller! So glad I managed to catch you!' panted the Major. To the best of his knowledge, he had not run a step since he had last seen a tiger.

'I'm afraid there's been the most terrible mistake.'

'There certainly has, Major Mapp-Flint,' replied Georgie, icily. 'A very serious mistake on your part.'

Major Benjy sagged. There on the table was Georgie's uniform, beautifully folded and pressed by Foljambe. Beside it, a pair of sergeant's stripes, splendidly embroidered in yellow gold, seemed to grin at the Major like the yawning jaws of a shark.

'You haven't told your wife about this, have you?' panted the Major.

'It was Mrs. Pillson who revealed to me the extent of your treachery, Major Mapp-Flint. You have attempted to use me as a pawn in a sordid intrigue.' Georgie paused. Did one use pawns in sordid intrigues? Never having been in one himself, he could not say. 'As a result I cannot accept the appointment. I wish you success in your search for a suitable candidate.'

'It was all my idea,' said the Major desperately. 'Elizabeth knew nothing.'

'Your chivalry seems somewhat misplaced, Major,' returned Georgie coldly. 'I am surprised that a distinguished solider like yourself should be capable of using the commission entrusted to you by the King in such a frivolous way. I expected more of you, Major Flint.' This phrase reopened the barely closed wound, and with a passionate throb in his voice burst out, 'You said I was a civic leader! It's too unkind! Good day to you, Major Mapp-Flint!'

He swept out of the Institute and slammed the door behind him. It could have been a fine, dignified exit had he not caught the hem of his cape in the door and had to reopen it to twitch it free.

'Tar'some thing!' he exclaimed, and was gone.

'Damn',' said the Major. 'Now what shall I do?'

For once, he knew the answer to that question. He rose to his feet and from a crate marked 'Explosives' he drew a bottle of whisky. He had often had recourse to such explosives during his career as a Home Guard commander, but even this secret weapon did not seem likely to do more than ameliorate his own condition. Gloomily he trudged back to Grebe, kicking a small stone in front of him. He knew how it felt.

'No luck,' he confessed, as he came into the presence of his wife. 'He's found out. Pillson was quite rude to me.'

'Well, that's that,' said Elizabeth. 'We shall have to sell this house and move away. I can't face what people will say, I really can't.'

'Cheer up, Liz, we aren't done for yet,' said the Major, trying to sound nonchalant, and failing. 'You'll have to tell everyone the truth. I don't think Lucia is all that popular these days.'

'That's true,' mused Elizabeth. 'She's trying to stop them playing Bridge and wants them all to learn the piano. Diva was urging me to defy her only the other day.'

'And the Padre says he's going to preach a sermon on Tolerance on Sunday, with a veiled attack on Lucia in it,' remembered the Major. 'Or was it Hitler?'

'And even the Wyses say that they're too set in their way to learn the piano, and they don't think Bridge at all frivolous. Benjy, I think we have a chance after all. Ah! and I have an idea.'

'Well done, old girl! Tell me about it.'

'She's sure to invite them all to dinner tomorrow night to show them the invitation. Very well, then. I'll speak to them all in the morning at marketing hour and tell them my story. The truth, I mean, and then I'll say how much Lucia's tormented me, and that's why I haven't been able to put a stop to this no-Bridge nonsense. If I stress that bit, they'll all take my side because it'll be me against Lucia about Bridge. We can't lose!'

'Brilliant!' exclaimed the Major, deeply impressed.

'And so courageous. You're a marvel, Liz.'

Elizabeth smiled and reflected that if her account was not yet strictly true, it would be so indistinguishable from the truth that no one, except possibly Lucia, would ever be able to tell the difference.

The invitations were sent out; the word Bridge was missing from the left-hand corner. Elizabeth rejoiced, for the enemy had played directly into her hands. Her apologia was received with more sympathy and understanding than she had dared to hope, and this encouragement enabled her to rise to unprecedented pinnacles of the dramatic art. She was hurt, wounded, ashamed, repentant and defiant, from Twistevant's in the west to Worthington's in the east, and the power and intensity of her performance reached such a crescendo that Mrs. Bartlett, who was the last to hear it, was almost in tears by the time she had finished.

Tilling hated mysteries, as Nature is said to abhor a vacuum; the mystery of Elizabeth's curious self-humiliation before Lucia had now been solved and was most thrilling. In fact, the simple act of explanation, had she known it, would probably have vouchsafed absolution for Elizabeth. As it was, her masterly reworking of the facts had roused Tilling to a frenzy of excitement, so that people stood in queues for things they had no intention of buying simply in order to discuss the news with someone else. Certain aspects of the tale puzzled them; chiefly they had wondered why, considering the innocence of Elizabeth's motives in opening the letter, she had not told Lucia about it, and how it was that she had been so worried by Lucia's threat to expose her as a fraud. For all agreed that no one would have believed such an unkind and patently false account as Lucia had evidently threatened to tell them; why, the story would not even fit the known facts. On one thing, all were agreed: it was so like Lucia. Not the Lucia they had known and loved all these years, but the new, tyrannical Lucia, the Bridge-banner, the piano-enforcer. 'Typical!'

they said. 'And how poor Elizabeth must have suffered!'

Whether they would have proved so gullible had not Lucia made such a terrible blunder, it is hard to say. But Bridge was indeed the very life-blood of Tilling; its deceptions, its speculations, its psychic bids were a microcosm of the town itself. Around the Bridge-table all the animosities of the last few days were reaped and threshed, and the seeds of new ones planted in their place, to grow to maturity in time for the next Bridge party in a few days' time. It was the communion of the tribe, the stylised re-enactment of their daily lives. As the ritual of Adonis represents the death and rebirth of Nature, so the Bridge of Tilling embodied in its time-honoured patterns of misunderstood bids, revokes and bitter recriminations the whole social life-cycle of the population. To threaten Bridge was to threaten the very fabric of their society, and if Lucia thought that a dull evening listening to her hammering out the same old pieces on the piano was any substitute for this vital and meaningful activity, she was very much mistaken.

Elizabeth, unaccompanied by Major Benjy, who was busy with his explosives at the Institute, was the last to arrive at Mallards that evening, and all considered this a hopeful sign. They all remembered the good old days, when she had made a point of always arriving last at any gathering. After Lucia's coming, it had always been a matter of honour that Elizabeth was the last to arrive at Lucia's house, and Lucia the last to arrive at Elizabeth's. Indeed, one fine evening, Elizabeth had walked four times round Church Square and read half the headstones in the grave-yard because she saw the Wyses arriving at Mallards just when she was on the point of going in herself.

The guests were ushered into the garden-room for a glass of sherry. There, on the mantelpiece, was the fateful rectangle of white card that must surely seal Elizabeth's doom. On either side of it were two dazzling flower-arrangements that even a person with poor eyesight could not fail to notice, flanked by a selection of books that Lucia knew her friends were eager to borrow: a book on spiritualism for Susan, *The Irish Setter in Sickness and in Health* for Diva, and a rare edition of Burns for the Padre.

'Diva, dear, how marvellous you look!' crooned Lucia, 'and Evie and dear Padre! Such thrilling news of our beloved Highland Regiments! Mr. Wyse, how elegant, and you, too, dear Susan. I declare I feel dowdy by comparison. Ah, there you are, Elizabeth, we were afraid you were not going to come. No Major Benjy? How sad! Still, it is such important work that he is doing, is it not? Up and down the Harbour, and in all weathers too.'

Elizabeth smiled like a shark.

'Essential,' she agreed. 'But so much easier now that he has found a man to be his sergeant.'

'How exciting! Who?'

'Hopkins the fishmonger has finally heard the call of duty,' said Elizabeth grandly. 'Major Benjy managed to persuade him at last. He can be so persuasive at times – no wonder hs colleagues in Burma used to call him Silver-Tongued Benjy! Of course, he interviewed so many men for the job – many,many eager applicants – but not one of them up to his very high standards. What was needed, we felt, was a man respected in the community. Only the best for our dear Tilling, I insisted, and he agreed with me. Dear Lucia, you should have seen some of the paltry fellows who thought they might have a chance. Of course, when Major Benjy told them what the job involved, they scuttled away with their tails between their legs.'

A tremor of excitement ran round the room. This was war. As far as Elizabeth was concerned, Georgie had applied to be sergeant and had been turned down in favour of Hopkins. This was better than any of them had dared to hope.

'Such a difficult choice,' squeaked Evie, daringly. She had been one of those most deeply moved by the proposed abolition of Bridge. 'So few people in the town capable of doing the job, so many of them believing that they could. Poor Major Benjy!'

'He said it was very hard to find words for a tactful refusal,' continued Elizabeth blithely. 'Some of them were quite angry and rude, and stormed off in a huff. Such bad manners!'

'Ah weel!' said the Padre, another inveterate gambler, ''tes a' well that ends well. And yon Hopkins is a fine figure of a man, what wi' haulin' around the crates of wee fishies.'

'Indeed,' said Lucia coldly. 'I'm sure we'll all feel much better knowing that the strong arm of Mr. Hopkins has been raised up to protect us.'

'Fie, Lucia, to be so frivolous' (that dread word!) 'about our brave Home Guard. I'm sure Mr. Georgie doesn't share your low opinion of them,' said Elizabeth, staring straight at the invitation and smiling yet more enormously.

'On the contrary, on the contrary,' muttered Lucia, totally confused. Were they all blind? Was the room too dark?

'What delightful flowers, Mrs. Pillson,' said Mr. Wyse solemnly, stepping over to the mantelpiece and burying his nose in the explosion of primary colours that Lucia had placed there. As he did so, his eye was but a few inches from the invitation, so that had he been half-blind he must have read it. But clearly he was far too well bred to peruse other people's letters, for he turned and said, 'Exquisite chrysanthemums. Or should one perhaps call them chrysanthema? Thus the Greek plural, although the ending " – um" is Latin. But then, chrysanthema would be correct in either case, would it not, Mrs. Pillson?'

Lucia's only reply was to gurgle inarticulately. To be sure, this was the erudite and learned conversation that she longed to hear replacing the endless cries of 'Three hearts!' and 'I thought you had no more clubs' in her beloved garden-room. But there was a time and place for everything.

'That's always puzzled me,' said Diva, who had never given the subject a moment's thought before. 'Greek name, Latin ending. Odd.'

'It is an established etymological phenomenon in botanical circles, I believe,' intoned Mr. Wyse gravely. 'Often the first of two scientific names accorded to each individual species is of Greek derivation, whereas the second is of Latin origin. Thus in the case of *Pyracanthus latefolia*, *Pyracanthus* is, I scarcely need remind you, formed from two Greek words, while *latefolia* is a Latin compound. Inddded, some names of plants are macaronic within the same word.'

'Gosh!' said Diva. She had not the faintest idea what he was talking about, but Lucia's face was a prettier sight than all the pyracanthuses (or pyracanthi) in Christendom.

' 'Tes often the case that a wee flower is clept after the wight that first discovered it. Dahlia. Fuchsia. Ah, 'twud be a gladsome thing to be thus remembered. Now, if I were tae discover a new azalea, a' mankind would ken wha it was that first identified *Azalea bartletti*.'

'What wonderful flowers they must have at Windsor!' snarled Lucia, crossing to the mantelpiece.

'Not nearly as fine as the gardens at Kew,' interrupted Evie. 'Kenneth and I visited them once. Such colours.'

With a deliberate movement, Lucia knocked the invitation off the mantelpiece. It fluttered to the ground and came to rest at Mr. Wyse's feet. Gracefully, he stooped and picked it up, smiled and then replaced it on the mantelpiece. Lucia stared at him.

'Ah, dear Padre,' she growled, 'here is a book I promised to lend you. Do come and see.'

'Thank ye, Mistress Pillson, but as it so chances I managed tae buy a copy o' the self-same edition only the ither week. Sich a bargain 'twas too, at only three shillings.'

'And here is a book I have promised you many times, Diva,' Lucia ground on remorselessly. 'About Irish setters, you recall.'

'Ah yes,' said Diva, and she flushed red. 'Just so

happens I managed to pick up a copy of that the other day myself. What a coincidence!'

'How fortunate! Now, here is one for you, dear Susan.' Lucia was beginning to sound like a Sunday-school prize-giving. 'I recall that you asked me for it only the other day, so I searched the house from top to bottom and here it is!'

'Oh I don't think so!' replied Susan. 'On the contrary, I think I offered to lend you my copy. I think you must have got muddled up. Fancy you having one too! Such a fine work! Such sensitivity!'

Lucia could feel sweat breaking out on her forehead, although it may just have been the warmth of the fire. Reluctantly she came away from the fireplace and drank her sherry rather quickly.

'I do hope Mr. Georgie has cooked something special. He has been working rather a lot recently on turnips. I believe he intends to name this particular dish after the King.'

'That's handy,' said Diva, 'seeing as how they're both called George. I bet he's really named it after himself. And why not? Interesting name, George.'

'Originally,' said Mr. Wyse, 'derived from the Greek word meaning a farmer. Its popularity in this country is, of course, due to its being the name of our patron saint. Yet St. George was originally a Greek saint. Perhaps you can enlighten us on that subject, Padre?'

This dazzling dislay of scholarship threatened to overwhelm Lucia, for she gasped and sat down hurriedly. Obviously they were all deliberately ignoring the invitation. But why? Just then Foljambe announced dinner and the assembled company made its way through to the dining-room. There Georgie was standing, as was his custom. It had been a delicate matter for him to decide, for since he cooked the food, he felt he ought to stay with it and to be on hand to sponsor its arrival, so to speak, rather than abandoning it to the charge of Foljambe once he had brought it to life. On the other hand, he could not bring himself to pass round the plates, feeling (and rightly so) that it would embarrass the guests to be waited on by their host. So he usually remained standing up at least until the soup arrived and ate his portion quickly so as to be able to dash off to the kitchen to inspect the next course and return to his seat before Foljambe produced it. This ritual not infrequently gave him indigestion, but he felt that that was right and proper, in a way; the artist must suffer and by his suffering ennoble the world.

Lucia took her place at the head of the table. She had, in her desperation, thought of bringing the invitation card in with her; but that would not achieve anything. For some reason, everyone was ignoring it. Again she asked herself why. What had she done?

'Hello, everyone,' said Georgie. He was amazed to see them all so cheerful, when there should have been an uncomfortable silence. But there was Elizabeth, kissing her hand to Lucia as she took her seat at the opposite end of the table. This placing had been intended to isolate her, to put her on view after her disgrace. But now she sat in state, like a one-woman government in exile, and it was Lucia who felt excluded. Georgie shook his head and turned round to see what had become of the soup. By Lucia's express command it was Brown Windsor.

'Why Mr. Georgie, what delicious oxtail!' exclaimed Elizabeth, and a chorus of approbation arose from her fellow-guests. Yet it was impossible to contradict such flattery; to him it tasted like Brown Windsor, but the artist is but one interpreter of his own work. To Leonardo, no doubt, the Madonna's smile was but a smile; to the succeeding generations it has meant much more. So if Georgie thought his soup was Brown Windsor, Georgie must be mistaken. It was all most confusing.

To Lucia, it might as well have been chicken broth. So far as she could think coherently in this disaster, she was reconstructing all the possible causes for this drastic peripeteia in her fortunes. Had she perchance, walking in her sleep or under the influence of automatism, been overheard humming Haydn's Austrian Hymn? Had mysterious lights been seen at the windows of Mallards? She resolved upon one last attempt; should that fail, she decided, she would leave Tilling for ever, to end her days as a hermit on some rocky Scottish island, singing madrigals to the unheeding breakers.

'Tell me, Elizabeth,' she nearly shouted through the buzz of conversation, 'when you were at Windsor. . . .'

Simultaneously, Susan Wyse (on her left) and the Padre (on her right) began to talk to her loudly and rapidly; both, as it so happened, declaring what a comfort it was, in such dark days as these, that they still had the simple pleasures of life to console themselves with – such as a game of Bridge among friends. Like the stichomythia of the Attic drama, they recounted celebrated Bridge-games of the past – the distant past, in fact, for without exception they dated from before Lucia's arrival in Tilling.

'I remember when Elizabeth made two slam decorations in a row and won them both! Such daring! It cost me six shillings, but I begrudged her not a penny! Before your time, I think, Lucia dear. A pity. You should have seen it!'

'Ah, right weel do I recall it, Mistress Wyse. And do ye recall that evening in this very room, when Mistress Mapp – as she then was, drew a hand of a' four aces and three kings? That was a canny no-trumps hand and no mistake!'

Like the motifs in a piece of music, these themes recurred again and again; the pleasure of Bridge, Bridge at Mallards, Mallards before Lucia. Gradually, the whole table except Lucia and Georgie took up the refrain until it resembled some intricate figure in which the vital elements are so closely interwoven that they emerge one with another; Elizabeth, Bridge, and no Lucia.

Only then was it that Lucia realised what had happened and it took her breath away. Because she had suggested, gently and hypothetically, that every hour of every day need not be spent in playing cards, the whole town had deliberately resolved to take no notice whatever of one of the most sensational incidents in the history of Tilling since its capture by the French in the Hundred Years' War. How was I to know? demanded Lucia of her much enduring soul. As the voices raged around her like·the sea, she could think of nothing that might alter this situation. If all the town was united against her, there was an end of it.

It hardly seems necessary to add that the rubbers of Bridge that followed this ill-starred meal, for follow they did, were of a quality scarcely if ever seen before in Sussex. At times, four aces seemed to be the absolute minimum in a pack of cards. When diamonds were trumps, each player's hand resembled some Rajah's crown. Doublings and redoublings were legion and if the president of the Society for Psychical Research had been present, he would have gloried in the innumerable and successful psychic bids. Even the normally impassive Mr. Wyse was gripped with excitement. For all that Georgie had developed a substance indistinguishable from nougat chocolate, Diva was so enthralled by the conflict that she scarcely touched the second plateful. Finally, when the smoke and din of battle was lifted, Elizabeth rose from the tables no less than eight shillings richer, while Lucia's purse was lighter by an exactly corresponding amount. Everyone else had broken more or less even, so the significance of the omen was obvious.

'Such an enjoyable evening,' exclaimed Susan Wyse as she climbed into her cockpit of sables for the three-minute walk to Starling Cottage. 'Such excitement! Why, I confess that I was so carried away by the excitement of the card-play that the war slipped from my mind like a bad dream!'

'I too was transported back to the long-dead past,' agreed her husband. 'I never thought to spend such a light-hearted and carefree evening again.'

179

'Although Hitler has taken from us our food and our clothes, our loved ones and our tranquillity,' declared Elizabeth (and all agreed that Mr. Churchill could not have said it more sonorously), 'he cannot take from us the everlasting pleasures of friendship. Thank you, Lucia, for an enchanting evening. I shall treasure the memory of it always,' she cooed, as she departed with a twinkling wave.

'What happened?' asked Georgie as he and Lucia stood on the threshold of Mallards contemplating the empty street.

'Bridge, Georgie, Bridge. Because I suggested – purely a sounding-out, a testing of the waters, that we might do very well with a little less Bridge and a little more Poetry and Music, they have conspired together not to notice Elizabeth's deceit. They have taken her side against me!'

'I warned you,' said Georgie softly, 'but you wouldn't listen.'

'I know,' said Lucia, 'I should have. Well, there it is.'

They stood awhile and reflected on this stark reality, until Mr. Rice, the A.R.P. warden, passing by on his bicycle became aware of light flooding the street from the open portal of Mallards.

'Shut that blooming door!' he roared. 'Do you want the Germans to blow you to Kingdom Come, or what?'

Yes, decided Lucia, and shut the door.

12

Tilling remained aloof for some weeks and Lucia came
to feel that she was in the position of some savage chief-
tain – Caractacus, say, or Cetewayo – who, after doing
great damage to his enemies, is captured and made to
live among them, a turbulent warrior dragging out his
miserable existence with only the grudging respect of
his ancient foe. As she walked down the High Street, she
seemed to hear them say to each other, 'There goes
Lucia, who actually tried to put a stop to Bridge-playing
in Tilling. And she very nearly succeeded, too!'

So long as Irene Coles remained in Tilling, Lucia was
sure of at least one staunch ally. But the day came when
even that *fidus Achates* departed. She called at
Mallards at seven-o'clock one wet morning, clad in an
enormous duffel-coat and smoking an oily black briar.

'Alas!' she declared dramatically. 'We must part,
dear Lucia. Duty calls and all that, though it breaks my
heart to go!' And she flung her arms around her acutely
embarrassed friend.

'Now you will take care,' said Lucia solicitously.

Irene roared with laughter. 'Don't you worry about
me. I'll be all right. It's you I'm worried about. How can I
bring myself to leave you when Mapp is grinding you
beneath her iron heel? Never mind, you'll win through.
Serenely, beautifully, triumphantly, you just mark my
words.'

Lucia decided it would be best to move off this difficult
subject. 'And where will you be going? And who will you
be going with?'

'Sh!' hissed Irene. 'That's a secret. But I'll tell you. We'll be taking coal to Manchester along the Ship Canal. There's me and Lucy, of course, and Henry Porteous's sister Antigone. We call her Tiggers,' said Irene, in a voice heavy with gruff affection. 'Oh, if only you would come too, and leave all this petty turmoil. The open waters, the nights beneath the brilliant stars, the tranquil progress through that majestic industrial landscape! I feel I shall do some of my best work with such inspiration all about me.'

Lucia shuddered. It all sounded perfectly horrible. 'It all sounds perfectly delightful,' she fluted, 'but I am far too old and pampered to be of any use to you. But do have a simply wonderful time and paint hundreds and hundreds of beautiful pickies. Write to me and I'll send you some warm socks and balaclava helmets.'

'That's so like your beautiful, generous nature,' cried Irene, deeply affected. Then she embraced Lucia again, her eyes wet with tears. 'And how dare that miserable old Mapp be so beastly to you! I've got a good mind to teach her a lesson before I go!'

And what she did was this. Rushing back to Taormina (for she still had a little while before her train arrived) she telephoned to Grebe. Putting on a deep, musculine voice (something which came easily to her), she asked for Mrs. Mapp-Flint. There was a short pause as Withers fetched Elizabeth from her dressing-room. Putting in her teeth, Elizabeth replied, 'Yes?'

'Mrs. Mapp-Flint?' said Irene. 'This is the Warden of the Tower of London speaking.' Elizabeth at the other end of the line went white. 'It has come to my attention,' continued quaint Irene, 'as official investigator of cases of infringement of protocol and general lèse majesté, that you recently bluffed your way into an official reception at Windsor Castle, masquerading as your distinguished fellow-citizen, Mrs. Pillson of Mallards House, Tilling. What is your explanation of such deplorable conduct?'

Elizabeth began to babble hysterically about wireless broadcasts and letters opened in error, about how some people jumped to the worst conclusions and how she had been, after all, a sort of ambassador. . . .

'Come off it, Mapp,' said Irene in her own sweet voice.

At the other end of the wire terror changed to fury. Quaint Irene put down the receiver and left to catch her train.

Elizabeth's vengeance was swift and sure. Just as Major Benjy's independent action had seemed to call for punishment against herself, now Irene's interference, though no doubt unsolicited, must bring down retribution on Lucia's head. Elizabeth set about placing Mallards under embargo. So pleasant had she been to her friends in Tilling, and so great was her reputation as the saviour of Bridge, that they accepted her lead unquestioningly, while magnifying Lucia's brief spell of domination into a prolonged and barbarous tyranny. First, Elizabeth began to decline invitations to Mallards, whereupon her supporters followed her lead, supplying each other with the prior engagements necessary for this purpose. Then she removed Lucia's name from her own guest-list, an example followed at once by everyone else, so that an unprecedented state of excommunication existed in Tilling, a terrifying precedent for the disloyal and a crushing blow for Lucia.

Georgie was not included in this internal exile, and, although at first he put up a show of solidarity, his flesh proved too weak. He had never proposed to abolish Bridge; why should he suffer? On the pretext of bringing Lucia all the news, he began to attend the social gatherings for which his heart yearned. There he was met with a display of sympathetic understanding as if all pitied him that he was bound in chains of matrimony to that monster. No one, at least in his presence, voiced any criticism of Lucia, for no one mentioned her at all. It was as if she had never existed.

After a fortnight of this unendurable torment, Lucia

183

seemed quite broken in spirit. Elizabeth, determined not to err as Lucia had erred in failing to be at least moderately merciful to an overthrown opponent, then relaxed the blockade, so that Lucia was gradually readmitted to the social life of the town. This clemency was noted and approved of by Elizabeth's partisans and her supremacy was now undisputed, as it had never been in the days before the advent of Lucia.

Lucia endured it bravely, but in her heart she was close to despair. She could see no way out of this snare in which she had so foolishly allowed herself to be caught, but nevertheless, she continued to live peacefully in retirement, as it were, playing the piano, reading Dante and Aristotle (and the austere calf-bindings of her excellent collection of standard authors gave no clue as to whether these works were in the original or a translation, so that it must be presumed that they were in the former), supervising the production of foodstuffs in her spacious garden, and devoting as much time as the authorities of that institution would permit her to the service of the Tilling hospital.

One evening, as she made her way home through the darkness from an afternoon of reading to the elderly and confused, she noticed a brilliant light, as if of flames, down by the marshes. For a moment, her heart stopped still; then she ran to the telephone box and called up the Institute. No reply; and she recalled that Major Benjy and all his troop were away at Hastings, taking part in a training exercise with the Regular Army. She then telephoned the police station; but tonight was the police-sponsored War Charities Dance and, so she guessed, charity began at home for the defenders of the law in Tilling. In the background she could hear piano-playing of doubtful quality and raucous singing and the voice that answered her enquiry laughed so noisily and suggested that she should go and investigate it herself. Finally, she telephoned Mr. Rice, the A.R.P. warden. Mr. Rice was not there, said his wife; he was out on his bike snooping about after his blessed lights again, and his dinner going cold on the table, and she didn't know why she bothered, she really didn't.

'Typical!' snorted Lucia, and she slammed down the instrument. She sought about her effects for some makeshift weapon, but all she could find was a cucumber, intended as a gift for the elderly and confused, but which had been politely refused on grounds of indigestibility. She wrapped her scarf around the vegetable so that it vaguely resembled some concealed firearm, and set off with a firm step towards the marshes. Every shadow, in that uncertain twilight, seemed to hide the presence of an unseen assailant, every doorway and street-corner appeared to harbour some desperate enemy, but her blood was up; in some way she could not rationalise, she appeared to be hunting Elizabeth through the dark and treacherous town. Two or three times she stopped, convinced that the foe was upon her, and, making a clicking noise with her tongue and back teeth, she levelled the cucumber menacingly and rasped out: '*Kommen Sie hier!*' But each time her suspicions proved unfounded and she pressed on, only too aware that she was doing a very brave thing and unable to help speculating as to exactly how brave she was being. She very much wanted to be brave, but she was highly unwilling to be foolhardy.

Indeed, it is extremely unlikely that even the fearless Lucia would have gone headlong into such danger had not the thought of the glory that must inevitably surround her been constantly in her thoughts. As she tiptoed through the gloom, her eyes fixed on the flickering light before her, she could almost hear the excited gabble of the High Street, Evie's awestruck squeak, Diva's respectfully hushed twittering, the Padre speaking plain English in his excitement, and, of course, the shamefaced stammering Major Benjy, saying that Mrs. Pillson had done his duty for him, that Mrs. Pillson was worth the whole Home Guard put together; how he held himself entirely responsible for her tragic and premature death . . .

As she came to the edge of the marshes, she could

distinctly see the cause of the fire. An aircraft had crashed nose-first into the ground, so that its tail was raised up towards the sky, silhouetted and darkened by the brilliance of the flames that played about it. It was a single-seater fighter, and although she could not identify it by its darkened tail, she imagined that it was a Messerschmitt, possibly a night-fighter that had lost its way over France and run out of fuel over the Sussex coast. As she speculated thus over the origins of the wreckage, she became aware of a human figure slumped in an attitude of resigned despair just outside the circle of flickering light.

Lucia dropped to her knees and crouched behind a small undulation in the ground. From where she was she could see that he appeared to be unarmed; there was no holster at his side or weapon in his hand, although he was a large, powerful-looking man, no doubt capable of snapping her neck like a pencil. He seemed entirely preoccupied, however, wtih the fate of his machine; perhaps he was actually grateful that, for him, the war was over. She had read that most Germans did not believe in the war, although one did not trust all that one read in the newspapers.

Like one of Major Benjy's tigers, she crept forward, the cucumber thrust out in front of her, taking care to be absolutely quiet. Often she paused; still the airman remained motionless. She nerved herself for the moment of reckless courage; the flames seemed to hiss encouragements to her, the cinders glowed red – red as Elizabeth's face would be when she learned what manner of woman it was that she had tormented. . .

'Hände hoch!' she cried and made the clicking noise again. 'Halt, oder ich schiesse!'

'Schiessen Sie nicht! Ich bin waffenlos!' wailed the airman with tragic resignation in his voice. He did not turn round but raised his arms slowly in the air.

Lucia had thought no further beyond this moment, for she had hardly dared hope that she would get this far. What was she to do now? What was the German for 'On

186

your feet!'? She racked her brain for some periphrasis, silently scanning in her mind the pages of opera libretti, for to such works was her knowledge of German confined. But alas! in neither *The Magic Flute* nor *Parsifal*, not even in the entire *Nibelungs' Ring* does one character say to another 'Get up slowly and no funny business.' She made a wild guess.

'*Zu deinen Fuss!*' she snapped. '*Schnell!*' The airman remained where he was. '*So standen Sie aus?*' she suggested. '*Bitte?*' she pleaded.

The airman turned around and looked at her, evidently mystified. She waved the cucumber threateningly and motioned him to rise. He did so.

She pointed to the town in the distance and said, '*Eamus,*' before she remembered that that was not German but Latin.

'*Bene!*' replied the airman in the same tongue.

This, thought Lucia, is a stroke of luck, until she recollected that she still had no idea how to say, 'Make a sudden move and I'll blast you,' even in Latin.

The little procession made its nervous way into the town, which was quiet and deserted. The airman, who had been silent all the way up from the marshes, began to babble as he saw the town, so that Lucia was compelled to dig him in the back with the cucumber.

'England!' he cried. '*Britannia!*'

'*Mehercle!*' replied Lucia. There is no simple way of saying 'yes' in Latin. Doubtless, she thought bitterly, Algernon Wyse could think of a more elegant or idiomatic way of putting it, but then, Mr. Wyse would be hiding under his bed by this stage if he were in her shoes. Hah!

'*Cantium,*' said the airman. That was the ancient Roman name for Kent.

'*Non est Cantium,*' replied Lucia distractedly, '*Est Sussex.*'

The airman once again started to jabber in his barbaric tongue. It was most unlike the German of Lucia's experience, but she (fortunately) had never claimed to be a German scholar. Her acquaintance with the filthy language had been made at Covent Garden and, for all she knew, the airman had a Bavarian brogue. She began to wonder whether anyone would ever appear to take this obnoxious person off her hands. But the town seemed to be entirely deserted and she was alone with her captive in the darkling streets.

'*Amicus sum*,' sobbed the airman in desperate tones. Lucia smiled grimly, for she had anticipated trouble. Fortunately they were at the top of Malleson Street. Surely the Home Guard must be returned by now, for it was quite dark, bringing with them every conceivable kind of lethal instrument to guard this miserable enemy. She directed her captive, who was pleading with all the eloquence of a Cicero that he was in no respect an enemy, down the street to the Institute. The blacked-out windows let out a few chinks of light and, oddly enough, there was a sound of singing.

'Fifteen men on a dead man's chest,' sang Major Benjy, as she thrust open the door. 'Yo ho ho and good Lord it's Mrs. Pillson. What are you doin' roamin' around this time o' night? An' hoozat with you?'

'Major Mapp-Flint,' said Lucia contemptuously, 'I have captured a German airman.' And she thrust the prisoner into the throng of bewildered tradesmen. Several of them tried to hide under the table.

'By George!' cried the Major. 'It's a Hun! Don't fire till you see the blues of his eyes! All got blue eyes, these fiends,' he explained.

'There is no need to fire,' shrieked Lucia, for she was standing directly behind him. 'He is unarmed and the British do not shoot their prisoners.'

'That's true,' reflected the Major. 'Sergeant Hopkins, restrain the prisoner!' The burly fishmonger clapped a hand on the airman's shoulder and thrust him into a chair. 'I shall telephone to Hastings at once,' continued Major Benjy. 'Prisoner. Damn' Hun. Send an armoured car.'

After a somewhat confused conversation, the Major

satisfied his interlocutor in Hastings that a prisoner was to be collected from Home Guard Headquarters, Tilling and drew towards him a crate marked 'Explosives'. Lucia, who had read of the punishments meted out to prisoners in the Indian Mutiny, cried out in alarm, but the Major drew forth a bottle of whisky and chuckled.

'This calls for a li'l drink,' he said.

Lucia snorted. 'If I were you, Major Mapp-Flint, I should not impair my faculties with liquor while there's a dangerous prisoner to be guarded.'

'Celebration,' guffawed the Major. 'Just a li'l drop to wet the prisoner's head. Here, you guard him, you seem to be better at that sort of thing than the rest of us. By the way, where did you get that gun?'

'It's not a gun,' mumbled Lucia. 'It's a cucumber.'

'That's a good one,' carolled the Major. 'Resourceful, if you like! Captures a desperate fiend with a cucumber! Here, you'd better take my revolver.'

He drew the weapon and dropped it on the floor at the airman's feet. Everyone froze in horror; everyone, that is, except Lucia. With the speed of a leopard, she struck the airman over the head with the cucumber, so that it disintegrated into fragments, while Hopkins retrieved the Major's pistol and pointed it at the prisoner, who had not moved.

'Nice work, Mrs. Pillson!' exclaimed the fishmonger, with a world of respect in his voice. 'We could do with you as Officer Commanding. Better than some I could mention, anyhow.'

Lucia's face glowed with pride. Now there was a thought! She turned over this possiblity in her mind during the silent half-hour that followed, until the roar of engines and the screech of brakes heralded the arrival of the Regular forces from Hastings.

A young man in Lieutenant's uniform, flanked by two massive sergeants, burst through the door.

'Right then,' he said, 'where's this German airman of yours?'

'There,' growled the Major, 'in that chair. Fiend!'

'That,' said the young man impatiently, 'is an R.A.F. Flying Officer.'

'He can't be,' gapsed Lucia. 'He speaks German. With a Bavarian accent.'

'And who might you be?'

'Emmeline Pillson. I captured him down by the marshes. His aeroplane crashed there. A Messerschmitt.'

'Well,' drawled the Lieutenant, 'you may be interested to know that you have captured a Wing Commander of the Polish Squadron, Royal Air Force, as you would have no doubt have observed if you had taken the trouble to look at his insignia. Excuse me, sir,' he enquired of the bemused Pole. 'Can you speak any English?'

The erstwhile German gazed at him despairingly.

'Apparently not. We'll drive him over to Hastings. There's an interpreter there.'

The Lieutenant took the airman gently by the arm and ushered him towards the door.

'Beats me how you could have taken him for a German. Doesn't sound a bit like German, Polish. And what's this slimy stuff all over the floor?'

'Cucumber,' piped up one of the Home Guard. 'Mrs. Pillson hit him with a cucumber.'

'Did she indeed?' sighed the Lieutenant. 'Poor chap must wonder whose side you lot are on. Lieutenant Flint, no doubt you will hear from your superior officer in the morning. Our time is not without value. In the meantime, might I suggest that you and your band of pirates go and guard that wrecked plane until someone arrives to take care of it? Good evening.'

He saluted precisely and slammed the door.

Major Benjy, it was rumoured, did indeed receive a reprimand from Headquarters; but it was understood that clemency was extended owing to factors beyond his, the Major's, control, notably the outstanding stupidity of a certain civilian, Mrs. Pillson. Had she contacted the proper authorities instead of taking it upon herself to take action a great deal of embarrassment might have been spared all round. However, the Polish officer had decided not to press charges of assault, following Mrs. Pillson's striking him with a cucumber, and so the matter was best left there.

'The odd thing is,' said Elizabeth to Diva, as they stood in line at the fishmonger's, 'she's supposed to be perfectly fluent in Polish. Entertaining the Polish nobility to lunch every other week, hobnobbing with princesses and counts. I suppose Wing Commander Sobieski must have had a thick regional accent that rendered him incomprehensible to our dear friend, although, since he is related on his father's side to the Polish Royal Family, I find it difficult to accept. Poor Lucia! Caught out yet again in one of her little deceptions. She does bring trouble on her own head.'

'Another thing that strikes me as odd,' mused Diva, 'is Major Benjy not recognising an Air Force uniform like that. Strange.'

'Poor Benjy! We are all fallible, are we not? But then, the exhaustion of the day's manoeuvres, the exposure to the noises and fumes of the explosives' (here she was closer to the truth than she knew) 'and then to be confronted in a dimly lit hall with a hysterical woman and a foreigner. He never claimed to be a linguist.'

Diva had her doubts, and, as Elizabeth, by military prerogative, bore off the last of the skate, she speculated whether it was not so much the dimly lit hall as the brilliantly lit Major that had been at least partially to blame. Deep in her vacillating heart, she felt a twinge of sympathy for Lucia. It had been very brave of her, with only a cucumber, to confront an unknown airman on a dark marsh, even if the airman had turned out to be a Polish nobleman. Admittedly, she had lied about knowing Polish, but then, nobody had believed her, so it was not a particularly heinous lie. Lucia was a show-off and a fraud two-thirds of the time; she admitted this readily.

But Elizabeth was the same for three-quarters of the time and so much more malicious. True, Lucia had tried to put a stop to Bridge, and as a true Tillingite Diva abhorred this. But, on the other hand, Elizabeth had tried to put a stop to Lucia, and had effectively succeeded. No true Tillingite could let such a thing happen; life would be so much less exciting without her.

She was roused from her reverie by Mr. Hopkins' assertion that there was no more mackerel either.

'I bet Major Flint doesn't have to worry about where his next mackerel is coming from,' she snapped. 'All right then, it'll have to be herring again.'

If only the balance could be restored, she reflected, as she scuttled back to Wasters to resume her position at her watching-window. If only we could get back to where we were, with neither of them completely dominating the other. Life would be so much more fun that way. As it is, she thought bitterly, we'll have to put up with Elizabeth's airs and graces for ever. And Mr. Georgie's cooking is so delicious.

Fate paused, high above the straggling clouds, and in her hands she raised two sets of golden scales. In one were placed the destinies of Britain and Germany. In the other, slightly smaller, set were the fortunes of Elizabeth and Lucia. The golden instruments wobbled for an instant, and then fell decisively.

Now then, mused Fate, if only I could combine the two. . . .

13

It was a dull autumn day in the second month of Lucia's exclusion. Elizabeth opened the back door of Grebe and walked out on to the cinder-path to inspect her garden. The ground where the tangled thickets of potato-helm had so recently slumped was now black and bare, and the red and golden hoard of Catriona and Majestic lay, secured against frost and damp, in her cellars. Although she had never quite managed to acquire the same enthusiasm for potatoes as she had for the *jolies fleurs* which had previously resided there, she felt deeply satisfied that something had been gained and nothing lost in return. Even the apples seemed to smile at Elizabeth, their little faces blushing in anticipation of the jam-jar and preserving bottle. She had taken thought for the morrow, unlike the attractive but essentially impractical lilies of the field. They, poor dears, would shortly be nipped by the cruel frost. Not so Elizabeth Mapp-Flint.

With her basket on her arm, she began to walk at a leisurely pace along the flat road to Tilling. Out on the marshes she could see a couple of lorries pulling away the last remains of Lucia's Hurricane, a hurricane which had swept away (so she thought) all that was left of her rival's establishment. She smiled and waved at the lorries, but they were too far away to notice. Soon she could clearly see the Landgate, the church-tower and the brown roofs of the town, with their sagging lines and unexpected windows. Quaint, decided Elizabeth, as she did every morning, and quite charming.

Georgie had decided to resume his sketching of the

Landgate. Since he was not a civic leader he could do what he chose, and so, with a fresh sheet of paper and a selection of pencils, he sat down to contemplate his subject. But he was destined, it appeared, never to preserve Tilling's outstanding monument in the amber-drop of Art (like a peach in syrup, he mused poetically) without interference from the disquieting forces of Grebe.

'Good morning, Mr. Georgie,' said Elizabeth brightly, 'such a pretty picky! May I look?'

(How did she know if it was pretty if she hadn't looked? Infuriating woman!)

'I declare I'll never get the hang of the thing,' he sighed, 'though I sketch it for a hundred years and more. It always seems to be falling over backwards, and then you have to move the road round. If I move it any more you'll have to walk out to sea to get back home this afternoon.'

'But Mr. Georgie,' she crooned, 'it's perfect. Such perspective! Don't change a thing. Well, a little more shading there, perhaps, but otherwise quite delightful.'

'Where? I thought the shading was the one thing I got right.'

'Just there, I should say. Where the V is set into the stone-work. No, perhaps you were right,' she said as his swift pencil flicked a few lines across the paper. 'Better in that corner there.'

'Now it looks like a croquet hoop,' moaned Georgie. 'How tar'some of it. I shall have to rub out the whole of the inside, and that will leave such a mess. What a bore!'

'Never mind, Mr. Georgie. You're nearly there. And now I won't disturb you any more. And how is Lulu today? Quite well I trust?'

'She's started doing callisthenics again,' replied Georgie. 'Positively overflowing with health. It tires me just to watch her.'

'Dear Lulu, what a marvel she is,' chirped Elizabeth, as if Lucia were a hundred and four. 'How we are all fuelled by that wonderful vitality! Age cannot wither her,' she concluded, and with a little wave was gone.

What age could not do, she thought, I can.

There was now no danger of being enfiladed by Irene at the junction of the High Street and West Street, and she strolled past that once dreaded spot with a relaxed stride. Diva, as ever, was at her window; as ever, she was sewing away at something (she always sewed *at* things, as the sea drives at the cliffs but never moves them). This time, it was a dull, russet object, resembling nothing so much as a mailbag. . . .

'Good morning, Diva,' she called. As ever, Diva tried to duck out of sight, and, as ever, she was too late. Years of practice and all to no avail.

'Hello, Elizabeth. Can you spare a moment for a cup of tea and a chat? Or are you in a hurry?'

This was said without much hope, and Elizabeth duly ascended the stairs. Diva braced herself for a comment on her needlework that would make her wish to rend the inoffensive garment into pieces.

'Such a pretty sketch Mr. Georgie is doing of the Landgate,' said Elizabeth. 'I feel we ought to revive our little picky exhibitions. I cannot now recall why Lucia cancelled them in the first place.'

'Well, the Institute is needed pretty well all the time by the Home Guard,' said Diva. 'Wouldn't do to turn them out just for a few pictures, especially with the cold weather coming.'

'I shall have a word with the officer in charge,' said Elizabeth coyly. 'I know him quite well, as it happens. He's such a gruff, soldierly man, but he has a heart of gold. I expect he can find us a little corner for our pretty pictures.'

Poor Major Benjy, thought Diva, he'll get no peace until he agrees. Then watercolours all over his cartridge boxes.

'And what is this going to be when it's finished?' asked Elizabeth charmingly. 'A new skirt? No, here are the sleeves; it must be a jacket. How silly of me. It will go well with your pink blouse. Most inventive, dearest. I wish I could find time for such things. Any news?'

'I saw Susan Wyse going down Malleson Street when I popped out for some thread just now. No sables. What could she be wanting?'

'Well, I don't think she's going to enlist,' drawled Elizabeth, 'so we can rule out the Institute. The house-agents, perhaps? Letting Starling Cottage while they take a holiday! Most unlikey. Ah! I have it! The station. She must be meeting a train, except that there isn't one due for an hour and besides Mr. Wyse would go with her. They would probably regard it as a special occasion and take the Royce. The post-office, then. An important letter, perhaps, and she cannot wait for the postman. Or perhaps,' said Elizabeth sardonically, 'she simply wants some stamps.'

'That must be it, then,' said Diva sadly. 'Never mind. I'll get us some tea. Janet!'

'Don't trouble on my account, dear. I simply popped in to wish you good morning. We meet at the Vicarage this evening, do we not?'

She's seen something, thought Diva, as the footsteps on the stairs receded, or she'd have stayed for her tea. What is it? From the window, she saw the Wyses deep in conversation with the Padre and wee wifie.

'Forget the tea, Janet!' she called, casting down her sewing. 'I'm popping out for a bit.'

'A quite remarkable escape,' declared Mr. Wyse, as Diva and Elizabeth joined the group. 'Ah, good morning, Mrs. Mapp-Flint, Mrs. Plaistow. I fear we shall have some rain very soon.'

'From what?' demanded Diva. 'The escape, I mean, not the rain.'

'Such joyful news from Italy,' said Susan. Diva snorted. She could read about the war in the news-papers.

'Our dear sister Amelia,' explained Mr. Wyse. 'She has escaped from Italy after a truly remarkable series of adventures, and has arrived safely in England. She will be coming here very shortly.'

''Tes a miracle, by a' accounts,' declared the Padre.

'The seas divided for her, as for the Children of Israel; she has come out o' the land of bondage and is safe in bonny England.'

'We were so worried,' continued Mr. Wyse. 'Francesco di Faraglione, you see, had so vigorously opposed the Mussolini *régime* that he was placed under house-arrest at the beginning of the war. Naturally, Amelia was determined to stay at his side. But then,' his voice faltered, 'he disappeared suddenly one night.'

'No!' squeaked Evie. 'How horrible!'

'Later she had word that he had made his way to some friends in the South and was leading a band of desperate guerillas in raids against the enemy.'

'And with his bad knee,' added Susan. 'So courageous.'

'He left instructions with Amelia, telling her how to escape to England and rejoin her family. She disguised herself as an old peasant woman – so distressing for one of her refinement, yet in her letters she tells us that she felt a strange exhilaration – and joined a crew of *zingari* – gipsies, Mrs. Mapp-Flint – and they travelled north, singing and selling clothes-pegs as they went. Dear Amelia, so she says, took the *rôle* of a teller of fortunes and soon became quite proficient in the use of the crystal ball and *tarocchi* cards. Apparently she had borrowed a book on the subject from our Mrs. Pillson on her last visit to these shores, and she took this book with her. She declares that it has saved her life. Finally, they made their way to the Swiss frontier, and my sister bribed an aged shepherd to conduct her across the mountains on a donkey. But her adventures were not over; they were stopped by a German patrol, and to divert their attention she read their palms – apparently she had read about this also in Mrs. Pillson's book. The Germans seem to have been impressionable ruffians and were so pleased with the brilliant prospects of plunder and promotion which Amelia saw in their hands that they let her pass unhindered. And now she is in London, and will shortly be travelling to Whitchurch to spend a few days there, before coming to Tilling for the duration of the war. But, she declares, she is much changed by her experiences. She vows that she is quite finished with Italy and all things Italian; she will not speak another word of that accursed tongue for as long as she lives. And she is most anxious to meet Mrs. Pillson and return the book to which, she swears, she owes her continued existence.'

Elizabeth ground her beautiful teeth. It seemed as if Lucia's tentacles extended to the four corners of the earth.

'So fortunate!' she exclaimed. 'Truly a remarkable tale. I shall look forward so much to hearing it from her own lips. But oh! what a terrible place this world has become, and how wicked people are!'

''Tes the blackness o' the murky sky that makes the wee stars to shine so brightly,' murmured the Padre. 'Come, Evie, we must gang awa' tae the fishmonger's.'

Georgie, of course, was unaware of all this excitement. He had tried to adjust the shading of the interior of the Landgate (which had completely satisfied him until Elizabeth sowed seeds of doubt in his mind) with the result that everything inside the arch now was cast into Stygian gloom. He decided that the sketch would have to become the Landgate at night, and should be postponed until his creative powers had had time to recuperate.

He made his way back to Mallards and let himself in. Lucia was sitting in the drawing-room, staring at a letter. The envelope had fallen to the ground.

'Lucia!' he exclaimed. 'What is it? Not bad news, I trust.'

'Read this,' she said, without any expression. So he read it.

'Lucia,' he said, in a voice full of wonder and awe, but could not continue.

'And in our house, Georgie.' She pulled herself together with a massive effort. 'Not a word to anyone. No one must ever know. It must be our secret.'

'Not even Elizabeth?'

'No one.'

Georgie sat down, and his sketching things joined the envelope in an unheeded heap on the floor.

'So like Lord Tony,' he said, 'to have thought of us.'

'No, Georgie,' said Lucia with deep sincerity, 'it is all your doing. See what he says in his letter: ". . . a beautiful house in a sleepy little town and absolutely the best cook in England." '

'Oh Lucia,' he said, 'it is true, isn't it? All of them coming here. If only we could tell Elizabeth. She would burst into flames and burn herself into ashes.'

'There are more important things in life, Georgie, than scoring points off Elizabeth,' said Lucia gravely. Georgie looked her in the eye. She had meant every word she said.

The autumn was beginning to grow cold now, and the days were getting shorter. Encouraging news from the front set tongues wagging almost every day and a general air of optimism filled the town. Diva, after several false starts, tentatively gave the mailbag its *première* and was most annoyed when nobody noticed it, a most unTillinglike occurrence. The Wyses awaited with mounting excitement the arrival of Amelia di Faraglione (who now answered to no name but Amelia Wyse-Faraglione), who had declared that she could wait no longer to be reunited with her saviour Mrs. Pillson.

Only Lucia and Georgie seemed withdrawn and abstracted, as if something of great importance were hanging over them, blocking the trivia of everyday life from their sight. For the scintillating pleasures of Tilling they had no appetite. Georgie, it seemed, passed all his time in the kitchen of Mallards, and Lucia with him, emerging after the shoppers had left the High Street, to buy necessary provisions. Yet no invitations were issued, no unknown guests seen arriving or leaving. It was not offence or dudgeon that had caused them to withdraw from society; it was just that they were both entirely preoccupied with something, and nobody could guess what it was.

One evening, the guests assembled for dinner and Bridge at Starling Cottage. Elizabeth and Diva met in West Street and paused to enjoy the evening air in the twilight before going on to their hosts. As they stood there, they heard the purr of motors coming up the street behind them, a most unusual noise in those days of petroleum rationing. A procession of enormous Rolls-Royce cars went by, and the two women gaped open-mouthed at the occupants clearly discernible in the early evening light. There was a tall, distinguished-looking man in the uniform of a French general, his striking profile familiar from a thousand newspapers. Another car contained a large, powerfully built man in American uniform and, beside him, an Admiral of the Royal Navy – and not just any Admiral. That last motor in the procession. . .

With trembling knees they passed on to Porpoise Street to relate what they had seen.

'How long have they been talking, Georgie?' asked Lucia, perched on the edge of her chair in the drawing-room.

'You mean since his chauffeur went in with the maps? Ages. Isn't it glorious!'

There was a knock at the door. Lucia put down the tray from which she had eaten her supper, sprang to her feet and lunged at the door-handle.

'We have to come to congratulate the *chef*,' said the intruder. 'I trust you do not object to cigar smoke?'

At Starling Cottage, the debate had raged all through dinner and all through the rubbers of Bridge that followed; when the cards were finally cast aside the debate had hardly started and still they had come to no conclusion.

'They must have been going to Hastings,' insisted the

Padre; of Scots there was no trace in his accent, and he spoke in the tones of his native Birmingham.

'But why should they go that way? It's nowhere near the road to Hastings,' cried Diva, weary from repeating this obvious point. 'Nor the London road. The only place it leads to is Church Square.'

'Or the Norman Tower,' urged Mr. Wyse. 'It is an excellent place for a conference.'

'Nonsense, Algernon,' said his wife. 'The Town Hall. They were holding a conference in the Town Hall.'

'It's no use,' said Diva. 'We'll have to go and look.'

So Evie and the Padre, and Mr. Wyse and Susan, who forgot to put on her sables, though the night was cold, and Diva and Elizabeth and Major Benjy, who in his excitement had drunk nothing at all save three glasses of wine and a spot of port, all set off to see what they could see.

They did not have far to look. As they rounded the corner they saw, in the brilliant moonlight, the illustrious guests, the demi-gods, the pillars of the free world, shaking Lucia and Mr. Georgie warmly by the hand and climbing into their motors.

As they stood and stared a stocky figure in an unmistakable black hat grasped Lucia's hands in both of his and said, in a voice whose orotund tones echoed in the narrow street as they will echo forever throughout history:

'A thousand thanks, my dear Lucia, for so graciously allowing us to take over your delightful house for a whole evening. And let me say this. Never, in my vast experience of the culinary art, have I dined so well as I have tonight, nor ever tasted anything to rival your splendid lobster *à la Riseholme*.'

He tipped a little ash from his cigar, and then he too was gone.

'He called her Lucia!' whispered Evie.

'Well, I'll be blowed!' exclaimed Major Benjy.

And there they stood, like trolls who have been caught out by the dawn, standing as still as if they would never move again.

THE END

Queen Lucia
E.F. Benson

'We will pay anything for Lucia books.'
NOEL COWARD: GERTRUDE LAWRENCE: NANCY MITFORD: W.H. AUDEN

Queen Lucia is set in the middle-class, garden-party world of the 1920's, a society dominated utterly and ruthlessly by the greatest arch-snob who has ever existed. Lucia and her cohorts – Georgie with his dyed hair, embroidery, and piano duets, Daisy Quantock with her passion for the new and exotic – capture the mood and flavour of a whole period, and the nuances and rivalries of English life are described engrossingly and with a rapier wit.

If the pens of Evelyn Waugh and Jane Austen had mated, Lucia would have been the offspring.

'At long last, here she is again, the splendid creature, the great, the wonderful Lucia.'
NANCY MITFORD

'My greatest reading pleasure in 1967 was the discovery of E.F. Benson's 'Lucia' novels . . . I enjoyed them so much that I borrowed (and was tempted to steal) two more of the series: and I confess myself a Lucia addict.'
TERENCE DE VERE WHITE

'To describe her as a snob would be to describe Leonardo as a talented man.'
MICHAEL MACLIAMMOR

0 552 99075 2

BLACK SWAN

Lucia in London
E. F. Benson

'We will pay anything for Lucia books.'
NOEL COWARD: GERTRUDE LAWRENCE: NANCY MITFORD: W. H. AUDEN

Lucia, Queen of provincial society, now launches herself on to
the London scene. The *creme de la creme* of social climbers,
Lucia never falters as she dons her real (seed) pearls and
prepares to attack the beau monde, wheedling her way into
parties where she has not been invited and coaxing the rich
and titled to come to tea.

Lucia in London is the second of the famous Lucia books by
E. F. Benson. Comic masterpieces, these novels of manners
are brought to life by sharp, satirical social observations and
are as deliciously funny today as they were when first published
in the 1920s.

'He was a master of a certain kind of light fiction, and he can
delight even though one knows that his satire is ultimately
friendly . . . He is clever and funny, but he writes for his
victims'
THE SPECTATOR

'The flow of his comic inspiration never dwindles'
ELIZABETH HARVEY

'Here she is again, the splendid creature, the great, the
wonderful Lucia . . . I must say I reopened these magic books
after some thirty years with misgivings: I feared that they
would have worn badly and seem dated. Not at all; they are
as fresh as paint. The characters are real and therefore timeless'
NANCY MITFORD

'One of the supreme comic novelists of the English language . . .
Although set in the world of prosperous, idle people in their
golden age between the beginning of the century and the
Second World War, the novels of E. F. Benson really belong,
in their witty, camp and destructive style, to no age but our
own . . . I defy anyone to read any of these books without
being enchanted . . .
AUBERON WAUGH, DAILY MAIL

0 552 99076 0

BLACK SWAN

Miss Mapp
E.F. Benson

'The flow of his comic inspiration never dwindles'
ELIZABETH HARVEY

Here is the redoubtable 'triumphantly arch of all arch
villainesses', Miss Elizabeth Mapp of Tilling – a schemer,
a woman of fine habits and low cunning who spends her
days in the delightful bow window of her delightful period
house, light opera glasses in hand, noting and annotating
the business of her neighbours. Not a thing escapes her
gimlet eyes, from the purchase of a basket of over-ripe
red-currants, to the unfortunate drinking habits of
Captain Puffin.

Miss Mapp is the third in the sequence of the famous
Lucia novels. Deliciously funny, outrageously U,
quintessentially English, Benson's comic characters have
come alive again for another generation.

'He was a master of a certain kind of light fiction, and he
can delight even though one knows that his satire is
ultimately friendly . . . He is clever and funny, but he
writes for his victims'
THE SPECTATOR

'My greatest reading pleasure in 1967 was the discovery
of E.F. Benson's 'Lucia' novels . . . I enjoyed them so much
that I borrowed (and was tempted to steal) two more of
the series. I confess myself a Lucia addict'
TERENCE DE VERE WHITE

0 552 99083 3

BLACK SWAN

Mapp and Lucia
E. F. Benson

'I have not laughed so much at any novel as *Mapp and Lucia*
since I read the early Waughs'
TERENCE DE VERE WHITE

At last they meet — the two most formidable ladies in English
literature collide in genteel and deadly enmity. Lucia, now
widowed, shakes the dust of Riseholme from her elegant feet
and, with Georgie Pillson as devoted courtier, prepares to
conquer the high society of Tilling. She brings her musical
evenings, her Italian, her poetry, and her ambitious snobbery.
And Miss Mapp, her features corrugated by chronic rage and
curiosity, can only prepare to defend her position as doyenne
of Tilling. The town is split in an exciting and scintillating war
of garden parties, bridge evenings, and staggeringly simple
little dinners.

Mapp and Lucia is the fourth of the Lucia novels, a chronicle
of life in two English country towns described with malicious
delicacy and wit.

'I might have gone to my grave without ever knowing about
Lucia and Miss Mapp. It is not a risk anyone should take
lightly'
AUBERON WAUGH

0 552 99084 1

BLACK SWAN

Lucia's Progress
E.F. Benson

'I might have gone to my grave without ever knowing about Lucia or Miss Mapp. It is not a risk anyone should take lightly'
AUBERON WAUGH

Once more the society of Tilling is locked in exquisite trepidation as Lucia and Miss Mapp – now Mrs Benjamin Mapp-Flint launch themselves into a fresh foray of deadly civilities. For Mrs Benjamin Mapp-Flint, triumphant from her honeymoon in Monte Carlo, is *too* triumphant, and Lucia has delicate designs of Borgian dimensions to reduce Tilling's new bride to her rightful place.

Lucia's Progress is the fifth of E.F. Benson's delicious, satirical, sparkling and malicious Lucia series.

'I reopened these magic books after some thirty years with misgivings; I feared that they would have worn badly and seem dated. Not at all; they are as fresh as paint. The characters are real and therefore timeless'
NANCY MITFORD

0 552 99087 6

BLACK SWAN

Trouble for Lucia
E.F. Benson

'Whenever I stopped reading to laugh aloud, I measured
the pages still unread, not to see how much more I had to
accomplish, but from a simple fear that my pleasure was
drawing to an end . . . A Cranford of 1930'
TERENCE DE VERE WHITE

Lucia's lofty ambitions are at last to be fulfilled. For as
Mayor-Elect of Tilling it seems she has come to her
highest calling. The tearooms of Tilling quiver with
delicious gossip as she reigns from Mallards – formerly
the home of Mrs Benjamin Mapp-Flint – with dear
Georgie Pillson as her consort.

But Lucia's position as the town's *premiere* socialite is in
danger. For, concerned with her civic dignities, 'Dear
Worship' is inclined to forget the subtle nuances and
quaint customs of Tilling society.

Trouble for Lucia is the last of E.F. Benson's Lucia novels,
a delicious study of outrageous snobbery, essentially
English and consistently entertaining.

'The art of these books lies in their simplicity. The jokes
seem quite obvious and are often repeated; we can never
have enough of them'
NANCY MITFORD

0 552 99088 4

BLACK SWAN

Lucia Triumphant
Tom Holt

'We will pay anything for Lucia Books'
Noel Coward: Gertrude Lawrence: Nancy Mitford: W. H. Auden

Lucia, twice-elected Mayor of Tilling, with her dearest arch-enemy, Elizabeth Mapp-Flint, ousted from the Council, is strangely wearied of her mortal span. For she feels she has accomplished everything — what else is there for her to do?

But the times (and Elizabeth Mapp-Flint) have events of catastrophic proportions in store. Lucia has hardly launched her project of The Tilling Tapestry (to do for Lucia what the Bayeux did for France) when Elizabeth sweeps through Tilling society with her Monopoly Set, putting sewing, bridge, and dinner parties to rout, wooing even the obedient Georgie to the delights of buying Vine Street and the Water Works.

Lucia throws off her lethargy and prepares to conquer Tilling anew.

'Might have been dreamt up by Benson. Tom Holt has provided manna'
THE SPECTATOR

'He never lets us forget that the people even at their most absurd are human and vulnerable. I thought, after six Benson novels and two TV serialisations, that I was tired of Tilling — but I laid this book aside with real regret'
DAILY TELEGRAPH

0 552 99281 X

— BLACK SWAN —